Praise for *Hunting for a Husband*

Beautifully written! A heartwarming tale of finding love unexpectedly. Mindy's characters come to life on the pages of this sweet story where family, romance, and faith blend together for a story that will linger with you long after "the end." *Hunting for a Husband* left me with a smile. I absolutely loved it!

— Mary Alford, *USA Today* Bestselling author of *Amish Country Kidnapping*

Mindy Steele's *Hunting for a Husband* is a heartwarming story rich with fascinating details about Amish daily life—the author's appreciative understanding of the Plain lifestyle shines on every page. The sweet, slow-burn romance between Joe and Leah is beautifully crafted and gently infused with inspiring elements of faith. Steele deftly tops off the story with a dollop of danger, creating a book you won't be able to put down. A surefire hit for fans of Amish romance!

— Laurel Blount: bestselling author of *Shelter in the Storm* and Love Inspired's Hickory Springs Amish series

Some stories can feel like a cup of hot tea on a cold winter's night. Mindy Steele's *Hunting for a Husband* does just that, giving reader's a healthy dose of happily ever after for characters you can't help but cheer on. Tackling the difficulty of change and all the struggles that entails while highlighting hope amidst despair can be difficult, but Steele does so beautifully as she showcases God's goodness in all things. This sweet Amish tale will have you smiling and turning pages!

— Beth Pugh, author of the Pine Valley Holiday Series

THE HEART *of* THE AMISH

Hunting for a Husband

MINDY STEELE

Hunting for a Husband ©2025 by Mindy Steele

Print ISBN 979-8-89151-145-3
Adobe Digital Edition (.epub) 979-8-89151-146-0

All rights reserved. No part of this publication may be reproduced or transmitted for commercial purposes, except for brief quotations in printed reviews, without written permission of the publisher. Reproduced text may not be used on the World Wide Web. No Barbour Publishing content may be used as artificial intelligence training data for machine learning, or in any similar software development.

All scripture quotations are taken from the King James Version of the Bible.

This book is a work of fiction. Names, characters, places, and incidents are either products of the author's imagination or used fictitiously. Any similarity to actual people, organizations, and/or events is purely coincidental.

Cover Design: Kirk DouPonce, DogEared Design

Published by Barbour Publishing, Inc., 1810 Barbour Drive, Uhrichsville, Ohio 44683, www.barbourbooks.com

Our mission is to inspire the world with the life-changing message of the Bible.

Printed in the United States of America.

To Mike, for keeping love interesting.

To Esther, for enlightening me.

To Charlotte, for your knowledge.

*The preparations of the heart in man, and the answer of the tongue, is from the L*ORD*.*
P*ROVERBS* 16:1

NOTE TO READERS

I often write about the Amish of northern Kentucky, as I can't imagine any setting better to share with readers than my beautiful surroundings. However, there are times I find inspiration elsewhere without looking for it. For this story, inspiration found my husband. During my first reader event in Pennsylvania, we came across an Amish deer farm. It was not a public destination, but there were deer, and my husband couldn't resist driving up the long lane in hopes of getting a closer look. After introducing ourselves, we were blessed to learn more and get closer to those beautiful animals. What an amazing livelihood, and what a perfect setting. Thus, the Wickey sisters and their family found their way into my imagination.

Hunting for a Husband is a continuation of my novella, *Leaving Lancaster* in An Amish Lancaster Christmas Anthology, which was released in September 2024. This is one sister's story and a closer look into both physical disabilities and examining our hearts. The Amish have many unique trades, as you will soon read about, but their faith is inherent in their ability to accept God's will.

I hope you enjoy,
Mindy

GLOSSARY

ach: oh
aenti: aunt
boppli/bopplin: baby, babies
bruder: brother
bu/buwe: boy, boys
daed: dad
danke: thank you
dawdi: grandfather
dochter/dochtern: daughter, daughters
dok/doktor: doctor
EE glech dee: I love you
EE kaw sell nit glauba: I cannot believe that
Ei. Ei. Ei.: an expression of astonishment or frustration
Englisch/Englischer: a non-Amish person
Es ish ke fershtant: used often when speaking to a child that something is not sensible
fraa: wife
freinden: friends
Gmay: an Amish church community as a whole
Gott: God
grosskinner: grandchildren
gut: good
Gut mariye: good morning
haus: house
huck yersht ahna: just sit down
hund: hound or dog
Ist gut: it is good
jah: yes
kaffi: coffee
kapp: prayer covering
kichlin: cookies

kinner: children
komm ena: come in
maed/maedel: girl, young woman
mamm/mammi: mom, grandmother
mei: my
menner: men
mutter: mother
nacht: night
naet: not
nee: no
onkel: uncle
schwester/schwestern: sister, sisters
sell ist goot: that is good
sohn: son
verra: very
Vort a klee: asking one to wait patiently
Was iss letz?: What is it?

PROLOGUE

Sometimes in the midst of falling snow and a newly kindled fire it's difficult to decide which to linger in. Not willing to make another poor decision, Leah Wickey remained in her assigned seat next to her twin at the wedding table and watched as Beth smiled at her new husband with such affection that Leah wanted to burst into tears.

Only two months ago they had both watched their eldest sister, Louise, marry their lifelong neighbor. Marcus was a fine man, and Leah already thought of him like a brother, but no sooner had Louise wed than *Daed* purchased a farm in Kentucky and had the whole family pack all their belongings. Land was cheaper in Kentucky than in Pennsylvania, giving the family more acreage for their growing deer farm.

Two months ago was the same time Leah's intended had also disappeared into the night, leaving his family in shocking grief as well as breaking Leah's heart. Even now, sitting behind two long sheet cakes with pink roses perched on white icing, Leah couldn't bring herself to look up for fear of another penetrating look from Conner Brinker's *mamm*. Though no one blamed Leah for Conner's poor choice, Leah felt the burden of guilt for not swaying Conner to stay within their faith.

Now Beth was married to Daniel Fisher and was having the happiest day of her life, and Leah wanted nothing more than to run into the snowy fields outside just as they had a thousand times growing up. But she remained seated, clinging onto Beth a little longer. The separation would soon come—and be something else Leah was forced to accept.

Little by little, Leah completed all her duties as Beth's sidesitter—seeing that the *eck*, or wedding table, was decorated just as Beth wanted and sitting near her all throughout the day, including the wedding meal—while a heavy February snow fell outside, turning all of Ronks and Lancaster County, Pennsylvania, into a winter wonderland. It wasn't until after the late supper that Leah found a moment to herself as folks began leaving. Slipping on her coat and wrapping her heavy woolen shawl over her head and around her shoulders, she aimed for the side door, where fewer folks would notice her leaving.

"Where are you going?" *Mammi* Iolene's voice clipped, causing Leah's hand to still on the door latch. Despite age and a limp, Mammi Iolene had the keenest senses where her six *grosskinner* were concerned.

"Getting some air. I'll see to the cleanup as soon as the bishop and his family are gone," Leah replied, noting the bishop's *fraa* still deep in conversation with Mamm at the kitchen sink. Though everyone would do their part to help put Louise's home back in order, the van driver who would be returning Leah and her family to Kentucky insisted they leave no later than midnight ahead of a winter storm.

"He's not here, if you are thinking to go looking for him."

"I'm not," Leah said, lifting her chin to assure her grandmother she thought no such thing. She was quite aware that Conner hadn't been in attendance today. In fact, Leah was thankful he hadn't come. How could she ever again face a man who held to her heart for three long years, then tossed it back in a blink?

"There's nothing to do but look ahead *for you*, for a happier season. But not to worry, for I will see you just as happy as Beth and Louise when we return home," Mammi Iolene said with signature confidence before quickly disappearing around a corner.

Leah wasn't ready to call Kentucky home yet, but Mammi's profound wisdom once again was wrapped in sharp, pointed promises. Leah needed no reminders of her bad choices. Even moving to a new community where no one would know of her failure, the chances of finding someone who made her heart as complete as Conner was unlikely. It would be spring before she'd feel a warm breeze on her cheeks, and likely the shortest day that darkened the hours at both ends of a clock, the celebration of the Lord's birthday, before Leah could imagine some measure of hope for her own future.

Outside, she quickly made her way around the side of the house, avoiding the young men gathering at the hitching post and barn. Leah suspected all three of her young *bruders* would be there, saying final farewells to friends. Leah forced back the threat of tears. She wasn't stubborn, but she'd not bid farewell to Alma, her dearest friend, no matter how far Daed moved them away.

Passing the clothesline that would never again dry her dresses, Leah picked up her pace. She would be living in a whole new state, among cousins she barely knew, leaving behind two *schwestern*, a best friend, and a man who stole her best years. *Nee,* she'd not cry. She'd walk. Walking always made even the biggest of problems shrink somehow.

The boundary line between the Wickey and King farms was board fencing, but Daed had installed two short gates for all the traveling the families did back and forth to each other's house over the years.

Leah opened the gate, slipped through it, and latched it back before facing her last Lancaster sunset.

Snowy fields, dipped in rows from the last harvest, stretched for what looked like miles ahead before the roof of the Kings' house and barns were visible. She'd not go far, but take in this lasting scene of her childhood before she'd have to leave.

Two cardinals picked under the snow in hopes of food, and Leah couldn't hold back her vast run of emotions any longer. The tears spilled out so fast, she couldn't have stopped them even if she tried.

"I'm so sorry," she cried. Perhaps she shouldn't have packed up all the bird feeders, leaving her feathered friends to survive on their own. Chances were that Louise wouldn't even consider feeding the birds as Leah had. Not since Blinkers, Louise's buttercream cat, had a habit of making a meal out of them so regularly.

The cardinals darted off as she drew near. Something else she'd be leaving behind. "Lord, I'm so happy for my schwestern. I am. But I feel as if nothing will ever be the same again."

It wouldn't be. She didn't need *Gott* to tell her that was true. So many changes in two months, it was a wonder she hadn't been a mess of tears since December.

Continuing toward the sunset while snow sprinkled her scarf, Leah focused on the silence. Winter was a gift, quieting the world, and right now, Leah craved quiet.

"There is hope in tomorrow," she told herself encouragingly. "If we have joy in the morning, we will have peace in the *nacht*." Had that not been a proverb Mamm had spouted many times over?

"If only I weren't so…uncertain and…afraid. I've never done many things without Beth or Louise, and now that…" Leah couldn't say his name, but Gott knew, and that's all that mattered.

"Guide me and help me be strong. If You have a different plan for my life, then I will be willing to see it."

Praying and walking came hand in hand, but before Leah knew it, she had traveled halfway across the Kings' farm. Stopping, she gave the Lord a proper amen and turned to face the house she once called home. A red sunset burned on the white vinyl, flashing in the window glass. She drank in every shadow, every detail, storing it to memory.

Memories could be a blessing or daunting, but each one she'd cherish and hold on to.

Wiping away the cold dampness on her face, Leah let out a long, slow breath. She'd had her cry. She'd talked to Gott. There was nothing left to be done but to straighten her shoulders and bid farewell to her schwestern and the only life she had ever known.

Looking down, Leah found herself oddly smiling. No one had crossed the fields since the snow began falling, and only her steps left a mark in the new fallen snow.

There was something about treading on fresh snow no one had stepped on yet to give a woman a reason to look ahead to a better tomorrow.

CHAPTER ONE

Everyone thought that Leah was heartbroken after Conner Brinker threw away three years of courting to live among the *Englisch*. She wasn't so delicate. Though if asked, she'd admit that her heart was bruised. It was best that Leah discovered Conner's lack of faith and love for the world sooner rather than later. Worse than never being married and having *kinner* of her own was having both with the wrong person.

That had been five months ago. Five months and ten days, to be exact, but who was counting? Not Leah. She'd not look back. Only forward. She'd be no pillar of salt of the past.

Moving to Kentucky had become an unexpected blessing. She liked being part of a new community where few knew your flaws yet. She liked her new part-time job too, being a mother's helper. Still, Leah did miss working at the Bird-in-Hand Restaurant, her best friend Alma, and her eldest sister, Louise, who had always been best for giving sound advice.

Right now Leah wondered if Louise thought it wise to trust Mammi Iolene to set her up on another date. Leah did want what every other *maedel* wanted.

A family.

Mammi Iolene had lived a great many years and surely knew more about such tender subjects than Leah. Leah was eager to give love another try. If change was good, she'd cling to it with hope in her heart that even she might find love despite living in the middle of nowhere, Kentucky.

The small community was growing on her. The rolling countryside charmed the senses. Folks were friendly, and there were the Wickey cousins to spend time with. Most women her age were already married. At twenty-four, Leah was considered a spinster among her new community, whereas in Lancaster, few married so young. Mamm fretted that Leah was pining. She wasn't. She was simply having a hard time relating to any of the men here. They either felt as uncomfortable as she did or talked about her family's deer farm the whole visit. Neither made for a fine date.

Her parents' choice of livelihood was not common. Raising deer to sell and breed and for bottled scents and antlers drew a lot of attention. The first two months after moving into the older home with more cracks than her strawberry muffins, folks came by car and buggy to gawk at the high fences in hopes of catching a glimpse of one of the five bucks her father had invested in.

Leah was no stranger to boldness, as folks had at times snapped a photo when she waited on tables, but having cars pull into your driveway at all hours was terribly rude. There were plenty of deer in Kentucky, from what she'd read. That's why Daed put up a No Trespassing sign, warding off any further onlookers.

Her cousin Joel had not been secretive at all in introducing her to Jacob Lemmon during Rulen church, which took place twice annually in her new community instead of once a year as she had been accustomed to before. Rulen church was on the second Sunday in March and again in September, when ministers of the community went over the *Ordnung*, or rules, of the church.

Jacob was kind. He had a slight stutter. Leah didn't mind but suspected other maedels had, considering he wasn't already married. Everyone was flawed in some way. Were they not? Leah was willing to look past simple flaws and get to know him better, but after one ride home, Jacob informed her that he had no interest in courting. It was for the best, she told herself, considering Jacob Lemmon ran an animal sanctuary for a living. Leah couldn't imagine a life living with so many strange animals. As it was, she wasn't too happy to be living with eighteen deer, twelve chickens, and three bruders.

Determined to find her own match, Leah had accidentally smiled at Ruben Paul Smoker during her first youth gathering. His light hair and rich blue eyes had caught her off guard. *Just like Conner's.* It had been a simple mistake, and in truth, he smiled at her first. Now Leah lost any chance of a budding friendship with Barbara Yoder, his intended. Being a newcomer was a complicated state to maneuver.

Thankfully, Mammi Iolene saw Leah's plight and forced her to offer a second helping of cherry pie to Abel Lambright during the fellowship meal last Sunday. Abel was tall and handsome, kind speaking, and forgiving when Leah spilled the whole slice of cherry pie directly over his shoulder. The thought made her giggle. Instead of scolding her, Abel asked to drive her home—much to her grandmother's delight. Who knew clumsiness could be rewarded?

The Lambrights ran a mushroom and berry farm at the far end of the community. Leah liked mushrooms and berries and had been over-the-moon excited to get to know the handsome man more that evening, but then Amos had gone and twisted his ankle while shooting baskets with some of the younger boys. Showing off, no doubt, and Leah had to see him home safely.

Talk about a bird without wings. Leah was embarrassed after having to explain to Abel why she couldn't stay and visit with him. Three times, she counted, that Leah considered jumping from the buggy and into a ditch to avoid Amos' teasing on the ride home.

But Gott offered second and third chances, Leah was discovering. Abel understood the importance of family and agreed to meet her today at the benefit auction. That's why despite being late, she was smiling as the Englisch driver, whom everyone called Driver Dan, raced along the narrow country road to reach the local auction house in time.

"For as one door closes, Gott opens another," she whispered as the van rounded a sharp curve. Signs marked the auction site long before Leah noted the gravel access. Trucks, vans, and buggies were cluttered chaotically throughout the soft meadow like cookies tossed in a jar. The auction started at nine, but even after the late noon hour, there were crowds of folks milling about between two long metal buildings.

Driver Dan pulled to a stop near the auctioneer's office. Leah thanked him, offered up two matching bills, and hopped out. The sun aimed toward Sugar Mountain, doing little to ward off the chilly spring wind.

Leah gave her *kapp* a finger's touch for straightness, and her new blue dress a quick brushing, before aiming for the nearest building. Two long barns sat at an angle on each side of a private drive currently being used for loading cattle trailers and trucks with recent buys.

She was late. Not her doing, but since accepting work as a mother's helper, Leah found it was harder to predict her schedule than before. Especially since the new mamm was the local Amish *doktor*. Folks didn't always get sick or need advice between the hours of seven a.m. and five p.m. Surely Abel would forgive her tardiness.

She'd not run, looking desperate, but she picked up her pace, passing a group of women carrying trays of tomato plants, flowers, and a crate filled with small rabbits. Three young boys in spring violet-colored shirts trailed behind them. There were many Amish and Mennonite communities nearby that Leah wasn't familiar with yet, but by quick inspection, she concluded they were New Order Amish. Such colors would never be permitted among the Amish here. Neither was the heart-shaped kapp she had worn all her life but had to put away.

Stepping into the barn, the scent of livestock permeated the air. A table of pies was displayed at her left, where two older women chatted about the unusually cool temps for May. Leah scanned the many straw hats and faces but couldn't find Abel's tall build nor sandy blond hair among the crowd. With a sigh, she looked to her left, where another cluster of Amish men stood, but saw nothing of the man she felt God had placed in her path for a reason. One who followed the Ordnung and didn't seem at all interested in leaving their faith.

Moving toward the center of the arena, she smiled as young kinner gathered to poke and *aww* at small animals in cages, boxes, and crates. Aside from greeting winter cardinals or late spring hummingbirds, Leah was not a fan of critters, small or large. Growing up in a big family, full of people who doted on everything from menacing felines to antlered wildlife, Leah had long ago tired of cuddling small things that only grew up to be sold or traded—or died.

An auctioneer's voice broke her fast-moving stride, and she noted the flat wooden wagon in the center of the arena. Her twin, Beth, stood in the front of the crowd, stars in her eyes, as she watched her husband point to a tray of overly grown tomatoes. Married not three whole months, Beth and Daniel had stayed with his parents for the first weeks of marriage before joining them in Kentucky. Daniel had accepted a few auctioneering jobs locally, meaning Leah would have her sister with her for a few blessed weeks. Plans had already been made for them to head north to Indiana and Michigan soon.

Leah was tempted to stick around and make a bid herself, for who didn't like tomatoes at any stage? But Abel had said to meet him at eleven, and here it was already well past noon.

The spring mud sale was rumored to draw a large crowd, but it was nothing like the simple charity suppers in Lancaster. According to Delilah and Mary Elizabeth Glick, money raised here would be added to the community medical funds. No matter where Leah planted her feet, the sense of community within her Amish faith always filled her heart with such belonging. How Conner had never felt that, she might never understand.

It's just a smaller community, she reminded herself. Smaller didn't mean less than. Not with open buggies, fewer strangers, and no one sneaking pictures of you every time you offered them a glass of water. It was a lot to adjust to, but Leah did find riding in an open buggy with the wind in her face a pleasure.

"Here ya go, folks. You'll be picking tomatoes by June first!" Daniel waved a hand before tossing Beth a wink. "Three times your money, raised and cared for by the local greenhouse."

Beth, the twin who liked adventure, wasn't afraid to speak her mind, and ached to try on new things, was blessed to have married a man who loved all the same things she did.

Leah rolled her eyes, watching the two ogle one another in public. Leah's love life had been met with opposition from the start. Three long years courting Conner Brinker, who only had eyes for leaving his faith, his family, and her behind to live among the Englisch. She'd not begrudge Beth's happiness one bit. It filled her heart with joy to know both her sisters had found men who loved them so well. It was just confusing to wonder why such happiness eluded her.

The tomatoes disappeared into the clutches of two middle-aged Englisch women before Daniel's voice boomed again, trying to pull in bids for a five-drawer ladies' dresser.

"Come on, folks, this isn't a slapped-together stick piece but a handmade, sturdy dresser. We're here to raise money for a good cause, with fine craftsmanship up for bid. Now we're at 350. Who will give me 375? 375. 375. Now four!" With a microphone in his hand and a glint in his dark eyes, Leah could see how Daniel had charmed her twin into marriage. *A man who is content is a man who will bring contentment.* Mamm always said as much.

Across the lot, another auctioneer was stirring the crowd into laughter while selling a corn picker. Leah spotted her father just a few feet away, arms crossed, watching Daniel with piqued interest, and worked her way to him.

She nudged his shoulder. "Hiya."

"I thought you were coming with the Glicks. I haven't seen you since we arrived this morning." He lifted a dark and questioning brow.

"Dok Stella had folks showing up one after the other. I couldn't very well leave little Viola with Lena." Viola was Dok Stella's three-month-old *dochter*, and Lena her aging mother-in-law who needed no looking after, but Leah knew without being asked, she too was part of Leah's new job, as Lena's eyesight was beginning to decline. Leah didn't mind. She loved snuggling, holding, and spending time with Viola, and she did as much as she could to help Lena with simple chores and company too.

"You know Lena's hands can't hold a healthy *boppli* for long." Lena loved seeing over her own, but now that Viola grew rounded at three months, it was becoming a chore for her to manage for long periods of time.

"I thought the dok only did business on Monday and Tuesday." His hat concealed what Leah knew was an expanding bald spot. Her father was not a proud man, but few outside of the *gmay* had ever seen him without a hat.

"She's thinking to open a few hours each Friday to help even further. I don't mind the work." Leah never knew a woman to work outside her home with young kinner before. Many had small cottage shops selling jams or quilts, but such would have been frowned upon in Lancaster. Of course, some worked to solely support their families when there was no man to do it for them, but Stella was married to a bishop who had his own smithing business. Thankfully Daed had no quarrel with the arrangement.

"It is better to have work than *naet*. If you are looking for someone in particular..." Daed paused, a grin tugging at the corner of his mouth. "I saw him head to the next arena."

Leah's face warmed. She had never talked of such matters with her daed before, though she was plenty aware Mamm gave him regular updates on all his kinner.

"I happened to sneak into the kitchen early for some of your mamm's cinnamon rolls and walked straight into their planning of your future." He chuckled.

Her schwestern didn't like having anyone planning their futures, but Leah was blessed to have a family invested. Hopefully they would no longer have to. Abel surely had a true interest, or he would have never tried for a second date. "Well, perhaps they should have planned on me being late."

19

"Will you be riding home with this young man?"

"*Jah,*" Leah replied, lowering her gaze. Nee, she didn't like talking about private matters with the first man to win her heart any more than he liked asking to know his kinner were accounted for. Her father grunted and gave a nod.

"A storm is coming," Daed warned before putting his focus back to his new son-in-law and a hope chest with a large, engraved horseshoe on top in front of him.

Leah scurried away before her father had any other questions to ask. She'd not once remembered a time he spoke to her about Conner.

In the next arena, animal pens lined both walls. Most were empty, with the exception of a couple of horses, three young lambs in need of a bath, and one very noisy tom turkey. She spotted Abel behind a set of bleachers with a cluster of young folk from their district. He was right there. How wonderful to know he had waited for her when he didn't have to. She went to make her way to him, but as folks were leaving or heading to the concession booth, the short hall leading into the room overflowed with too many folks. Leah didn't want to push her way past so many. Surely there was more than one entrance.

Turning around, she veered around the corner and made her way around the side of the building. The sound of voices indicated this would lead her in through another door. Briskly, she hurried along the outside of the arena wall and toward the opening. A large round bale of hay stood in her path, and Leah was just about to skirt around the bale of hay when a voice called out.

"Stop!"

"Get down!" another voice said.

Leah abruptly followed the commands, dropping to the ground on instinct. That's when she heard a wisp and a thud pass over. Still flat on the dirty earth, she looked left and spotted a group of young men near a fence line, all wide-eyed and staring. She recognized her cousin Andrew standing in the front. He'd barely turned eighteen and looked as if someone had just knocked her over. He ran to her side.

"Leah. He almost struck you!" Andrew's voice pitched and shook uncontrollably. Offering a hand, he helped Leah to her feet. Now she was dirty and later than ever.

"Struck me with what?" she said, perturbed. Andrew pointed. Behind her, Leah could see the arrow that had blown by her, buried deep within the hay bale. Suddenly realizing how close she'd come to being struck, she turned back to the men.

"You could have killed someone!" she yelled at the spectacle of onlookers. Not an innocent one in the bunch.

"Joe was just letting Barry try out his new bow. I'm so sorry, Leah, but you came out of nowhere."

"You should look where you're going, girl," an Englisch man called out. His dark gaze narrowed on her as if she had been to blame for his poor judgment.

"You should be sure of your target and your surroundings," a deeper voice replied sternly, and a sudden chill ran up Leah's spine at the sharpness of it.

"Forgive us. We shoot here all the time but should have been paying better attention," the man in a wheelchair continued to add. He had dark hair—part controlled, part unruly, under a wide brim. His tone had shifted from firm to bending and remorseful as quick as an arrow flew. Leah didn't know every face looking at her now, but she did this one.

Joseph Shetler was part of her new community, though she had only seen him a handful of times during the biweekly church service. He had stolen a glance at her that first Sunday but hadn't spoken to her once.

His beard was thin and well trimmed. Another oddity Leah had not quite grown accustomed to living here. Joe wasn't the only unwed man in the community to have a beard, whereas back home only married men abandoned their clean-shaven habits.

Joseph gripped the wheels of his chair and made his way toward her. "We truly are sorry. Are you okay, Leah?"

Leah wasn't one for staring, but when their gazes collided, she couldn't help but feel his concern. He had a look to him, she concluded—then chided herself for even noticing at all. He wasn't much older than she was, and her heart tugged noting his wheelchair. Had he suffered a terrible accident? Leah knew never to ask such things, even if they pulled at her heartstrings.

A rooster crowed from the neighboring arena. A low chuckle gently spilled out of someone's mouth, forcing her back to the present.

"I am," she replied, brushing at her dress once more and lifting her chin. She wanted terribly to reprimand him. *Them*. But as his sincere gaze studied her for evidence of a wound, she felt her temper soften. *Accidents happen*, she reminded herself. His dark eyes shifted to hers once more. She wasn't sure what words he was keeping to himself, but Leah was certain he was saying something. She instinctually touched her kapp. It felt straight. Perhaps she had a stain on it from her fall to the earth.

"I'll take it, Joe," an Englisch man said. Joe flinched as if suddenly realizing there were others about.

"Let me see you inside," Andrew insisted, reaching for her arm.

"Nee, I'm meeting Abel, and I'm already late. I should be happy to make it at all, considering you're all playing bows and arrows like kinner." She darted the men with a sharp reprimand.

"If you did get hit, it would have been your fault. Who walks through a target range?"

"I didn't know it was a target range," Leah defended. The taller *Englischer* simply liked to argue.

"Perhaps this is a good lesson to each of us, and we would be better off shooting elsewhere from here on. I'm not one for repeating mistakes." Heads nodded in agreement with Joseph's wisdom. At least no more lives would be in danger.

Leah did feel her own guilt for not paying better attention. She also nodded, proof that she too was capable of learning from past mistakes. It was no excuse, however, for why they chose so close to the arena for such foolish play. "You are all forgiven, and I'm glad you made the sale," she said with a bit of pluck in her tone before rushing to the nearest door and straight to Abel. Surely nothing else would stand in her path today.

CHAPTER TWO

Joe Shetler felt his heart leap into his chest the moment the arrow was freed from the bow and a woman hurried into its path. Thankfully, she didn't hesitate to follow a blind command. As he stared up at Leah Wickey, his newest neighbor, he could see she was contemplating her next words as she studied his chair and the small lot of enthusiasts who had gathered while he and Barry Anderson, owner of Bucks and Beards Hunting Reserve, tested out the new Matthew's Lift compound bow.

Joe didn't like pity, even if it came from a pretty newcomer. Nee, pretty was an insufficient word. Too simple, and it lacked direction, assurances, or exclamation. Flowers were pretty. Stars were pretty. Leah Wickey was something dreamed up in the imagination. And he almost killed her by letting Barry shoot his bow into a hay bale conveniently sitting next to the south arena.

Blue eyes looked down on him, laced with a hint of empathy and mingled with a touch of fury. Her folks had more than their share, buying up more land than anyone could, and he doubted she experienced many struggles of her own.

Rueben and Lilly Wickey were a bit interesting, Joe had thought upon first meeting them last fall when they attended two church services. They had scouted the area before purchasing a 394-acre parcel with a run-down house that would serve them better as kindling while they built a home that might last.

He'd met the eldest son, Amos. *A mirror of the father.* The boy could go on for hours spouting about deer genes and breeding and some critter named The Fed. Apparently the Wickeys owned one of the massive buck's offspring, and that meant something. Joe didn't know much about deer aside from the fact that they made good jerky and stew, but most of his customers were avid hunters, so he tried to pay attention. No matter, he couldn't see spending money to breed a bunch of does all because some buck had a silly name.

Amos was just old enough to attend gatherings, had big thoughts and wants, and never shied away from how easy either was to obtain. Joe had been taught from the cradle that there was no room for pride or boasting, but it was plain to see that not all Amish communities were alike. While some had so little, some had more than plenty. He didn't know much about deer farming, but clearly there were big bucks in. . .well. . .big bucks.

One corner of his lip hiked at the pun. Deer, to him, meant hunters. Joe knew something about that since he owned Shetler Outdoors & Archery. He sold crossbows, bows and arrows, knives, and other same such to equipment enthusiasts—from the yearly bowhunter to the avid sportsman who liked to compete on occasion at the local 4-H fair.

It wasn't a common trade among his plain community, but Joe didn't consider himself common, and he was a fine shot with a bow. The match was made after the former shop owner retired, and it suited him better than working part-time for Willis Wickey's cabinet shop. Despite being in a wheelchair, Joe had learned to master cutting materials, assembling parts, and varnishing wood, but it was at his shop where he felt most at home. Where a day's work kept his mind sharp and didn't send his body into spasms and fits.

Joe knew that aside from Leah, there were two other girls in her family—and both newly married. Joe's mamm was adamant on keeping him up on the latest news. It had wondered him why Leah wasn't already taken up too. Yet, according to his bruder, Levi, she was. . .complicated. Joe didn't know much about that. She looked hurried, a little shaky from a near-death experience, but not so complicated. Then again, what did Joe know about such things? He'd stopped going to youth gatherings long ago when it was clear that no one wanted to marry a man incapable of standing on his own two feet.

Levi had been courting Elizabeth Wickey for almost a year, and Lizzy revealed Leah had stepped out a couple of times. Accepted a ride home from the scant available men their age.

Joe's closest friend, Jacob, said she was in search of a husband. Jacob found her friendly enough, but Jacob wasn't in the mindset of courting. Joe felt sorry for Jacob. For as much as Joe's life had been altered by one bad decision on his part, Jacob's had been changed forever when his parents left the faith just months after his only sister died in a car accident that had taken the lives of many in the community.

Joe tried to adopt such a mindset, but the truth was he wanted a family. He longed for someone to fill the quiet moments in his life and kinner to cradle of his very own.

He studied the pretty face above him. Ivory soft skin, speckles of red dotting her cheeks from her frustration, and lips that mimicked Mamm's blooming hibiscus flowers. Then he glanced down at his legs, useless now, though at times he welcomed the ache they brought on. That was when he knew they weren't completely lifeless.

He'd only been fifteen when life changed course and delivered him a hard blow. While other youngies old enough to take part in activities did so, Joe and his closest friends roamed to the back of Ervin Graber's farm. The creek beds were swollen, but the current was gentle enough no one had to fear being carried away. The day was so warm that swimming was everyone's first thought.

Joe wanted to be the first. He'd always wanted to be first at most things. Bragging rights were utmost at that age. Despite how that decision changed his life forever, Joe was grateful he was the first to jump. If Jacob, or even his own bruder, had gone first, they'd be sitting in this chair now, not him. No one knew of the dangers that lurked just below the water's surface. How heavy rains forced objects from their natural place.

He remembered jumping. The fast fall, followed by the enormous pain that barreled through his body. He cried out, but underwater no one heard his cries. Thankfully, those with him had a clear view above of the moment his body made contact with stone.

Jacob had been the first in the water, while Levi ran for help. The following days were a blur of surgeries and medications that made him drift in and out of consciousness, numbing any further needs to cry out. The following week came the tests. Joe never forgot the look on his mother's face when doctors said he'd never walk again. Breaking bones was far less painful than a mother's tears. Everyone told him to keep the faith, so Joe was determined. He prayed feverishly, but nothing changed, and that's when Joe learned that not all prayers were answered.

Doctors worked hard, pinning together all the shattered pieces of his hips, pelvis, and legs. Still, after all that piecing together, mobility continued to elude him. He'd been a skinny kid who quickly grew stronger so his upper body could handle maneuvering himself in and out of his chair. After six long weeks, he was finally able to go home, as long as he continued his weekly appointments with physical therapists.

What a waste of a man's time. No matter how hard Joe worked, the pain head-butted any last hope the doctors might be wrong. It kept him awake long into the nights and visited him each morning. Months shifted into years. A teenager still, he tended to have no tightly held reins over his emotions. Too much change going on to wrangle one thought over another. During those early days, anger came quickly upon mounds of frustration.

Why him? Why had he, after so many jumped into that creek, been met with a different result? Where was God when his mamm cried and when he begged for mercy?

Thankfully, years tamed that angry boy. His father was not only a fine minister to the community but to his family as well. Daed had bestowed great patience, helping Joe with understanding and then acceptance.

There were times even now when Joe felt a wave of shame wash over him, recalling those first two years. The blame he pointed out. The anger he fed. The sudden slipping of faith when miracles didn't appear and he wasn't made whole again. But as with any man's plight in this world, the temper drew cold, and acceptance found its footing. Sometimes the answer was simply no.

God had spared his life that day. He was grateful for that. He allotted him a mother who prayed and cared over him, a bruder who stood at his side, helping him along the way, and a father who reminded him daily to look to Gott for all answers and guidance. As years disappeared behind him, the aches and pains lessened, only rearing their ugly heads if he overexerted himself or put his body into too many uncommon positions.

He'd carved out a life for himself, a home of his own, and a business that provided him with a fair livelihood. He'd never lean on the community again after all they had done to see him through those trying times.

Joe shifted in his seat as he watched Leah, her *lopa*—that ruffle of fabric sewn to the back of her dress indicating one's baptism—pointing outward on her dress, race toward the arena opening. She'd mentioned Abel. *Abel Lambright?* Of course, there was no other Abel in the community. As she disappeared inside, Joe wondered what it would feel like to know someone was that eager to see him. That someone would run to him.

"Hi, Abel," Leah greeted as she drew near. He wore a light green shirt and a fresh-shaven face among a cluster of friends who all turned when she spoke. Barbara Yoder took one look at Leah and strolled off, Ruben Paul after her. Oh how Leah wished Barbara would accept her apology.

Abel's forehead creased as he looked at her. Suddenly, Leah felt the air still. Beside Abel stood Elaine Shetler, the local schoolteacher. Leah's bruder Mitchel was in his last year of school, and already she had written Mamm two notes that he very well might need to repeat his final year. Leah knew her youngest brother learned at a turtle's pace, but outside the classroom, he thrived at learning. Had she not taken such in account?

"I'm sorry I was late, but you wouldn't believe. . ." Why was Elaine standing so close to Abel and looking as if she might have swallowed a gnat?

"*Was iss letz?*"

"Sorry, Leah, but. . ." Abel looked to Elaine, who quickly displayed a pale blush before ducking her head. His face too had suddenly grown a deeper shade of red.

"I asked Elaine if I could take her home." Abel removed his hat, stepped forward, and lowered his voice. No doubt the look of shock on Leah's face was the reason. Those standing within earshot averted their gazes, as if watching folks leave was more interesting than witnessing public rejection.

Leah inhaled a deep breath, appreciative of their willingness to not make this harder than it was. "Oh," Leah commented. "I see."

"This is the second time we planned to meet, and though not your fault," he politely expressed, "things didn't work out." His shoulders lifted toward his ears. "Perhaps this is for the best for both of us."

There was no judgment or resentment in his tone. Did she dare mention that none of this was her doing? Abel was kind and forgiving. He was the perfect example of a husband, but he was also. . .designed for another. Leah's hopes that real love had finally found her were swallowed up when he began to fidget with the brim of his hat, digging a thumbnail between the twisted straw braids. She let out a silent breath. She was familiar with awkward moments. Conner had schooled her well in them. How many times had he forgotten to pick her up for a gathering or missed a supper because he was too busy with his *Englisch* friends?

No matter. Leah would not begrudge love, even if it continued to elude her.

"Perhaps it is. Have a nice evening, Abel." With head held high,

Leah turned to walk away. She'd not think of Conner. She'd not dwell on how many times she felt God put someone in her path only to discover they were just passing by. She'd not scrutinize what made Elaine more worthy of Abel. Surely they had known each other their whole lives. She was a newcomer. God made all kinds. Did He not?

Careful of her footing over the uneven arena floor so as not to fall and ensure further embarrassment, Leah walked away—and kept walking until she found the darkest, quietest corner to hide in.

"Lord, I'm not sure what part of Your plan Abel was, but when will it be my turn?" She just needed a few moments to regain her composure. No matter, she'd not cry. Nee.

He was out there. . .her perfect match. . .somewhere.

Leah had only meant to stay hidden until she was certain Abel had gone. She wasn't going to face him a second time today, but when the sound of rain began beating on the metal roof above her head, she knew she had let too much time pass.

"Oh no!"

Hurrying out of the dark corner, she noticed few people remained. Folks were clearing out in a hurry. At the opening, she groaned, very unladylike, as the rain fell harder. Under the eave, she could barely make out shadows racing to cars under fast-moving waves of the downpour.

"Daed!" she called out, finally realizing her vulnerable situation. Abel no longer was seeing her home, but hopefully her parents were still there. Ducking her head, as if that would make getting wet less likely, Leah raced out of the opening and to the arena next door where her family had been earlier.

The wagon that had been in the center of the room sat full, but Daniel no longer stood in the center of it. There was no sign of her twin sister or Mamm, but a few folks were packing up folding tables in the far corner.

"Is it over?" she asked.

"Jah. They are calling for a bad storm, and it hit sooner than any of us expected. Best be getting on now." The older Amish man waved her on.

At the sound of a door slamming outside, Leah noted the large gray truck heading for the road. In the passenger seat was Daniel.

"Wait!" Leah waved both arms and ran toward them, but it was no use. Neither the driver nor her family saw her.

Lightning cracked the air, causing her to jolt. It was storming. She was alone. And though she didn't believe in wasting tears on stupid things but true heartbreaks and the death of loved ones, Leah let the tears fall.

CHAPTER THREE

"I thought the storm was holding off until tonight," Edsel Eicher grumbled as he stared up at a darkened sky. "Best get on now."

A few raindrops landed on Joe's straw hat. He didn't mind a little rain. He was happy to make a sale. He watched Barry dig through his wallet. The Englischer never flinched at having the newest and best.

"Here ya go, Joe." Barry handed him a handful of one-hundred-dollar bills. "I'm sure this one will bring me another big trophy for my wall."

Joe nodded and tried not to mention that hunting should be for providing food for his family, not for sport, but Barry Anderson lived to outshine those around him. His authoritarian tone, mixed with that of a man who often competed and won the yearly archery competitions, told Joe he'd be wasting his breath mentioning it.

Joe tucked the bills into his pocket as the rain beat down in a heavier cadence. It was best he left now too, considering he hadn't reserved a driver today.

Saying farewell to the men, Joe made his way to the nearest building front just as the clouds opened more fully. Folks rushed to their cars and vans. Perhaps he shouldn't have lingered so long over a few hundred bucks.

Joe watched a stretch of vehicles and buggies leave, as puddles began quickly forming in the lowest areas. Hadn't the Englischer who visited his archery shop yesterday told him sunshine and sixty today?

With a second groan, Joe lifted his collar. The weather had already been cool, but now it sent a sharp chill over him. Levi would be upset if he knew Joe came without safe transportation, but Joe could handle the short trip between his house and the auction barns. *Until now,* he concluded.

"No rain, the man said," Joe muttered. He should have never trusted a man who stared more at his phone than his purchases with the weather. Living close by had been handy in getting here today. He'd taken the road just like everyone else. Now it might prove more of a challenge.

He'd wait it out.

For the next hour, Joe watched vehicles tear up fields and umbrellas top every open buggy as folks aimed for home. The clouds didn't seem in any hurry to move on. It was best to get wet, take his chances now, and get on home before it grew any darker. The weather didn't seem to care that Joe would have to push his way up the muddy drive, down the narrow pavement, and up his own gravel lane before reaching the safety of his home.

Pushing his hat down firmly on his head and hooking all the eye hooks of his coat together, Joe pushed under the river of water pouring down from the arena roof and aimed for home.

After so many years, he and the chair had a good friendship, working in tandem. He was glad he had spent the extra for all-terrain wheels. His arms had grown muscle where his legs failed to do so, and he made it to the top of the incline, just fifty feet from the blacktop. That's when Joe realized his mistake.

The Englisch vehicles and their heavy weight had turned everything to soup here. If he had only tried crossing the meadow leading to his property, he would have been much better off.

"Let me help," the voice called out over the rumble of thunder and downfall of rain. Suddenly, Joe felt his chair jerk forward then backward. A weak attempt to get him out of the muck.

Peering over his shoulder, Joe nearly swallowed his tongue. Leah Wickey, soaked to the bone and grunting with all her might, was trying to get him unstuck. If ever he felt less than, it was now.

"I can get it. You better get back in with your driver. You'll be in mud up to your knees out here." He probably shouldn't have mentioned her knees, but Joe really didn't want to see her get any wetter than she was.

She must not have heard him, because she only tried harder, yanking his chair backward, shoving it forward. Mud made for a struggle. Especially the sticky kind that clung relentlessly. "You're just sinking us deeper!" Joe brushed her hands away and made another attempt.

"I'm helping you, and I don't have a driver. I can't get any wetter, and neither can you. Now, put some of those muscles to use and push!"

Joe flinched at her sharp demand. Levi had failed to mention Leah Wickey was also bossy. However, common sense told him that if he was going to get out of this rut, he was going to have to accept her help. He liked to think himself on the rescuer's side of things. Not the damsel. Dignity set aside, Joe gripped the wheels firmly and pushed with all his might. Leah shoved as well, and despite the mud now clinging to his hands, the wheels finally made a connection with packed earth once more.

"We did it!" Her voice rang out in exhilaration. No one had ever sounded so happy to be covered in mud and standing in a rainstorm.

Joe turned to face her. "*Danke.*" He blinked back water from his eyelashes. Just as he feared. Both of her shoes were barely visible under a thick layer of wet clay that made up most of the area. It was a farmer's nightmare to grow at this end of the valley.

One strap of her backpack, or purse—considering a few of the unwed *maeds* recently started wearing purses on their backs instead of over their shoulders—hung off her left shoulder. The blue of her dress had changed from the bright blue that brought out her eyes to a deep shade of murky water. Still, it didn't take much away from the look of her.

"I was in the lower arena hoping to wait out the storm when I saw you." She swiped water from her forehead.

"What are you even doing here. . .alone? Everyone's gone." He cocked his head. "I thought you were riding home with. . ." It was none of his business, and she'd not need to know he caught that bit of information she'd told Andrew.

"I thought you had a ride home," he corrected and sat straighter.

"He changed his mind," she said angrily. "My daed left before I could stop him, and well. . ." She bit her lip before her eyes collided with his again. "I don't really know that many folks yet to ride home with just anyone. A woman should be ever careful."

Joe admired her logic yet found it equally stupid. "Most are kind enough," he replied for a lack of knowing what to say. He respected her brave willingness to stay behind as opposed to asking for a ride with a stranger, but alone was not so safe either.

"Do you think one of the neighbors here will let me borrow their phone? If not, I can likely walk from here. It's only a few miles."

She craned her neck, as if to determine which of the three neighboring homes was closest. A thick strand of hair clung to one side of her neck, and he quickly averted his gaze. "I live next door. You can use mine to call a driver."

"*Sell ist goot.*" Leah smiled, and a sparkle in her blue eyes triggered a burst of interest that Joe hoped she didn't notice. If only he were the man he was before he jumped into the river. If only he were a man capable of saving a damsel in distress.

"I can't leave you out here alone. Besides, there might be more mudholes on the way." He shrugged.

"That is kind of you, Joseph Shetler."

"Joe," he corrected. Only Mamm still called him Joseph.

"Joe," she said, smiling despite them both getting wetter by the minute. "For the sake of the next mud puddle, I accept."

She knew his name, and he liked hers.

"Let's go," she said, not needing a second invitation, and started pushing his chair toward the blacktop. "I sure hope Driver Dan will let me in his van looking like I do."

"I don't think he'll mind at all." In fact, Joe couldn't imagine anyone turning her away.

As soon as they reached his drive, Joe directed Leah to the phone box at the end of the lane. There wasn't enough room for both of them, but he urged her to seek shelter inside and call her driver.

A few moments later, Leah emerged wearing a worried expression. "He doesn't answer his phone. Do you know of another driver I may call?"

Joe pointed to a piece of paper hanging on the wall nearby, the list of local Amish drivers that most folks kept at hand. Watching her dial each number, he hadn't noticed the rain had long stopped until she stepped back out.

"Not one driver is available. *EE kaw sell nit glauba!*"

Joe found it hard to believe as well. There was always someone available when his regular driver was tied up. "Let's head for the house. Get dry. We can figure this out." If he had a horse and buggy, he'd happily see Leah home safely. Sadly, Joe did not. Levi took him to church each Sunday, but Joe usually hired a driver for common necessities. A buggy proved too cumbersome to get in and out of alone, and there was still the need to stow his chair. Not many horses would bow down to his level to be harnessed up either.

If only he were fifteen again. But time could not be erased, and bad choices held grave consequences.

"What about your buggy? I mean. . ." She paused, as if realizing now if he had a buggy they both wouldn't be soaked and muddy. "That was foolish of me. I'm sorry. I didn't mean. . ."

"Folks think because the legs don't work so well, the rest of me doesn't either." He paused, giving her a serious look. "I don't have a buggy because it would be too costly to own a horse and buggy I'd seldom use, but I do fine without it."

"In Lancaster, plenty folks don't have one either," she offered with the same pitiful look she gave him just a couple of hours ago.

"Some ride electric bikes, some scooters." She shrugged.

Perhaps he'd overreacted. "They ride tractors in Indiana and Ohio." He appreciated her not making him feel different.

"They do?" She straightened and then walked beside him all the way up the wide, circle drive. She was being kind, but Joe knew she was not in a position to be anything else. She was stranded and needed his help, just as he had needed hers earlier.

When they reached the concrete porch of his house, Joe asked Leah to wait while he fetched them both a towel. She'd probably find his plain home even more so than most. More furniture meant more obstacles to move around. Only the essentials were necessary.

Before pushing himself back outside, he snagged his raincoat hanging nearby. If she thought to walk home in this weather, at least she'd not get any wetter. Outside, Joe noted Leah admiring the collection of bird feeders aligning the porch. He enjoyed watching the varied winged creatures and anticipated when the hummingbirds would arrive.

"You have a lot of feeders. Do you like bird-watching?" She accepted the towel.

"I do. The shop keeps me busy enough, but I live alone, so it helps pass the time." She moved about his porch, seemingly content to admire feeders that were in need of refilling.

"My best friend Alma and I used to go bird-watching with a group in Bird-in-Hand. I saw an indigo bunting recently."

"They're common here. Did you know the youngsters learn their songs from nearby males but not their fathers? Buntings live a few hundred yards apart, yet they all belong to the same community. Each community has a song, but they may learn the song of the neighboring community. A local song can be sung for almost twenty years, with little changes and variations."

"I didn't know that," she said, looking undoubtedly impressed. "I thought I knew a lot about birds."

He wasn't fishing for compliments and knew nothing of how to talk to a woman alone, but Joe had to admit, he did like the way she smiled at him now. "I'm sure there's plenty I've to learn yet too." Joe quirked a grin. He hadn't smiled this much in years.

"Did you know, if you see a black-eyed junco, winter is just three weeks away?"

Now it was Joe's turn to smile. "Nee, but now I do. . . Oh! I have my nephew's scooter in the shed," he suddenly recalled.

"A scooter?" She hugged her middle. "I don't like being such trouble. I can. . ." She looked beyond his small parcel. Four acres of pasture, yard, and structures. Not a flower even planted, but the fences all looked good. It had taken three times as long than if Levi had done it, but Joe proved he was capable of doing more than ringing up a sale and reading more than most by nailing and painting each board.

"It's just a scooter, and I can go with you so you don't have to make the trip alone." He'd be happy to go alongside her, extending any time he could have with her, no matter the terrain or difficulty.

Did she realize how expressive her pretty face was? "Unless you're worried someone will see us. . .together?"

"Nee," she quickly replied. "It's not that." She pulled in her bottom lip and continued clutching her middle.

"Then what is it? It's because of my chair, isn't it?"

"Nee, I don't doubt you would see me home fine. It's. . .I don't do well on bikes," she admitted.

Joe couldn't help but chuckle a little. "It's a scooter. Safer than a bike, and I'll be at your side, unless you want to wait out the rest of the storm and risk both our reputations." Joe pointed to a dark horizon.

"I should have never gone to the auction today," she muttered, still looking uncertain.

"We can't know how the day will be." Though right now, Joe was plenty happy that was true. "I have half a mind to speak to Abel about this. Even if he changed his mind, he was responsible to see you home."

"I don't think there was enough room in his courting buggy for me, him, and Elaine."

Joe suspected Elaine had eyes on Abel for some time and was just waiting for him to ask her for a ride home. Still, it shouldn't have been the day he promised a ride to another. "She's my cousin, and nee, there wouldn't have been much room. Elaine tends to have her way when her mind is set on it."

"It matters not now. Things happen for the best I guess, but. . .it's not easy being looked over." She stared at him in such a way that Joe felt her inner struggle. Being a newcomer wasn't easy. Being disabled wasn't either.

"No, it's not." His dark gaze bore into hers. They had more in common than birds and rainstorms. They knew the sting of rejection.

"Fine. Where is this scooter?" She moved off the porch and aimed for the barn.

Joe started to make his way down the ramp when she turned.

"Joe, I can get home from here. No sense in you taking me and risking being on the road so late. I'll return the scooter tomorrow." And she disappeared into the shed.

Joe sat on his porch as clouds churned overhead, waiting to let out another flood, and watched Leah push down the drive and up the road. She considered him, and that meant something. He didn't even care that he was still soaked to the bone. Those blue eyes saw him, and it was recognition he saw. Not pity. He watched until Leah reached the short dead-end lane of Robin's Nest Road before his lips curved into a frown.

If only he had two legs and a buggy.

CHAPTER FOUR

Tardiness was becoming a problem, Leah realized as she pushed herself along the blacktop. Hadn't she always been dependable before? The moment Leah found herself alone, she'd suddenly felt like a kitten without a home. But she wasn't the only one left behind and welcomed the stranger's help.

"Not really a stranger," she told the wind. Joe lived only a mile away.

Sitting on his porch and looking as if she had just swum the Atlantic only confirmed that she had to try harder to secure a husband. Surely no sensible woman ever found herself stranded before. She *must* try harder. Even if that meant hours of unwavering baking with Mammi Iolene. That was a deal breaker for most men, Mammi Iolene insisted. Conner had never minded her lack of experience in the kitchen. *He never* minded *anything*, she reminded herself as the scooter wheels crunched on the gravel road. He ate like a man without taste buds and found rules to be something one conquered, not submitted to.

Leah wondered if Joe ate well. With his disabilities, who baked for him? He lived alone. Did he like cake or pie or muffins?

He was not hard to look at, though Leah tried not to entertain staring at handsome men after what happened with Barbara Yoder's intended. But the way Joe grinned up at her formed a bubble of joy around her heart. He was kind and attentive, insisting she wear his raincoat despite being wetter than a fish already. Conner never even remembered to keep an umbrella in his buggy all the years they'd courted.

She made her way into the drive, a lantern in the window setting her nerves at ease. There was enough mud caked on her shoes, socks, and dress to start a pottery company. In a sea of bad days, this was certainly rising to the top. Another rejection. Left behind. A storm that came much too soon.

But you weren't alone.

Nee, she wasn't, and Joe's laid-back demeanor had been just what she needed. His plight, stuck as he was, reminded her that everyone got into a fix from time to time. Leah wasn't alone. Joe was there. From the moment Leah spotted the shadow in the distance, she hadn't hesitated to lend a hand and get him out of his predicament. She could never imagine a life where she couldn't come and go as she wanted. A life where she had to rely on the kindness of others to get her through.

Joe was also a man of few words and of curious long looks, as if his mind tended to travel elsewhere from time to time, but helping him had certainly been the best decision she'd made in the last three years. His gratitude shone in his wood-brown eyes, but he didn't shy away from thanking her more than once. It was nice to be appreciated.

Leaning the silver scooter against the porch steps, Leah hurried up the back porch seconds before the clouds burst open once more.

The two-story home was half the size of the home she had been born in. The attic smelled of mold and neglect, and the basement was no more than a tiny box to hide in, though no one dared with as many spiders that lived there. It was nothing like the home of her dreams, or even the second choice she penciled out when she thought she'd become a fraa. But the old house, with the help of her mamm's touch, held a strange coziness she had come to enjoy.

Soon, all those little forgotten upkeeps would be amended, as Daed had informed them last night over supper that he had sold Jo Jo, a young buck bred out of Timber King. With finances replenished, he'd have more time to focus on painting and restoring the house. To Leah's delight, he'd already turned the ground for planting a garden. Mamm was eager for a new summer kitchen, considering Beth and Daniel were currently living in the one already here, while Leah was excited to get her hands in the dirt. Leah might not excel in the kitchen, but she needed no instruction in a garden.

Through the kitchen door that squawked instead of squeaked, Leah inhaled the strong aroma of fresh bread and garlic immediately. Mamm would be upset as her new rule was that Leah help with every meal until her cooking improved. Who knew when that might be?

"What happened to you?" Beth was the first to notice her dripping all over the mudroom floor and quickly came to her side, offering Leah a hand towel.

"What a small cure for a large problem," Leah teased and swiped the towel over her face, arms, and neck. "It's raining, in case you didn't know," Leah added.

"You look dreadful." Beth grinned. She was adventurous, not practical. It made sense why Daniel Fisher was the perfect choice for her. Her heart-shaped kapp made Leah ache for her older sister Louise. Leah would never return, she'd promised herself that very day in the Kings' snowy field, but one still yearned for familiarity when surrounded by uncertainty, did they not? Nee, Leah would never risk facing Conner Brinker ever again or all the places that would remind her of him. Nee, she'd recover and move on.

"Did that *bu* forget to pack an umbrella?" Mammi Iolene planted two fists on her healthy hips and scowled. "I might have made a mistake there. If he has no more sense than. . ."

"Did he even drive you home?" Mamm hurriedly put in. Mamm lifted a questionable brow as she slipped on two oven mitts Louise had sewn for her last Christmas. The bold red mitts stood out among the plain home and dim lighting of a drab day.

"Nee, he didn't forget," Leah said. She didn't really want to relive the whole day. She'd rather eat.

"Did you offer him some of those strawberry muffins you made yesterday?" Mammi Iolene shook her head. "I told you that your cousin

Hunting for a Husband

Irene says young men like pie. No upright man wants a muffin."

"Perhaps we should let Leah answer the first question." Beth turned to Leah. "You cook just fine now. Even I've noticed. Mammi is just teasing. *Huck yersht ahna.* Just sit down," Beth encouraged, but a look of concern wore on her brows.

Leah plopped down in a nearby chair near the doorway. She was a disaster. No man would ever marry her. Her cooking skills lacked flavor and doneness. Her sewing skills barely reached acceptable under Mamm's trained eye. Other than smiling and being kind to others, she had nothing to offer a husband unless he was a fan of tomatoes.

That's why Abel had been a great choice. He didn't mind flaws. Or so she'd thought. Leah had been honest in mentioning she had much to learn yet, but Abel only laughed and told her he was terrible at a great many things too.

And he took Elaine home instead of you.

"I don't understand it. Mammi Iolene was right. He checked all my boxes!" Leah was too old to make lists and hide them under her pillow, but she'd memorized every trait that bode well for a husband.

"Daniel certainly didn't check any of my boxes, as you recall, but I've never been happier." Beth floated her husband an affectionate grin.

"If I had boxes or lists, you'd check all of mine," Daniel replied playfully, causing her twin to blush even more.

"You two aren't helping," Leah remarked. "It's my fault, really."

"How so?" Mamm didn't often encourage confidence, but she didn't ignore the lack of it.

"I was late meeting him...again."

"That's not like you." Beth's nose crinkled. She had childish features that always made her cute and adorable, even as they grew into young women. Leah favored their daed, with high cheeks and a pointy nose.

"The first time was our bruder's doing. Today, the dok had to see over a few folks, so I had to help watch over Viola and see that Lena didn't get scratched fussing over her rosebushes." Leah didn't mind watching the boppli at all. In fact, it had been the best part of her day, cradling a boppli in her arms.

"Well, perhaps you can invite him over for supper. No man can resist your mamm's rosemary chicken and roasted potatoes," Mammi Iolene encouraged. "It will give us time to work on your bread baking." She winked.

"I don't think the local schoolteacher will like me asking him to supper, Mammi, considering. . .he took her home." Maybe she was a little sore. It wasn't very Christian to harbor resentment toward others.

Mouths opened, forming O's as each woman registered what Leah was saying. Daniel simply pretended his shoes needed to be tied to avoid eye contact as the kitchen grew silent. That's what he got for lingering in here instead of outside with the rest of the men.

"You can call Cousin Irene or write to her." Mammi Iolene strolled to the hutch and pulled out a notebook. "I have her address."

"Leah doesn't need advice from Cousin Irene." Beth rolled her eyes.

"Then. . ." Mammi Iolene seldom looked frustrated. Proof Leah was challenging her more than Beth ever had. "We can call on Hazel Fisher. Word is she knows about these things. Folks say one visit to her bakery, and she'll find your match."

That sounded too good to be true, which meant it probably was. "I'm not visiting a matchmaker. I'm tired and wet and need to change."

"Don't be opposed to an arranged marriage. You don't have to accept on the spot. Just let Hazel see if there is a match for you."

"I don't want anyone choosing a husband for me."

"There is no shame in it. I hear Irene is seeking advice from a matchmaker."

Irene again. Leah rolled her eyes. Cousin Irene couldn't be very good at courting if she needed a matchmaker, Leah wanted to say.

"I thought she was courting Isaiah Bontrager," Beth put in, but Mammi ignored her as she often did when her mind was set on one thing.

"You need a husband, and he will be blessed to have you no matter how the match is made."

"Leah will find her match in time. There is no rush, but I'm curious: How did you get home?" Mamm prodded as she pulled a large pan from the oven. Leah was cold, wet, and hungry for the pizza dish.

"Joe Shetler was there. He had some trouble, and I helped him. He lent me a scooter." The matter that she spent the last two hours with him would only persuade Beth to tease her and Mamm to fret over her more than she already did.

"Joe." Mammi Iolene tapped her chin in search of recognition. "The minister's *sohn* owns a scooter?"

"It was his nephew's."

"That was kind of him," Mamm added as looks passed among everyone. Leah appreciated that Mamm didn't mention Conner as she so often did. But Leah quietly realized Conner Brinker would have never been as attentive as Joe had been.

"It was." Leah got to her feet, not the least bit interested in another conversation about forgetting Conner. In fact, it was mighty hard to forget someone with so many constant reminders.

She hurried toward the stairs around the corner before her brothers arrived and would no doubt tease her. Amos and Mitchel poked enough without seeing her in disarray tonight. *Not Caleb,* Leah thought with a smile as she raced up groaning, whiny stairs and into the last bedroom down the hall. Caleb tended to be a worrier, like Mamm, and would never poke fun at anyone.

Quickly worming her way out of the damp clothing, Leah washed away as much mud as she could before slipping on a dry dress. Downstairs, muddled whispers said her family was already discussing who they'd match her with next. Why was love so complicated?

Ignoring that it was May, she put on a pair of thick socks. The weather seemed about as in sync with the season as she was. Her hair was in desperate need of a washing, but that would take longer than she had before supper, so she quickly combed away a few of the tangles, twisted it into a fresh bun, and placed a kerchief over it before slipping back downstairs just as her father and brothers entered the house.

Once the food was all laid out, Leah took a seat next to Beth and bowed her head for the silent prayer. She'd missed Beth and was already feeling an ache of separation knowing she would be leaving soon.

Food was passed in orderly fashion, and forks went to work faster than usual. Mamm's pizza casserole seldom left room for chatter until the dish was clean.

"I forgot to mention it, but a letter arrived for you today. . .from Alma." Mamm looked to Leah and half smiled, knowing a letter from her best friend was the perfect ending to a miserable day.

"I've missed her so much," Leah said.

"She is just a post stamp away," Daed replied, his fluffy beard flowing with his movements, and one ragged suspender had her wondering if he'd caught it on something.

"Louise called as well," Mamm announced with an extra twinkle in her eye. Leah set her fork down, as did Daed. Any word from Louise was welcome news.

"I sure hope Marcus got the planting in. Almanac says a dry spell is coming," Daed mentioned. He didn't normally follow weather predictions, but since his eldest had married a farmer, he now subscribed to two farming magazines as well as purchasing the *Farmer's Almanac*.

"He did," Mamm replied. "I feel we should go visit them, come time for harvesting."

"I don't want to spend fall harvesting peppers or cabbage. It'll be breeding season here. Louise can pick a pepper as easy as she can make jam," Amos said, sounding none too happy about the idea.

"We can all help. Louise may not be. . .able to do so by then." Mamm's eyes twinkled again.

"*Ei. Ei. Ei*," Mammi Iolene muttered. "She will need plenty of rest, considering she is now in the family way," Mammi Iolene revealed, earning her a darted look from Mamm.

Leah was overjoyed with the blessed news. Louise was expecting a boppli. Leah was going to be an *aenti*! Turning to Beth, Leah couldn't help but notice Beth's smile looked forced.

"That's *gut*. That's gut," Daed said, sitting taller now. His smile was not to be contained.

"You'll be grandparents," Daniel put in. "I know that makes you both happy." Daniel jerked then quickly shoved a forkful of pepperoni smothered in stringy cheese into his mouth. If Leah wasn't mistaken, Beth kicked him under the table.

"Hope it's a bu. We have too many girls already," Mitchel remarked.

"We have the same amount of both," Leah reminded him.

"Jah, which means we have too many girls."

While her bruders made jokes, Leah played a picture in her head of Louise and Marcus' upcoming arrival. What beautiful kinner they would have. What a blessing to know Louise was loved and now would become a *mutter*.

"Whose scooter is by the back door?" Amos lifted his forkful, his beady eyes aiming Leah's way. Leah quickly resumed eating.

"I already told you it's Joe Shetler's," Caleb spat. "You got corn in your ears?"

"Nee, but I'd love to hear the reason behind it, since he's not at the table with us, and I don't see how a man in his condition would ever need one."

"Amos, that is not kind to say, and food is for eating, not wasting," Mamm scolded. "Your schwester simply needed a different way home from the auction this evening."

"I knew it!" Amos pointed his fork at Leah as if uncovering some great mystery. Brothers were a thorn.

"Abel Lambright wants a fraa who can make pancakes without burning them," Mitchel teased, as he often did. Mitchel let out a yelp, followed by Beth's wide grin. Leah's twin was getting terribly physical this evening, freely kicking shins under the table.

"Leah never had to repeat the eighth grade," Beth muttered.

"I thought you had a way home," Daed said with a mix of confusion and regret. "We would have never left if you didn't."

"Plans changed."

"As plans tend to do," Mammi Iolene sang. "One cannot predict what the Lord has in mind. We are grateful the minister's son was in need, just as our Leah was. At the exact moment, let me say."

Leah fought off the urge to roll her eyes as all three bruders sat to attention, eager for details. She'd not have them feeding any rumor mills with her tragic evening, but Daed's brows lifted a tad higher, demanding more—they were not as full as most men's his age and tended to insinuate much in their sharp exclamations.

Beside her, Beth giggled. No one wanted to hear all the details, so Leah only shared the necessary ones. How she found herself without a way home, finding it best to wait out the rain then seek out a phone. Seeing Joe in the distance, struggling. His hands had become so wet that he slipped, completely losing his dignity, as he struggled to move the wheelchair.

"He was as stuck as a person can get," she concluded.

"It's gut to help others, but I'm of the mind to warn the teacher that Abel Lambright is not a man of his word." Leah hoped Mammi Iolene didn't pursue the matter, making the whole encounter more embarrassing than it was. She already had one maedel being unfriendly with her.

"He took another home?" Caleb asked, before pinching his lips tight.

At that, Amos' expression hardened without the common laughter that usually shone anytime Leah failed at something.

"Jah, we are all thankful for good neighbors," Daed made sure to add. "We got to know Joe when we first came to visit. He and his bruder Levi helped with the fences and hired others to see it done to regulation." There were many rules and regulations raising deer domestically, and each state differed. "For a man in a wheelchair, he can do more than three sons." Daed passed the boys a knowing look.

"I will see to thank him come our next church service. Amos will see the scooter returned tomorrow morning before fetching the new windows I ordered."

Leah nodded her appreciation, surprised when Amos said nothing of the added chore. She quickly ate, eager to read Alma's letter and the comings and goings of Lancaster. Hopefully she'd have time to write her back. Did she dare mention Jacob or Abel?

"You should make him a pie," Mammi Iolene said abruptly. "He came to your rescue, and you saved him from dying of pneumonia!" Leah wished to add that they helped each other, but Mammi was not one to let her thoughts be overlooked. And that's when Amos and Mitchel started laughing and couldn't stop.

CHAPTER FIVE

The outdoors target range was soft and damp thanks to overnight rains, but Joe never turned down a chance to shoot a few arrows or make a possible sale.

"I wish you'd enter. The prize is over twenty-five hundred dollars this year." Brandon Carlton was barely old enough to drive a car, didn't own a pair of pants without holes in them despite his family's wealth, and spoke so fast that Joe often struggled to keep up. But he was a regular customer, a hunting enthusiast, and worthy of trying to understand.

"I don't compete. What do you think of this broadhead?" Joe angled the arrow to present the Iron Will S100. It was pricier than the Magnus Hornet, but Brandon always wanted the best. Joe shifted in his chair, hoping for a sale instead of more talk of competitions.

Every year, the third week of June, the Outdoors Field Archery Competition, or OFAC, was held at the local 4-H center. Joe simply loved the feel of a bow in his hand. The tension of the string as his eyes trained on a bull's-eye. It was controlled and precise when few things in life were. That moment when a man exhales and a swish quivers his gut as contact is made. But competing stroked pride, a sin he would never entertain again. It didn't mean a few Amish men didn't. Prize money often conflicted with men who struggled and young boys not yet baptized. They'd pay a fee to enter and, at the end of the day, walk away empty handed, humbled, and beaten.

"You're the best shot around. Barry has been practicing nonstop with that new bow you sold him and still can't outshoot you."

Barry was a good shot, winning two years in a row, but Joe didn't require validation. He simply was good at what he enjoyed.

"Don't tell me this is an Amish thing." Brandon rolled his eyes. His close relationship with Barry Anderson was only in hopes that Barry would hire him as a new hunting guide, but even Barry knew the young man talked himself up more than he could deliver.

"It is. We don't believe in competing." Not once one was baptized, that was. Before his legs had been knocked out from under him, there were basketball games, swimming races, and shooting arrows with his cousins. "Pride is not something we go seeking. It's hard enough not letting it in when shooting against you two."

Ricky, Brandon's new friend who had accompanied him, asked, "You ever seen any of those bucks your neighbor's got? Sure'd be nice if a couple would jump that fence come fall. My brother-in-law, Vance, drove by the other day and saw two with racks larger than anything we've seen around here in years, and they haven't even started real growth yet."

Joe had seen them over winter for a few weeks before shedding their antlers, but considering deer started growing fresh antlers in spring, he reckoned those velvety horns were turning a few heads. "I don't go gawking, and they're more like pets you gotta feed." No sport in that. "But I assure you, they won't be jumping any fences."

The sound of that familiar *clippity-clop* on pavement drew everyone's attention. Joe turned as it slowed. A high-stepping gelding trotted up the drive with wide eyes, fighting restraint, eager for freedom. The animal had worked up quite a lather, indicating it had been working harder than necessary to travel the short distance between the Wickey farm and his.

In the seat were Leah's brothers. Joe had hoped Leah would return the scooter herself but knew better than to hope for such. With that, the vision of her flickered through his thoughts. He didn't like being vulnerable to others, and Leah finding him stuck in a storm certainly constituted vulnerability, but her kindness and his concern for her overshadowed what would have normally been an embarrassing tale. In fact, Joe didn't need to be stubbornly independent with her. He only wished he was, because of her.

Why had he been so quiet when he could have gotten to know her a little more? He was an avid reader and a decent conversationalist, according to Levi.

"Excuse me, fellas." Joe handed Ricky his bow and the extra arrow. It was safer in Ricky's hands than Brandon's after spending all morning lining up the sights that Brandon had a habit of getting out of line.

Making his way to the barn opening that sat adjacent from his shop, Joe watched as Amos, Caleb, and Mitchel climbed out of the buggy. His gaze traveled once more to the horse. A beautiful animal. He had excellent conformation; a flat, long back; and a well-shaped head. His jet-black coat shimmered under a frothy heat. He wasn't a typical Amish buggy horse. This was a horse for impressing girls. A racetrack cull. Not practical at all.

"Hiya." Caleb was the first to greet him. "Hope we didn't interrupt anything." Unlike the eldest, this one had a softer look to him that spoke of a kindness that matched his schwester.

"Nee, just sighting in a bow and trying to make a sale. Danke for returning the scooter. My nephew will be glad of it."

"No problem. We were heading to the bulk store anyhow. Mamm has a list." Amos grinned as he lifted the scooter from the back of the buggy. His horse sidestepped, spooked by the sounds of the scooter being removed. Amos dropped the scooter and quickly wrapped a hand around the horse's bridle.

"I got it," Mitchel said, and pushed the scooter under the eave of the building.

"New horse?" Joe asked with a hint of chastisement. Three young men had no business with such an animal. It was an accident waiting to happen.

"Jah, he's the best there is. Got him straight from Indiana. He's a bit lazy climbing hills, if you ask me," Amos replied as he held tighter to the horse.

Joe shot him a stern brow. "Perhaps he's not a fan of pulling a buggy. More for racing, I'd think."

"He'll learn."

Joe suspected Amos had a stubborn streak to run parallel with his prideful one. "If you need help training him, I suggest you speak to Silas Graber."

"I don't need help training him." Amos glared. "I've been riding since I was old enough to walk."

It was clear the youngie didn't want to take advice from a man who hadn't ridden a horse in over ten years, but he had no idea the dangers of such an animal on the road. It was one thing to put yourself at risk, but Joe, in good conscience, couldn't ignore that Amos had his brothers with him.

"Leah had to work today but asked us to give you this." Caleb reached into the buggy and collected an apple pie.

"It's a thank-you, and though it's from Leah, no worries, Mammi Iolene baked it." Amos winked.

"I'll sure find a spot for it, no matter who made it." Joe grinned. Did the Wickeys know he had a thing for pie? Joe wouldn't be surprised if his own mamm hadn't slid that somewhere in conversation. She had a habit of talking up all her kinner to anyone willing to listen.

"Joe, I'll take those new broadheads, but Dad called and needs the truck. Can we come back later and finish shooting targets?"

Joe waved his approval. Brandon smiled widely before he and Ricky climbed into the new Ford and drove away.

"You have a target range out there?" Caleb inquired with a glint in his pale eyes.

"I do. Customers like to try out the best fit for them before buying." He looked to Amos once more. "The best isn't always the best," he said before turning back to Caleb. "Buying a bow isn't one size fits all. Folks need one they're comfortable with and serves their purpose correctly." Joe suspected the Wickey brothers were much like Brandon. Capable of buying expensive things but not capable of keeping the sights in place.

"Can we shoot?" Mitchel asked, craning his neck between the archery shop and the single-story home. It wasn't practical to have a home larger than he did. He'd never maneuver stairs, but the dark gray, acceptable within the Ordnung, was a bit boring. Joe liked color. Perhaps he would take his mamm and schwester up on letting them plant flowers.

Concrete aligned much of the property walkways, as well as a wide path to the shop and barn, thanks to his folks. Joe didn't like that they insisted on paying for such an expense but had to admit it made getting from one place to another easier, especially in foul weather.

"You own a bow?" Joe asked.

"I do, but it won't shoot straight no matter what," Caleb informed him. "Our old bishop didn't like us using them, so it only got moved around a lot and barely used. Not even sure I'm any good at it."

"Well, we're still waiting on a bishop," Joe replied to the younger bruder. Since the split of two growing communities, this end of Cherry Grove fell in line with the northern side of Miller's Creek. "But none of the three ministers mind us hunting with them."

"We aren't into hunting," Amos said.

Why the young man went out of his way to be difficult, Joe hadn't a clue. "I need to close. My bruder is picking me up. It's my mamm's birthday, but bring your bow by the shop sometime, and I'll give it a look. We'll have it splitting hairs in no time," he told Caleb. Yes, this one did put Joe in mind of Leah.

As the brothers made their way out of the drive, Joe couldn't help but shoot up a prayer for their safety. He remembered the days when he too didn't want to listen to others. Glancing down at his legs, he wished he had.

CHAPTER SIX

Joe wrapped an arm around Levi's shoulders as his brother helped him into the buggy seat. Levi was not only built sturdy, he was also a stickler for punctuality. Once Joe was seated, Levi secured his wheelchair on the back and bounced into the seat next to him.

"I don't think you helped at all that time," Levi teased and took up the reins. He'd helped Joe from buggy to seat since they were boys, never fussing for seeing Joe to gatherings or carting him to the store. God might have not given Joe the life he imagined, but he had given him much in his brother.

"Maybe you're getting weaker," Joe teased in return as the buggy moved onto the blacktop. Cherry Grove dipped and rose and twisted in a smooth cadence. Joe glanced toward the Wickey farm, barely catching a glimpse of the top of the new roof under an evening sun. He wondered in passing if Leah was readying supper, but the pain in his hip overtook pleasant thoughts.

"Maybe you're eating too many of Mamm's cherry pies."

It was always that way between them—playful. Passing the schoolhouse, Joe thought of their younger years, when Levi had relied on him. If that boy Joe had once been knew what the man he now was knew, he would have never been so unruly, so eager to try brave new things.

Levi had always shadowed him. There was barely a year between them, but thankfully, Levi hadn't followed close behind him that day.

He was clean shaven, tired from his work on the construction crew, but still had an eager glint in his matching dark eyes for what came next.

Joe appreciated Levi, but sometimes Levi could be a fusser. Much of his family was of the same mind. *Not Daed*, he reminded himself. Joe clutched his independence tightly, learning to do as much as he could. No one wanted to be a burden, and more often than not, his devoted family insisted on helping. Overhelping set limits on disabilities, but who complained about having a family who loved you through so much?

"Mamm has no idea we all are coming for supper." Levi veered onto Hummingbird Lane.

Round bales of hay dotted an eastern field. Having lain all winter without being taken from the field, their nutrients were now dense. Along the ditches, bright red cardinal flowers bloomed. Jah, perhaps he'd let them plant flowers like those. "Little gets past our mother." Joe shifted in the seat in search of comfort. Pains came and went, as unpredictable as the weather.

"Like that time we tried to hide Jasper in the barn." Levi chuckled. Boys liked dogs, so when they found out their elderly neighbor had a litter of beagle hounds free to good homes, it was like expecting them to sit at a table of pies with a fork in each hand and not touch one.

"She was *verra* angry, but Jasper grew on her." Joe winked. Their mother didn't go anywhere on the farm that Jasper wasn't on her heels. The pup grew into a lazy *hund* who knew where the best scratches behind the ears and treats came from.

"Looks like Lester has a truck in," Levi remarked as they neared two large metal buildings and a quaint little brick home. The box van, which made monthly deliveries of food goods from the major wholesale grocer, was parked in the machine shop's driveway. "Should we stop and help?"

That was Levi, always ready to lend a hand. "Looks to be finished," Joe replied as Lester and the driver came walking out of the large gray building.

"Folks are mighty thankful he let them use his shop." The local machinist had spent a stint in the Englisch world before returning home with a son and no wife. It had been all the talk, but his kindness outshined his past. Lester Milford allowed for secondhand market foods to be delivered to his shop from the wholesaler so they could be distributed among those in need. Joe wished his past was as easily overlooked, but with one glance at him sitting in a chair, folks were easily reminded of the day he acted recklessly.

When the family farm came into view, Joe felt immediate ease. Though he no longer lived under his parents' roof, there was something to be said about coming home.

"Lizzy's already here," Levi muttered as he brought his buggy to a stop near the long, gray metal calf barn. Daed seldom left the farm anymore. His age and worn back were telling him it was time to retire from a life of hard labor, but Daed was not one to let a day go without accomplishing much, and exchanged his hammer for raising bottle calves, two hundred at a time.

"Did you think she'd not come?" Joe teased as they were immediately welcomed by bawling calves hoping for their afternoon feeding.

"Nee." Levi blushed as he removed the wheelchair from the back.

Getting back into his chair was easier than getting into the buggy. Joe used much of his upper strength—a hand on Levi and one on the buggy—and, from an upright position, lowered himself into the leather seat.

"I'm thinking about. . ." Levi clamped his lips tight as he unharnessed his horse and pushed the buggy under the extended eave of the barn. He clearly had a lot on his mind this evening.

"About not eating whatever cake Karen has baked? Me too. I love our schwester, but her baking skills have not grown with her family." Karen had four kinner, made the best noodles in three counties, but tended to have more lopsided cakes than those that could hold up under the pressures of frosting. Joe had learned to put together a few pies and cakes himself and didn't know what all the fuss was about. He liked cooking and baking. It wasn't hard when you cooked for one.

It *was* hard to eat alone night after night.

"I'm thinking to ask her to marry me," Levi finally said as he put his horse into the small lot and closed the gate.

Joe wasn't surprised by the news. In fact, he had wondered what had taken Levi so long to take the next step. A laugh slipped out of him. "Was that so hard to admit? It's wonderful news, bruder. I think she will make a fine fraa. I do worry, though."

"About what?" Levi's brows gathered.

"That you'll be a terrible husband. You still forget to wipe your boots clean when you come into my house, and just two Sundays ago, you ate a whole pack of Twizzlers while the minister preached obedience." Joe chuckled.

"Daed had me feeding calves alone, so I missed breakfast. I got hungry!" Levi gripped the handles of Joe's chair. "No one saw me. And just so's ya know, Lizzy doesn't mind my sweet tooth." Levi began pushing Joe toward the house, apparently not caring how much Joe disliked it.

Before reaching the house, Levi stopped abruptly. "I can wait, Joe. If you want me to."

Levi didn't need his blessing. "Why wait? Life is too short to wait on starting the best parts."

"But you're older. Matt and Karen have each married and have kinner. You should be next. Not me." Levi ducked his head.

"I see." Joe nodded his head and placed both hands on his lap. He should have known Levi would consider him first. Joe hoped Lizzy knew what a wonderful man she would soon marry.

"I'm also in this chair. What woman will marry a man who can't even walk her home or take her on a buggy ride? Don't you wait, bruder. In fact, you should both run to the bishop now. To have a chance at what you have, I'd be running."

"That's not funny," Levi clucked, never agreeing with Joe's humor toward his disability.

"But we really have to consider what this will mean for you. If I marry, I'll have less time to...help you. I mean, just a few days ago you got stuck at the auction house."

"And it all worked out." Joe wished he hadn't told Levi about the embarrassing rescue, but his bruder was his best friend. Levi also had to understand things happened, and he couldn't always be there.

"I have been blessed, for sure and certain, by having you as a bruder, but I'm capable of doing much on my own. I can call a driver if need be, and Jacob lives just down the road. He won't mind giving me a lift to church. Bachelors need to stick together so all you happy folks can grow families," Joe teased.

"I'm being serious, Joe. I can still help, it's just..."

"Once you marry, you will have a family of your own and a fraa to care for." Joe knew what it meant. Although part of him had relied on Levi too much, he'd not stand in the way of what Gott wanted for Levi's life. Joe shook a finger at his younger brother. Barely a year apart, but still, Joe was the elder here. "Don't you keep from the life Gott wants for you because of me. I could never live with that burden." He'd not stand in the way of happiness. The last thing anyone wanted was to be a stone in his bruder's path.

"It just doesn't feel right. Lizzy and I would be happy if you lived with us. I mean, I know she wouldn't mind," Levi added.

"I like my house," Joe said flatly. "It's plenty quiet, and I can read without hearing you two kissing or giggling like lovebirds."

"Then perhaps it's time you consider taking a wife too." Levi crossed his arms and stared down at Joe.

"Now who's being funny?"

"I mean it. You think that chair matters? It doesn't. You have much to offer too, and the doctor said you could still have a family."

Joe felt his face warm at the personal comment. "The doctor said I could but not that I should." Nee, kinner deserved a father who could provide for and protect them. Joe looked away from his bruder. He didn't like talking about this. In the nearest window, little faces pressed to the glass. Nieces and nephews waiting for them. Joe loved his time spent with them. "Let's get inside before Matt's kinner eat everything. I'm hungry."

"There is someone out there, bruder," Levi insisted as he opened the front door. A strong waft of bacon and grilled cheeseburgers filled the escaping warm air. "Gott has her all picked out for you."

Joe wished Levi was right, but in his heart, he knew God's plan for him was not the same as Levi's. His path was different, but as Levi pushed him up the ramp and into the house, Joe had a sudden picture of Leah in his head.

His parents' house was a bustle of activity. Mamm tried not to let her smile broaden too widely as she believed it stroked vanity, but one could see she swelled in having all her kinner together. "I can't believe you all planned this without me knowing." Linda Shetler was fifty-nine and didn't believe in anyone making a fuss over her just because she was another year older.

"Our kinner have always been good at keeping secrets." Daed winked. John Shetler was only five feet and ten inches tall, but his presence always put those around him at ease. He was a carpenter by trade, with hands as worn as one who worked the chaff regularly. Joe carried many of his father's traits. Dark hair, wide shoulders, and that sideways grin when something amused him. Joe also shared his father's love for reading. They often swapped books and shared their thoughts about something they'd read recently.

Paper plates were filled for the kinner. Matt, the eldest of the lot, wrestled three-year-old twins, Flora and Dora. They were picky eaters who relied on squealing if anything unsavory touched their plates.

After a silent prayer, Joe readied a warm hamburger on his plate and began adding lettuce, tomato, onion, and Mamm's sweet butter pickles. Beside him, nine-year-old Joseph watched with curiosity as he built his sandwich in the same order. Kinner learned by watching, and Joe loved watching them learn. Kinner also never minded his disability. They had never known their *onkel* before and found taking rides on his lap a simple thrill.

"I hear that Jacob is getting a buffalo," Daed said before adding two large spoonfuls of Karen's potato salad to his plate. She might not make the best cakes, but she did make a good potato salad.

"Jah," Joe said and quickly swallowed his mouthful. "The local warden said they seized two from a farm over in the next county. The owner passed away."

"Sorry to hear it, but buffalo are a might big for one man to look after alone."

"Few critters best him, aside from that bobcat he nursed last year." Joe always felt Jacob was gifted to see over God's creatures. It wasn't until he was put to task to care for the wounded feline that he faltered.

"He had new scratches every time I saw him." Karen clicked her tongue.

"Jah, but thankfully it's free once more. Jacob can handle the buffalo or he wouldn't have accepted." Joe knew his friend well. Jacob was not a man who tested the uncertain.

"How's the shop?" Mamm asked, slicing a second large garden tomato onto a small plate.

"Gut. The indoor range does even better than the one me and Levi set up outside." Joe glanced at his bruder, who was currently stacking two burgers under one bun. His appetite was always impressive. "Levi's convinced me to order a few more things."

"It's an outdoors shop. You need fishing gear," Levi put in before sinking his teeth into his creation. Mustard dripped out of the sides, sparking a giggle out of Lizzy. The two were just hopelessly smitten with each other.

"Fishing gear, huh?" Daed shook his head, his brows gathering as they often did when he was concentrating on something. "I reckon it would do well. Have you spoken to the ministers?"

Daed followed rules without veering and instructed his kinner to do the same. "Gabriel and Lewis are fine with it," Joe replied. In truth, all three ministers had been keeping to themselves the last few weeks. Soon, a new bishop would be chosen, and no man was eager to take on the position unless called upon.

After supper, Karen presented Mamm with a lopsided strawberry cake with butter frosting. Levi gave Joe's ribs a quick jab, but both managed to keep a laugh from escaping.

Talk soon shifted to the comings and goings of Cherry Grove.

"Barbara and Melvin had a son," Mamm shared. Talk of *bopplin* was celebrated throughout the community.

"Teacher Kevin is looking for a new teacher. Seems Elaine no longer wants to teach," Daed said with a frown.

"Because she's courting Abel Lambright," Lizzy put in. "He was to take my cousin Leah home after the auctions but had a change of heart." Lizzy set her fork down, her face twisted into disappointment. "She had no way home and was left there during the storm."

"Oh, that is terrible. I hope she was all right." Karen was mortified to hear Leah had been abandoned. Joe ducked his head and studied his slice of cake, which was more frosting than cake.

"She wasn't alone. Joe here was there." Levi didn't make eye contact with Joe, and that grin was mocking. "The way I hear it, Leah is quite the hero."

Joe gave his bruder a jab to his ribs. The last thing he needed was for Mamm and Karen to go on and on about it.

"Hero?" Matt's fraa asked. "Isn't she the maed helping out Dok Stella?" Heads nodded that she was.

"Joe?" Daed said, the question rising.

Joe let out a breath and gave Levi another jab before answering. "I didn't call a driver, so when the storm hit, I was a bit stranded too." Joe's appetite diminished. That much sugar was probably no good for him anyway.

"Ei. Ei. Ei," Mamm said. "Why did your bruder not take you? You could have told us." That was Mamm, always thinking Joe needed someone at his side every moment of every day.

"I don't understand why you keep putting yourself in these situations," she clucked.

"Levi has a life beyond helping me out. One day he will have to focus on a family of his own." Two could play this game. Joe lifted a challenging brow to Levi, but he'd not share Levi's intentions. Levi just didn't have to know that. Instead, Joe took the higher road. "We cannot know how a day will play out, but instead have faith that all will be well."

"Well said, sohn," Daed replied. "But I would like to hear of this. I've yet to get to know the family, except for what folks say. If she helped you out of a fix, it would be good news to hear."

"I'd rather eat Karen's cake," Joe mumbled and gave his right leg a rub. Since he and Leah weathered the storm together, he'd been shouldering a few extra pains. Leave it to Mamm to notice.

"Yer hurting."

"I'm only uncomfortable."

"Getting stuck in the mud has put you in spasms, I reckon."

It had, but Joe didn't want his family to worry. "I'll pick up some more pills from the herbal shop soon." Just the mention of the herbal shop was a mistake.

"You need an appointment with Dok Stella soon. Matt or your daed can take you. I'll call and make sure she saves a spot for you," Mamm said.

Joe could handle making a phone call all by himself. He didn't need Matt to miss work when Driver Dan never overcharged as most drivers. "I'll call her and make the appointment," Joe replied. If he didn't, Mamm would, and it was not such a bad idea. He needed to refill a few herbs and vitamins, and Leah did work there, did she not?

CHAPTER SEVEN

Spring had pronounced itself wet and cold but quickly raced into a blistering eighty-four degrees. All morning, Leah tried everything to console little Viola, but the boppli was no happier with the humidity than Leah as sweat trickled down between her shoulder blades.

"I think a bath will do you fine." How many times had she and Beth resorted to hiding in the basement or swimming in Ronks Pond on such smoldering days? Leah couldn't count. At the sink, she readied the water and placed a towel deep into the sink to cushion the three-month-old. The more Viola cried, the more her pale, plump cheeks reddened.

"Patience, little one," Leah consoled and began removing her gown and diaper. "Crying won't get the sink filled any faster."

"What a fine idea. A bath is sure to help." Lena appeared in the kitchen. Viola's grandmother lived next door in the small *dawdi haus*, but she came and went like a northern wind. Leah never knew when she might appear. It was evident her eyesight was failing, without Dok Stella having to mention it. Leah made a point to keep a close eye on her elder. It was no hardship, considering Lena spent most of her days stirring something simmering on the stove or knitting between naps.

"That's because it's what would make me happy right now." Leah watched Lena shuffle farther into the room with her knitting bag on one thin arm and two stacked plates in the other. "I promised Michael

I'd make these today." Michael was the bishop's son, whom Leah had only met in passing, as he was either in a rush to work, visiting friends, or hoping for time with Mary Elizabeth Glick.

"Verna and Ervin were fussy bopplin when teething too. A bath also helped," Lena informed her. "Did you remember to see to all the windows? It's a might warm in here today. I've half a mind to go home and not visit today."

It was warm everywhere. "Jah, and I opened the one in the attic so as to let the warm air escape."

Lena nodded. Her thinning silver hair made her forehead look large despite her small frame. "They don't make homes like they used to." Lena sat in a chair and pulled out her latest unfinished scarf. "My Aaron built sturdy homes. These days it's all about the hurry-up."

Leah had noticed most of the Amish homes in the area were long gray metal structures. A hurry-up-and-move-in kind of home.

"They say we are in for a long drought. My blackberries did not do so well last year. I had hoped that this year would be better." Lena spoke often of her blackberries and the flower garden she still worked in daily.

"Mamm wanted to plant some, but so much is yet to be tended to on the house, and Daed's focused on feedlots for the livestock now." Leah hoped if God ever delivered her a home of her own, there would be blackberries everywhere and not a deer in sight.

"*Ach,* Gott has already provided plenty for them to eat. I reckon taming them only puts more work into it."

Leah smiled. That was Lena, straight to the point. "When you fence them in, they do need seen after." Leah slowly lowered Viola into the tempered water. The boppli stiffened at the unexpected contact but soon accepted the change and began stretching her limbs in contentment.

"Land was scarce in Lancaster, so we had to feed them special feeds. Here, Daed can plant crops like alfalfa, beets, and so on. They have more land to move about freely and naturally. He's got plenty invested in them and takes their diet very seriously."

"I see." With thin fingers wrapped around two knitting needles, Lena went straight to work. Leah had never learned to knit. It looked much like weaving, but Leah wondered how Lena did so well with her eyesight failing her.

Leah cradled Viola's head as the little one splashed the water.

"You'll make a fine mutter. Why is it you're not married yet? A woman needs kinner to look after."

Leah agreed, which was why she agreed to be a mother's helper. Children were less complicated than finding a husband. They had no huge expectations. You simply watered them in love, sprinkled on a few laughs and hugs, and marveled in watching them learn. "Guess I have trouble with the first part."

"I see. You have not lived here long. Folks are only just getting to know you. I'm sure you will have plenty of young *menner* come calling soon enough."

"Until they change their minds," Leah mumbled, but Lena oddly had impeccable hearing.

Lena set her knitting needles aside at that. "I'm all ears. Now tell me. Who was the fool who changed his mind?"

Leah stifled a laugh. "Fools," she admitted. "One was named Conner, who found the world offered him more than I could. Then there was..." She'd not mention Jacob, since technically he wasn't interested from the start. "Then there was Abel." The rejection hit Leah with a hard second punch.

"Abel Lambright? You know his folks started that berry farm with starts from my berries," Lena said as she pointed a shaky finger toward the window. "Now they charge six dollars for a handful of them." Lena shook her head. "You might be better off with someone who doesn't need what grows in another's garden but is more interested in planting his own."

A smile slipped from Leah's lips. She wanted someone who preferred planting a future with her. Was that too much to ask?

The sound of tires crunching on gravel outside said another

appointment had arrived. "Someone else has need of our dok." Lena glanced out the window. A hot wind blew her kapp strings. Leah could imagine her as a young woman. Lena bore fine features—strong yet delicate.

"What a gift Gott has given my Simon and Michael. My sohn lost so much when his first wife and kinner died, and now look." Lena looked to Leah and Viola with love in her eyes. "He's restored his heart, because his faith was so strong."

With that, Lena went back to her knitting without another word. Leah hadn't known the bishop had lost a family, but as she worked a washrag over little Viola's shoulders, she agreed God did restore the loss.

Glancing out the window herself, Leah noticed this vehicle belonged to Driver Dan. *Why would he be here this early?* It was barely four, and Dok Stella often had appointments until five.

"That's my driver. I told Stella I would stay until five today, considering it's her busiest day." Wrapping Viola in a towel, Leah went to the screen door for a closer look.

"Dan Grider drives many folks," Lena replied and shuffled to the door as well.

A hot wind blew in as dust lifted and maneuvered toward the house. Driver Dan got out. He was not extremely tall but didn't look like other drivers who sat in a van all hours of the day. Most leaned on the heavier side. Leah believed him to be in his upper sixties, and he sported what many called salt-and-pepper hair. He always wore slacks, not denim, and carried a pen in his shirt pocket as if ready to write something down.

"Did you know he used to be a teacher? Taught at the college and has even written a few books."

Leah didn't know and started to ask what kind of books when he opened the side sliding door, bent to let out the flat ramp, and backed away. The straw hat was the first thing Leah saw as the wheelchair moved down the ramp. But it was a set of wide shoulders and a tuft of black hair that told her who Dok Stella's next appointment was.

"Looks to be Joseph Shetler. *Ist gut* he's finally agreed to let Stella help. We cannot know what he's faced these last ten years, but if anyone can help him, it would be our Stella," Lena said forwardly.

"Ten years?" Leah questioned as Joe looked their way before disappearing into the herbal shop.

"He was a rowdy, as my Aaron thought him to be. Always first into the pies and hiding folks' buggies when they weren't paying attention. Linda had her hands full with him, though Matt, the eldest, was a bit of a rule breaker too." Lena's thin lips curved into a grin. "Levi would follow him like a worried shadow, fretting if he'd get too far away. Joseph was near time to join the other youth." The older woman paused, a solemnness overshadowing her expression. "After his accident, there were many surgeries, yet none gave him his legs back."

"That's so sad." It was terrible, that's what it was. Here Leah was feeling sorry for herself because she wasn't married or growing a family of her own and she'd been blessed plenty.

Lena shook her head. "Many doctors and medicines I cannot remember so well now, but I remember well hearing they tried running electricity through his legs. Don't know how trying to electrocute a man can make things better, but I'm no doktor."

"So he'll never walk again," Leah muttered. If she lived to be as old as Lena, Leah still would never understand Gott's plans. Here was a kind man. Handsome and well spoken. Yet his future looked lonely. No fraa to help him about or kinner with those same dark eyes and mischievous grins.

"Not if Stella has a say in it," Lena replied with certainty. "She's been reading up ever since Linda Shetler called her two weeks ago. We just hope he will accept it. I'm shocked he even came at all, but the first step is usually the hardest." Lena turned to Leah. "Have you two met? Oh, listen to me. You live in the same district, and two handsome youngies like you have certainly met."

"We met at the auction." Leah laid Viola on the family sofa and put on a fresh diaper and light blue dress. Surely she was ready for her bottle and a nap.

"I'll fetch her bottle." Lena disappeared into the kitchen and returned a few moments later with a warm bottle. "Did you and Joseph talk while at the auction?"

"We did." Leah tried not to let the obvious prodding trouble her; Lena had so few visitors and simply enjoyed chatting. "I didn't have a ride home, and he went to the auction without a driver. Then...the storm hit. We...sort of helped each other out." Leah accepted the bottle and nuzzled a sleepy Viola in her arms.

"I see." Lena returned to her chair and picked up her knitting once more. "That must have been quite a story."

Leah shared her and Joe's brief encounter as Viola sucked and dozed lazily. "I was glad I wasn't alone."

"But we are never alone," Lena reminded her.

Gott's promise was absolute. Viola's eyelids fluttered. *Jah*, the bath had not only given her some relief but had also worn her out. Leah rocked the beautiful child a few minutes longer before placing her in her crib in the next room.

"I see you will be using the same driver as Joseph now," Lena said as she walked back into the sitting room. "He'll be finished up soon. Best you fetch your bonnet and purse. Men have less patience than we do."

Leah hadn't considered sharing a ride, but now that Lena mentioned it, it would save on the cost. Lena began gathering her things. Surely Joe wouldn't mind.

"Don't forget the *kichlin*, dear," Lena called out to her.

"*Danke*," Leah offered. "But I don't need cookies, Lena. I ate a large lunch."

"There aren't for you, silly girl." Lena chuckled, her eyes twinkling with playfulness. "They're for Joseph. He never could resist my peanut butter cookies. Perhaps you can share them. After all, you are new here and need all the friends you can get if you want to marry before you're an old maid."

CHAPTER EIGHT

Joe pushed his chair over the tiny gravel lot and onto the concrete sidewalk. He'd left a message on Dok Stella's answering machine that he'd arrive at four. The later the better. It was no one's concern if he was visiting today.

Graber's Herbal Shop was a plain gray structure, much like many of the shops that dotted the county, but this one welcomed folks with hanging herbs from under the wide porch eaves. The front of the shop had double doors that led to different shops. On the right, Simon Graber stored up merchandise he forged from the smithy that sat between home and barn. The scent of burning wood lingered through the air, though Joe could hear no pounding of hammer and anvil.

On the left was the herbal shop. Levi often stopped to purchase fish oil, turmeric, and other herbs useful for Joe's condition. Joe didn't want to make a habit of coming here. The only two times he had come, the dok tried to convince him a massage would cure all that ailed him. It was laughable, but he wasn't in the business of making others feel small, so he avoided coming altogether.

Reaching out for the door, Joe peered toward the main house and noted the two shadows watching. He suspected one was Leah. Since the auction, she'd been heavily in his thoughts. An attraction to her would do him no good, but he had been raised right and tipped his hat her way before going inside.

Along the far wall were three wooden chairs. His eyes scanned the shelves of bottled vitamins, oils, and even organic toothpaste. In the center of the room were four small shelves, put together to form a circle, with raw sugar, beet powder, and flat, dried-out burdock leaves. Joe lifted a curious brow. He'd visited the holistic centers of Ohio, but clearly Dok Stella was something of an enigma.

Behind a closed door, he heard voices. The herbal shop was only open a couple of days each week. Joe suspected she was currently helping another, so he moved to the far wall to seek out his muscle pills. They contained a strong blend of stinging nettle, garlic, and turmeric. Once found, he began studying the scant bookshelf nearest the door.

Laughter from behind the door told him he might be waiting for a spell. Nothing was hurried. With that knowledge, he selected a book on tree bark. He'd read plenty about reflexology, medicinal oils, and vitamins to fill his own library. Nothing helped, not long term.

He had just finished reading *The Forward*, an interesting story of how a man named Michael found trees fascinating and was starting to explore the American beech tree, when the door opened. A woman dressed all in black pushed a wheelchair into the main room. A sudden jab to the chest met him, seeing a child barely eight or nine in a chair much like his own. His straw hat sat lopsided over damp, sweaty, dark brown hair. His eyes winced, probably from being worked over. Joe recalled the feeling of therapists working his muscles, trying to offer him relief, when all they did was ensure more pain and often bruising.

The boy looked his way, noting Joe's chair with similar interest, and smiled. There was a time when Joe questioned God and how He could allow for pain and suffering. He put such notions away, accepting God's will, but to see a child suffer tugged within his chest.

"Joe," Dok Stella quickly welcomed with a hint of surprise before turning back to the child's mother. "He might be sore later. Drink lots of water. It helps the muscles from contracting more than necessary."

Dok bent to the child's level and spoke in sweet, motherly tones.

"Samuel, you drink your tea and take the medicine Dr. Rafide sent for you."

Joe recognized the name, but all spinal doctors were the same. They pinned you and patched you together but didn't put much stock in miracles.

As the woman and boy made their way out the door, the child gave Joe one last look. This time no smile accompanied it. Did he fear Joe was a forewarning of what was to come? Joe shot up an immediate prayer for the boy. No one deserved this life, especially one so young.

"He fell from a pony," Dok Stella offered, staring behind them. "Landed wrong. That was three months ago, but he will walk again." Her confidence was unnerving. She couldn't know that. No one knew that, he wanted to say.

"So. . .are you ready?" She motioned him toward the little room with nothing more than a leather cushioned massage table, a cluttered desk, and a chair that rolled around on wheels.

"I don't need more than a few bottles to replenish my stock and to ask if you have something. . .a little stronger."

"But your mamm already paid for the treatment. I'm sorry, Joe. I thought. . ." Her voice didn't sound sorry. In fact, from the expression on her face, Joe suspected she and his mother had lured him here on purpose.

Joe let out a breath. "Fine, but only because you took her money. In the future, please don't do that anymore."

The dok nodded as she bit her lower lip, probably to keep from smiling. He wasn't looking forward to the massage, as it could possibly send his current discomfort into something worse.

"Didn't your doktor let you keep a prescription for the pain?"

"He did, but I don't like not thinking straight. I have a watchful diet and"—he held up the bottle of pills—"take fish oil and these. I've been out for a little over a week," he admitted. "I put some strain on things a few days ago. Figured I'd pay for it."

"Those certainly will help with some parts of it, including

inflammation, which I suspect is part of the problem."

"I just overdid it." Joe shrugged. "Mamm thinks a session might help speed up the process and help relax some of the tendons, but I'd be fine with some more ointment."

Few things offered Joe relief. He feared taking too many prescription medications and had long since resorted to taking aspirin or Tylenol to dull his aches, but Dok Stella's concoction of peppermint, tea tree, rosemary, and eucalyptus offered him relief more often than not.

"I have plenty of salve and will gladly use it while working your muscles. *Komm ena*, Joe, and make yourself comfortable. When you fell, what were your injuries?"

Joe let out a breath. He hadn't fallen. He jumped. Moving into the smaller space, he shared with the dok the injuries resulting in that one mistake. The dismantled pelvis, shattered sockets, and wrecked bones.

Half an hour later, Joe opened his wallet and dropped three twenties on the desk for ointment and a couple bottles of herbal pills. He knew all well and good his mamm paid less than that for the treatment. He couldn't understand how the woman stayed in business, not charging near what Englisch doktors did. The sciatic nerve pain, as she called it, had disappeared. Even his shoulders felt loose, and he could move his toes without fear of what it would cost him later. She had been kinder to his body than the therapists he'd visited years ago. In fact, there were times Joe was convinced they were trying to kill him, as rough as they had been. Dok insisted that pain didn't reduce pain, but gentleness was a healing balm.

"Linda told me you had therapy before. You know the drill," Dok Stella said, making change from a leather bag for him. "Lots of water, and don't over-rest it. Folks often think resting after a session is best, but muscles that have worked hard need to keep moving a little. Practice those exercises I showed you." She handed him his change.

The exercises consisted of nothing more than running his hands upward at certain points of his legs and hips to stimulate the flow of his blood. Joe didn't understand how that would do much good.

"It's common for arthritis to set up in the joints after such a fall, and considering where your injuries are centered, you could benefit from getting an X-ray to see if there is buildup in those places. Nowadays, they can go in and scrape away scar tissue and such."

Joe politely listened to the dok. He'd heard all of this before, but there was nothing to be done for his joints, considering they were fragments of what they were before. Had not that been what Dr. Gorman had told him?

"Joe, have you considered making an appointment with Rafide? Many of our folks trust him."

"I'm not going back to all of that. Dr. Gorman told it to us plain and simple. I'm broken and will never walk again. It was a big enough burden on my folks back then, and I'll not lean on others like that. I'll never walk. I've accepted that. It's been ten years."

"Jah, your muscles have been neglected, but nothing is impossible with Gott. He makes a way for things to happen, even when we can't see it. He restores the lame just as He made the blind to see. I will pray He will do both for you."

Both? He knew the verse and agreed wholeheartedly anything was possible but not if it wasn't God's will. He wasn't blind. If God wanted him to walk again, He would have done so years ago. Nee, this was his life now. He'd not lose sleep, hoping for something out of reach. He'd accept contentment in this life and be thankful for the blessings he'd received.

"I hope you come again for another session. I'll help work your legs and keep them strong. Just once a week, though three is best, but it will help you."

"They can't do anything, so what's it matter?"

"No spinal injury is the same. Each case is unique, as Gott made each of us. Each journey to getting better is different too. Your injuries are centered at the joints. Your knees and hip have suffered, but you are having feeling and can move your ankles and toes. I've been reading up on injuries centered around the hips and knees. Many of our own are dealing with scoliosis, and it's good to know what I can. I've read about a new surgery that—"

"Why would I do all of that again?" Joe cut her off.

"Because no matter what you have been told, hope is always there. Sometimes doctors get it wrong. This Dr. Gorman cannot know what Gott does. New procedures come along and change things. There is reason for hope, Joe. You are feeling all this pain, which is evidence that all is not lost. Your bones have healed, but not as they should have. You needed replacement joints." She shook her head and sat behind the desk. "You should have started five years ago, but it is never too late for one to start over again." She tilted her head sideways, her eyes softening. "That's what Simon tells me all the time. I may not be the best person to help you, but I'm happy to learn more and try. If you don't think I can help you, then you can make an appointment with Rafide. Your daed said your last appointment was over six years ago."

Joe frowned, knowing his father too had been mentioning private details with her. Joe had every intention of talking to both soon enough. "Danke, Dok, but I best be on my way. I'm not one to question God's plan for me." Joe rolled to the door and turned the handle.

"I didn't mean it that way." Stella's voice was clipped with frustration. "Oh Joe, just think about it. I know it must have been hard for you then, but I didn't know you at that time."

"What does that have to do with anything?" Joe wasn't accustomed to being spoken to so boldly by others. In fact, most avoided such topics with him.

"I think you're here not just for pain but for help. We can do this together. You won't be at the mercy of strangers, but with someone who wants to see you healed. You are young yet. There is still time for you to heal and marry and have a full life."

"Help the bu. He's got time yet." Joe pulled open the front door a little harder than he intended, and there stood Leah Wickey looking like sunrise, and the breath went out of him.

"I. . .I. . .I need a ride home, and your driver is also. . .my driver."

She presented a plate of cookies and smiled. Such a nice smile, powerful enough to disperse foul moods. Joe hoped she hadn't been standing there long, listening to the dok try to spill her hopes over on him.

"I see. That depends." Joe cocked his head and grinned.

"On what?" she asked.

"If Dan and I get some of what you have there." He smiled, instantly forgetting about Dok's nonsensical ramblings.

"You can have the whole plate, Joe Shetler."

CHAPTER NINE

Leah had remained perfectly still while Stella tried her best to persuade Joe to try something she wasn't sure of. It was a private conversation. None of her business, but on the curb of what Lena had recently shared with her, it seemed Joe's condition was possibly not a permanent one. It was hard to fathom his reasoning for not wanting help.

As the van rolled out of the drive, Leah sat stiffly on the single seat next to Joe's chair. She'd only look as if she were avoiding him if she sat in the back. She noted the brown paper bag on his lap. *Herbs and ointments?* Just last week Leah had helped Stella gather nettle leaves to dry and learned not only did nettle help with magnesium, but it did wonders for circulation and joints. All things Joe would do well to consider.

"We can see Leah home first," Joe told their driver.

"Sure thing, Joe. A gentleman always delivers the lady home first," Driver Dan said with a chuckle.

"I don't mind if he sees you home first," Leah whispered beside him. Surely, after his time with Dok Stella, he'd need to rest, and no one needed to get the wrong impression of two unwed people riding together. Not even the Englisch driver. What would her grandmother think of her riding home with a man? *She'd probably insist that Irene Yutzy never accepted a ride with a man she wasn't courting.* Mammi Iolene doted on her niece despite how many beaus she'd been known to court!

"You've already seen my house." Joe tilted his head her way, sending her heart all aflutter. Leah's fascination with Joe made no sense. He was a few years older than her but acted nothing like the boys she'd known so far. No wonder Mammi Iolene suggested a matchmaker. Leah clearly was having too many irrational thoughts lately.

"You've seen mine too," she quickly added. "I just thought maybe you'd want to rest after. . ." She held the rest of the thought.

"I'm twenty-six. I stopped taking naps a good while back." His eyes flickered with playfulness.

"I haven't," she returned and lifted the plate of Lena's cookies toward him. "In fact, I'm rather looking forward to one right now. Viola was not happy at all today. Lena feels that she's teething, but she is barely three months."

"My oldest bruder, Matt, has six kinner, and they all cut theirs early, so. . ." He cocked his head her way, grinned, and swooped up a cookie. "Could be Lena is right."

Leah bit her lip, letting the plate rest on her lap. She'd read every book on raising babies before accepting a job as a mother's helper, and yet none of the books mentioned teething at three months. "I guess some things can't be learned in a book," she muttered.

"You like to read?" He sounded surprised.

"I do." It was a great way to escape from her miserable states of confusion, and one could always learn something new by reading.

"What kinds of books do you read?" Leah reached for a cookie of her own despite not being hungry. The chewy goodness almost made her moan. It was a simple conversation between adults sharing a snack, she told herself—and that's what she'd tell her family if they saw her return home.

"Bird-watching currently." Joe winked again, causing Leah to lose hold of the rest of her cookie. It tumbled into the floorboard. If Leah wasn't mistaken, Joe Shetler was a bit of a flirt.

"I like a good suspense. Those whodunit stories that have you digging back through the pages wondering if you missed something."

Joe's long arms reached down, claiming her lost cookie. He tossed it out the window. "No telling how many shoes have stomped these floorboards," he said in a low tone.

"I clean everything twice a week," Driver Dan called from behind the wheel, causing both of them to suppress a laugh. "Don't waste food. That's my second rule for riding in the van."

"Oh, we have plenty. Try one." Leah leaned forward, offering their driver a cookie. Why hadn't she thought to already? *Because the man beside you makes your thoughts scramble, that's why.*

"Thank you, young lady. I was wondering if you two were gonna share or eat them all." He chuckled. "My Greta wouldn't appreciate me eating dessert before dinner, but lunch was too long ago."

"What is the first rule?" Leah couldn't help but ask. Perhaps if there were rules no one had told her about, it was best to learn them for future rides.

"Seat belts," Joe quickly replied. "He knows we don't like wearing them, but his rig—his rules." Joe shrugged and took up another cookie.

"And no children on laps," Driver Dan added as he turned onto her lane. "If there isn't enough room in my van, then best find another. I won't be responsible for anyone being. . .irresponsible, and it's a law."

"Do you like suspense or romance novels like my sister Karen used to read?" Joe asked, reaching for another cookie.

"I like both. Anything really, within what is proper, of course."

"Of course," he said and then finished off the second cookie. Who would have thought Joe liked reading and bird-watching? If Leah believed in keeping a list any longer, Joe would certainly check a few more of her boxes.

"Do you like pets?" It was a simple question. *Two neighbors should know each other*, she told herself, not because it had once been a topic on her list.

"Odd question, but. . .no!" He chuckled. "I'm not a fan of fur or messes that are too difficult to clean up." He rested both hands on his legs as they leaned toward the door. He had large hands with a long callus on his first right finger. Perhaps he liked to whittle, considering his condition limited him to few things. Leah immediately thought of her grandfather and how he used to whittle, which brought a smile into her heart at the spawning of the old memory of him sitting on the covered porch on long summer days, whittling small animals out for her and her siblings.

"We had a beagle growing up, but he always took to our mother more than us boys." Joe floated her a questioning look.

He didn't mind her questions, which only prompted her further. "I don't care for animals much. Growing up, someone was always bringing something home. Louise, our eldest sister, stayed in Lancaster, got married, and loves her cat, Blinkers. I don't know why. He sheds on everything and likes torturing my birds at the feeders. My twin, Beth, loves anything with four legs. Even the deer," Leah said, rolling her eyes. "We are no more alike than the moon and sun."

"I met her during a fellowship meal. Daniel's a nice fella. Fast talker, for sure. Mentioned that they're heading for Indiana soon for the summer auctions. I didn't know you're a twin." He studied her face, this time with an extra ounce of scrutiny. Was he comparing her looks with Beth's? Why did his eyes cause her skin to become clammy?

"Other than the fact we finish each other's sentences, we have few things in common, but I will miss her terribly." Leah paused. "It's like she's taking part of me with her." She wasn't a little girl anymore needing the comfort of sisters, but now that both Louise and Beth had moved forward, she felt a little left behind.

"She's been blessed to have Daniel. I'm so happy for them." Leah forced a smile and offered him another cookie. How did they get on this topic anyhow?

"I see." Joe's expression tightened as if he did see her inner struggles. Leah wanted showers of blessing for everyone. She simply struggled knowing she might never have such happiness for herself. Joe liked books, had a sister and brothers, and had a hankering for peanut butter cookies. He was no longer the man she found alone in the storm. Did that make them friends?

"You've met *mei* bruders, jah? They're always looking to add something else to feed or muck after. Caleb once had a pet chipmunk. The little thing would eat right out of his hand. Of course, it bit Mitchel when he thought to make friends with it."

"I noticed Amos' horse." Joe's expression turned grim.

"Ransom. Jah, Amos bought him not long ago. That's why I take a driver," she shared. "We usually share a buggy, and Penelope, that's Daed's mare, was gone. She's easier to handle than Ransom. I don't even like harnessing him up."

"You're smart not to. He's not a buggy horse," Joe said bluntly. "He could use some proper training, but I think sharing that with your bruder might not have gone over well."

"I see." Leah grinned. When had Joe and Amos spoken? Had it been the day Amos returned the scooter Joe let her borrow? "You must have made an impact. Ransom is leaving in the morning in a trailer."

"Where to?"

"Someone named...Silas."

"Silas Graber," Joe said with an impish twinkle in his dark eyes. "He'll give that horse a chance." He said it with such sympathy that Leah wondered if, like her, he had a soft spot for the downtrodden and misunderstood. Had that not been why she remained with Conner even when all the warning signs were there? Leah shook her head. That was the old Leah. The one who thought she could make a difference and help Conner keep his faith. She'd learned she couldn't change a person's heart. She could only be certain to keep her own heart safe from future injuries.

"Caleb says your shop is for bows and arrows." Leah had never heard of such a livelihood.

"I always like shooting bows with my cousins, and after..." He swallowed, clearly not wanting to speak about the accident that changed his life. "It seems the best fit for me."

"I like being a mother's helper, though someday I do hope to have kinner of my own. Do you sell a lot of...arrows?" Well, now she was just rambling.

Joe chuckled. "I sell arrows, bows, and some of the bishop's knives he makes. I keep a great many things in stock for those who love the outdoors. Hiking equipment, books, bird feeders, and I line up bows for folks for the extra. I have two target ranges for those wanting to learn or practice."

"Books and bird feeders?" Leah had no interest in dangerous weapons, but some of what Joe said piqued her interest.

"Jah, folks who hike like books on identifying snakes, trees, and birds. I've read them all," he added. "I sell binoculars and camping gear. My bruder convinced me to add fishing gear too."

"Makes sense, and who doesn't like to fish? I've never been camping, but our grandfather used to take us fishing when we were all kinner. I always caught the biggest fish, even if Beth caught the most."

"Well, if you ever get a hankering to show me up, let me know. I have a pond out back that I stocked last year. I've been curious to see how big they've gotten."

"Don't tell my bruders that," Leah said in a serious tone. "They will clean that pond out in no time."

"Not if we don't tell them." He winked.

Leah simply couldn't make heads or tails of how easy Joe was to talk to. He had a mischievous grin and compassion for others, yet the yoke he bore was not an easy one. Lena mentioned everyone hoped to see Joe well again. She did too. It tugged at her heartstrings, knowing he'd never take kinner camping or hike Sugar Mountain, where she had heard many species of birds flocked through the seasons.

When Driver Dan pulled into her driveway, Leah instantly felt disappointed. She hoped she and Joe would talk again sometime. "Will you be visiting Stella often? Sharing a ride is half the cost," she quickly added.

"Nee," he replied flatly.

"Danke," Leah offered Driver Dan and opened the door. In her heart, she believed Joe would have done that for her if he could. He seemed like that kind of man.

"Daed was thankful you lent me that scooter," she said before taking a step out.

"It was the right thing to do. I only wish I had a buggy to take you home in."

His eyes held hers for a length of three long breaths, and she saw something there that told her he too wished they would speak again.

"Pedaling is good for the heart." Leah tried to ignore the way his gaze caused her heart to beat faster. "I needed help, and you were there. We can imagine all we want how a day will start and end, yet only Gott knows who we need to meet." She offered him a smile before exiting the van.

"See ya, Leah," Joe said after her.

Leah wasn't sure if she had crossed over too many personal boundaries in such a short ride, but she was certain she had at least made a new friend.

That night Leah sat on her bed, pen in hand. She couldn't wait to write to Alma all about her short ride with Joe. He was...interesting. She liked the easy way about him, though she detected he struggled with his limitations. His passion was easily noted in the glint of his dark eyes and the way he sat taller when talking up his outdoorsman shop.

> Alma,
> I'm sorry space has grown between you and Isaac, but I'm certain all will be well. You two have always had eyes for each other.
> I made a new friend today. He's funny without trying to be. He likes to read and would never find Blinkers to be a cute cat. He even likes birds. He owns his own shop. It's an outdoorsman shop with things for camping, hiking, and hunting. He also...

A dog barked in the distance. She hadn't noticed if her nearest neighbors had dogs, and she hoped not. Such frightening animals, especially when not loved and cared for properly. Setting down her pen, Leah strolled to the window. From this height, she had a clear view of the front of the barn and the deer-holding pens that cascaded over the hill where the young does slept securely behind high fences.

Glancing into darkness, she noted the stars, the sliver of a slanted moon, and the flickering lights dancing between standing timber at the base of the hill.

Narrowing her gaze, Leah made out what looked to be a flashlight by the way it swayed and darted in and out in the tree line. It wouldn't be the first time one of her bruders ventured out while their parents slept unknowingly downstairs. She had half a mind to go wake Mamm and Daed and let them know Amos, or possibly even Mitchel, had sneaked off. But why would either bruder venture into the deer lots?

When a second light appeared, Leah was certain her bruders were up to something. Just to settle her mind, she went to check their beds. With a lamp in hand, she quietly tiptoed into Amos' room and noted his silhouette right away.

"Amos, are you asleep?"

"I'm not now. What do you want?" His deep voice growled.

"I see flashlights outside. I thought you snuck out, but I guess it's Mitchel. Please tell me he isn't letting friends in the deer lot. Daed will have his hide." Mitchel, like Amos, liked to boast too much about their deer herd.

Amos rose up out of the bed with a start. "Mitchel wouldn't dare. Where are they?"

"Between the holding lot and the fenced-in woods. I saw them go up and down and back and forth."

"Let me see." Amos got to his feet, his sagging pajama pants dragging on the floor at his feet.

"It's just out there, see?" Leah pointed, hoping to direct Amos to where she saw the lights earlier, but suddenly a shot rang out in the darkness. A squeak spilled out of her. The lamp in her hand shuddered, but she gained control quickly.

"Poachers!"

Snagging a shirt hanging on his bedpost, Amos took off in a run down the stairs. Careful of the lamp in her hands, Leah rushed behind him. "Slow down! You'll break your neck!" she called out as doors opened behind them.

"Was that a gun?" Mammi Iolene appeared in the doorway, her kapp askew, draped in a blue robe, much too heavy for warm weather.

"Amos says it's poachers!" Leah called over her shoulder as more feet scrambled overhead. By now, everyone in the Wickey household was fully awake.

"Daed, we've got poachers!" Amos called out as he slipped into his chore boots.

"Slow down, Amos!" Daniel appeared in the kitchen. Bare feet and hair standing on end said he too had been fast asleep. He and Beth had set up a temporary living space on the long closed-in porch just outside the kitchen.

"Don't go rushing out there without me," Mitchel said, he too working into a pair of boots.

"Don't either of you think of going out there!" Mamm came from her bedroom. Her long braid of brown hair hung over her shoulder and past her waist.

"I heard them shoot! What if they shot Timber or Brax?" Amos said in desperation. Timber King was the offspring of the much-sought-after buck, The Fed from Indiana. Because of his bloodline, he alone was worth more than all the other deer they raised.

"We can't let them just shoot our deer!" Mitchel said.

"Nee, your mamm is right, kinner. We cannot risk one of you getting shot too," Daed said, bringing everyone to a halt.

The deer were their livelihood. In Pennsylvania, there wasn't any worry of poachers, just folks stopping to snap a photo from time to time. But the overpopulated area didn't allow for much cover for the deer or for dangerous men to lurk and have such opportunities.

"But we can't stand here and do nothing," Amos said in a panic.

"We'll call the sheriff," Daed finally said.

CHAPTER TEN

On the first Sunday in June, everyone gathered at the Fender's Bed-and-Breakfast for the biweekly church service. Minister Gabriel and his fraa, Erma, lived on a small parcel, but the large home provided plenty of room for the new community and visiting families in attendance today. The dining and sitting areas had been emptied, making ample room for benches to sit on.

Leah had tried to stay awake while Minister Gabriel spoke of Peter, the prophet. "We grow in Christ, and growth requires a mindful change," Gabriel began, his bushy white beard practically sitting atop his bulging middle.

Leah sat next to Cousin Lizzy as her nephew, three-year-old Jay, sat on her lap fidgeting with a rubber toy that only required one to push it from side to side.

Six days had passed since the sheriff and his deputies had visited the farm. Leah wondered if Daed was aware of the dangers of moving here. No one had ever fired a gun at the deer when they lived in Lancaster. The sheriff's assurances did not quench the concern in her stomach or help her sleep any better at night. One deputy had suggested they get a dog. Despite Leah's lack of fondness for animals, she did feel a hund would be an easy sacrifice if he could at least keep trespassers away.

She fended off yawns. Being awake most of the night had made Leah clumsy. While refilling the coffee thermos to fill cups of the men already seated, Leah left the spout open to empty onto the kitchen floor.

By the third seating of the fellowship meal, she was plenty ready to escape out the back door with the other maedels. Under the wide eaves of the two-story home, Beth stood washing dishes in one of the three dishpans set out on a table. Leah went to help, grateful to stand in the shade.

"Thought you were cleaning tables," Beth said, cocking a thin brow.

"Erma and Mammi Iolene are comparing phrases again." Leah rolled her eyes. "They have plenty of help, and you never did like doing dishes."

"I don't mind them now," Beth shared. There were many things Beth now enjoyed that she otherwise would have frowned upon. Laundry used to be her most despised chore, and now she hummed while washing, hanging, and ironing clothes for the whole house.

Everything changes, Leah was learning as she watched finches dart from one bird feeder to another. The Fender parcel was neatly kept and pleasing to the eye. Purple irises burst along both sides of the house. The small nearby pasture looked as if a blanket of white clover had been neatly laid over the earth.

"Folks keep asking about the sheriff paying us a visit," Beth informed her.

"Daed said it had to be poachers. He once found a dead deer near the creek below our farm, but it had no head. Mei bruder says some just kill them for their horns!" Delilah made a face.

Leah couldn't fathom such cruelties. To take an animal and provide for your family was one thing, but to leave it to spoil was certainly a sin.

"I would have been scared," Delilah remarked as she stirred sugar into a cup of *kaffi*. How folks drank kaffi in such weather was beyond her.

Their mothers had become close friends since moving here. Betty Marie Glick was a small, rounded woman with kind eyes. She was a widow who had married a widower, blending their two families that now counted seven. Leah was especially fond of little Fiona and spied her in the distance, barefoot and running into her father's arms.

Leah had made the mistake once of accepting a full glass of Betty Marie's fresh lemonade during the last fellowship meal, so when she offered it a second time, Leah declined, saying she felt the need to drink more water in the summer months. Betty Marie's lemonade was all tart and no sugar.

"I was, especially when Amos and I heard the shot." The memory of hearing that gunshot sent shivers down Leah's spine.

Glancing right, Leah noted the barn surrounded by marigolds, with a large sign that read FENDER's on the front. In a sea of black hats, she observed the group of young men with Amos standing center, arms waving as his lips moved. He enjoyed telling a tale or two, and Leah suspected he was currently telling his friends all about the poachers. She'd be happy to forget all about that night.

Suddenly, a tall figure turned her way, locking eyes with her. Under a black hat she could barely make out a tuft of light hair in the summer sun. She hadn't noticed him before and wondered if he was with one of the visiting families. For a moment, Leah thought of Conner. They bore the same blond hair and the same pale eyes. Conner often stopped during a chat with friends to seek her out, looking her way to show her that he was still there. A hard lump formed in her throat at the fleeting memory, and she quickly pulled her gaze away. She was over Conner Brinker, so why couldn't she simply forget him as easily as he had forgotten her?

"Who is that?" Delilah whispered.

"That's Elam Zehr. He's one of the Pine Valley Amish, but I guess he's visiting our district today. Got a nice look to him, jah?" Mary Elizabeth muttered beside them. Her blond hair was much lighter than Leah's, and she had eyes as blue as a cool morning sky. From what little Leah had gathered, Delilah's younger sister courted two men, one being Dok Stella's son, Michael, and the other rumored to be a young man from Miller's Creek. Still, her lips curved into an inviting grin as the newcomer smiled their way. Perhaps Barbara Yoder should be more concerned with Mary Elizabeth than she was with Leah.

"You should go say hello. He obviously isn't here with anyone, and I don't think he's family to anyone here. Plus, he's staring...at you."

"He is not." Leah scoffed at Delilah's bold comment, but when she glanced up once more, sure enough his pale eyes studied her purposefully. The community was small, with barely a dozen families within the new district lines, and most young men were ready to settle down. Leah had already counted at least six upcoming weddings within the districts rumored and two already published.

Oh how she wished she too could be sewing dresses and planning for her own special day. How she wanted kinner to grow up alongside Louise's. She felt a lift in her heart knowing Louise, who'd been like a second mother to all of them over the years, would be cuddling a boppli soon enough.

"I just heard about what happened from Fran Martin. Has the sheriff found who tried to shoot out your windows?" Susan Keim approached, carrying another large coffee thermos, her long face stretched farther with her mouth hanging open in surprise. Leah knew stories tended to vary as they traveled along the Amish grapevine, just as they had in Bird-in-Hand.

"They were trying to shoot at one of the deer," Beth corrected. "Fran should be mindful of repeating gossip."

Susan Keim lived with her two sisters. They made and sold homemade rugs and had delivered two personally to Mamm on second Christmas to welcome them. Leah found them to be far too beautiful to stand on while washing dishes, but Mamm always said if it didn't have a use, it was unnecessary.

"Thankfully, no one shot at our house," Beth added as she stacked freshly washed utensils from the fellowship meal in a tote to be loaded back into the church wagon that would go to the next hosting family. "And none of the herd was harmed."

Leah wished she was more like Beth, brushing off the incident as if it never happened. It was a terrible thing to know someone out there was capable of trespassing on someone's property to kill their livestock.

"Such a shame young men have nothing better to do than scare folks," Joe's mamm replied. With the new district still without a bishop, ministers from the neighboring districts often helped fill the needs of the community. Leah had no idea Joe's father was a minister until he stood to deliver the short sermon today. It was easy to see where Joe got his wide shoulders, dark eyes, and mischievous grin.

Linda Shetler was barely an inch taller than Leah, with dark hair laced with fine silvery strands under her kapp. In her arms was a sleepy child, her tiny cotton kapp hiding her face as she rested against her grandmother's shoulder.

"I asked Joe if he heard the shooting, but he had not," Linda continued.

"Your sohns Levi and Joe came to see us Tuesday and promised to keep an eye out for trespassers," Mamm returned.

Leah dried the remaining utensils and set them in the tote. She hadn't known Joe and his bruder had come to the farm, but she felt her worries lessen knowing Joe and his bruder were watching out for them.

"They are fine menner, jah, but I worry if this trespasser has not a care to shoot so close to your home, if he might not think to rob the outdoors shop. The path of sin widens if walked plenty on," Linda said, biting her lip. Her concern for her sohn was obvious.

Mamm quickly assured her. "We cannot know what such men think, but we can pray for their hearts and for the sheriff to discover who they are."

All kapps nodded. Leah hoped they didn't return or didn't think to rob Joe's outdoors shop. How would he defend himself from intruders? The scary thought caused her to lift her hands to her cheeks. "I shall pray they don't as well," Leah put in.

"Danke, I'm sure my sohn will appreciate that," Linda offered as the child in her arms stirred. "I best see to getting this one home soon."

"I see Levi waving me over," Lizzy said. "I'll see you all soon."

"She is smitten with that one." Beth chuckled. "It's such a fine day. I'd like to take a walk myself."

"Daniel is with Daed talking to the menner. Want me to fetch him for ya?" Leah offered.

"Nee, I'd like to walk with you, schwester," Beth replied.

"Because I have no one else to walk with?" Leah offered her a questionable look.

"Nee, because I love you and want to speak with you of something important."

Beth was an open book. What could she want to talk about? "Of course." Leah followed her twin. Was Beth possibly staying while Daniel worked the auction circuit? Leah hoped that was true.

"Don't you two take long. Mammi Iolene will be ready to go home soon," Mamm called out behind them.

"Mammi Iolene's too busy learning new words, and just before the fellowship meal, I heard her ask Betty Marie to teach her to make mush." Beth made a face before taking off across the gravel drive toward the eastern end of the property.

"What is mush?" Leah hurried to keep up with her twin.

"I have no idea, but you know I'm not a fan of fried foods." Beth rolled her eyes. "Is there a lake over there?"

"Jah," Leah replied. "The first church service we had was here, but it was frozen at the time. Alma's grandparents cater to lots of folks, so they even made little trails along the edges and through the trees. Alma used to talk of her grandparents' place, but I've yet to explore them." Leah had promised Alma she would seek out the landscape, but Leah had yet to find the time.

"Maybe we'll interrupt some of the young couples." Beth winked over her shoulder as she went along a narrow trail. Leah hoped not. In fact, she didn't want to stumble across any couples sneaking a kiss or holding hands away from the viewing eyes of the elders.

White board fencing separated pastures. Beth pushed through the self-closing gate and held it open for Leah.

"It's verra nice here. No wonder Alma talks of it so much." A phone shanty sat a few yards away, a worn-out trail leading to the neighboring property. It felt like midsummer in the open field, but a few steps farther down the incline, a cool breeze wafted up from the pond and rolling valley below.

"There's the shelter haus." Leah pointed. Large enough for a meeting but not so big it took away from the quaintness of the countryside. It took some getting used to rolling hills and sunken valleys after growing up with farms as far as the eye could see, but Leah found beauty in both. Gott carefully designed every inch of His creation.

A young couple sat at one of the picnic tables. Leah recognized Levi and their cousin Lizzy. Behind them, the pasture gate squeaked. More folks were having the same such idea of taking a Sunday stroll around Fender's pond.

"Let's not interrupt them. I do think Lizzy is hoping for a special question to be asked of her soon," Leah shared. It would be another cousin getting married and another wedding to attend that was not her own.

"Ach, I had hoped for such." Beth smiled endearingly. "They make a fine pair, for sure. There's a bench. Let's sit."

They made their way around the pond's edges, where willows hung heavily over the water, and sat on a concrete bench with chipped white paint. A school of minnows darted into the deep, and Leah thought of Joe. She wondered if his offer to take her fishing was because she was a newcomer or that he didn't find her nervous ramblings unbearable.

"So what's the big secret?" Leah turned to her twin.

Beth inhaled a deep breath, her blue eyes twinkling just as they had the day she married. "Daniel and I have special news to share, and I wanted you to know first."

It didn't take but two breaths for Leah to know what her sister was alluding to. "Oh schwester!" Leah wrapped two arms around her. "I'm so happy for you." Pulling away, she added, "This is why you didn't look surprised when Mamm shared that Louise is in the family way too. What news this will be!"

Both her sisters had found husbands and were building families.

Leah pushed aside that familiar tug to her middle for half of what they had. "Mamm is going to be doubly blessed, for sure and certain." Leah chuckled.

"I know Daniel and I are leaving this week, so we hoped to share the news sooner, but when Louise called and said she too was expecting, I didn't want to mention it yet. It didn't seem right."

Beth was so wonderfully considerate. "Mammi Iolene will fuss that you're filling us with hope and leaving."

"Nee, she's not a fusser over me any longer. You're her target now," Beth teased and gave Leah's hand a pat.

"She's probably talking me up to someone now. I fear she'll make me an appointment with the matchmaker soon. The other day, she pretended she forgot how to make raspberry muffins and dared ask if I'd go to Miller's Bakery and fetch some. I really wish she'd not do that."

"She only wants to see you married off. It's her goal in life," Beth said, waving an arm. "Oh, Leah, what if we have twins, and they can share all the best news and secrets together as we did?"

Leah smiled at the thought, then let her smile fall, knowing that despite the joys of having a twin, there would come a day when one would marry and leave home, leaving the other empty.

CHAPTER ELEVEN

Joe positioned his chair toward the back of the room, next to the men crowded on the long benches. The minister's home was spacious, and Joe appreciated they had installed a ramp entering the house to accommodate many of the guests who frequented the bed-and-breakfast.

The new community wasn't large. Folks had yet to even give it a name, still accustomed to the old ones. But a new bishop would soon be chosen from one of the three standing ministers, and that too would change.

The women, including Leah, sat in two sections across the room. She looked lovely, despite dark circles under her eyes. She'd not been sleeping well. Joe hoped the trouble last week hadn't disturbed her. Then again, he too had been missing sleep since that night. Joe made a point to leave his bedroom window open so he could hear any sounds not usual for an early June. He made his rounds each night to the end of his drive before double-checking the locks on his shop and small shed. He'd never worried about thieves or trespassers before, but considering recent events in the area, for the first time in his life, he locked his door.

Throughout the morning, he tried to focus as his father stood in the center of the room preaching trust and the blind faith of Bartimaeus from the book of Mark, but his gaze was drawn to her. The slant of her head as she listened, the curve of her cheekbones. He cherished their friendship and wanted to explore it further despite knowing better of it. His attraction to her wasn't waning. In fact, the more time Joe spent with Leah, the more he felt drawn to her.

She was an odd one yet, he mused. Like the moon during the day, or a double bloom on a plain flower. He suspected she knew that already and that she hid beneath her smile a few hurts of her own. He knew the stings of being set aside or just how loneliness could leave marks on the heart. He hadn't even realized the service had come to an end until voices lifted in song.

"I'm starved," Levi said, placing a hand on Joe's shoulder as women bustled off to ready the fellowship meal, and men began seeing over seating. With so many visiting this Sunday, there would surely be three, maybe four seatings before everyone ate.

When it came his turn at the table, Joe continued sneaking glances Leah's way. Nee, he couldn't ignore the attraction to her. Couldn't do anything about it either, he reminded himself as he munched on a sour pickle.

He'd not burden another person with his lot in life. Mamm and Daed had been burdened plenty during Joe's first years after his fall. Yet, no matter how angry he got for not being able to do simple chores or knowing the financial strain his foolish mistake had put on them, his parents never wavered in loving him. Levi had practically set aside his own life to see to chores Joe couldn't accomplish from his chair.

Joe shifted his attention to his bruder. He couldn't change much about his life, but there was one change he could take to help his bruder. Levi was ready for a life of his own. One that didn't require a fifth wheel taking up too much of his time.

Finishing off the pickle, Joe considered his best options. If he hired on help, even part-time, Levi would be free to start the family he'd been itching after. Joe could afford help. After all, he had no family to support.

But who?

Glancing around at folks eating and milling about, his sights landed on Caleb wandering over toward the barn. Joe liked the quiet fella.

He was easygoing, but did he have time or need work? Then again, Joe needed so little. Someone to keep the yard and fields mowed off. Maybe a day a week in the shop to help when Joe was teaching classes.

Drawing his gaze back to Leah, he watched as she hurried to fill a coffee pitcher. She turned, forgetting to lower the spigot handle, and coffee poured onto the ground before Betty Marie reached over to stop it. Leah's face went crimson before rushing out of sight. It was clear she was struggling to fit in.

When her twin went behind her, Joe relaxed. Leah spoke of their strong connection. It was revealed strongest to him when she spoke of her twin leaving soon with her husband. He'd detected the lonesome in her voice. Leah Wickey needed someone like Levi in her life, he concluded. Beth was leaving soon.

After the fellowship meal, Joe made his way to the barn where some of the young men stood. He noticed Elam Zehr and gave him a nod. Joe remembered when the ministers took up a collection to help the family a few years ago. It wasn't uncommon for someone from a neighboring district to attend church, especially if they had an interest. It was none of Joe's business whose eye Elam was trying to catch.

Center of the lot was Amos, weaving the tale of the visiting poacher into an embellished blend of facts and fiction. He boasted as if he'd single-handedly scared them away and planned on catching them himself if they dared return.

Joe wheeled himself next to Caleb, at his left.

"He always makes a day more exciting, does he not?" Caleb stood, arms crossed, a placid smirk on his lips.

"I'm certain it was troublesome having someone shooting on your property."

"It wasn't something we expected, for sure, but they were down the hill and didn't shoot at us. Amos just likes to stand taller than he is." Caleb looked to Joe. "Do folks really kill them just for their horns?"

"Jah, and some the size of what your family raises brings in big bucks," Joe replied. "Care to talk?"

"Sure," Caleb replied. He put both hands on Joe's chair and pushed him a few feet more from the lot. Joe never understood why folks did that. Did they not notice he got around well enough on his own?

"Over here is fine," Joe said, pointing to a patchwork of pansies. Erma Fender loved her flowers, and it showed in her wonderful displays.

"What's up?"

"Not sure you're even looking for work, not with getting your family's place in order and what's been happening over there, but I'm needing help at my place. Someone to keep the grass cut and hold the ladder if I decide to climb up and clean the gutters."

Caleb stifled a grin. Few laughed at his dry humor. *Aside from Leah.*

"The sheriff is certain they won't be back, especially since it's all anyone talks about. Can I shoot?" Caleb tilted his head and cocked a brow.

Joe chuckled. "Of course, but only when the work is over and I don't have customers."

"Then we got a deal." Caleb reached out and shook his hand eagerly.

"You haven't even asked me how much I'd pay ya."

"Doesn't matter to me. What do I need?" Caleb shrugged innocently before turning as someone called out his name.

"Looks like they need you." Joe missed playing ball with his friends and wouldn't keep the young man longer than necessary.

"Jah," Caleb replied humbly. "It's me or Amos, and between us, he talks better than he pitches." With that, Leah's bruder strolled off in long, slow strides toward the eastern pasture.

"Tuesday!" Joe yelled after him with a hint of laughter in his tone. Oh how he missed his youth and days when grown-up duties weren't the center of life. Now Joe needed to speak to Levi. His bruder might not like being replaced, but Levi deserved his own life.

It took some asking, but Joe soon discovered Levi and Lizzy under the shelter house roof. The pasture gate had been easy to manipulate, but Joe had to keep a firm grip on his chair wheels, maneuvering over the narrow path barely wide enough for his chair.

Their friends all looked up, waving him over. Most of them were married or soon to be. There were many things Joe had missed. Courting being the foremost on his mind currently. He found it a waste of time focusing on things he'd missed and tried to focus on contentment instead. However, that ache for more, he still longed for more...

"Hiya, bruder," Levi welcomed with a stern look.

Joe was sweaty from handling his chair over the path, but it was good Levi saw him capable. The blush on Lizzy's face said Lizzy had happily accepted to marry Levi. Since some things were considered private, Joe would have to wait to hear how Levi asked.

"Levi says you're putting fishing poles in your shop." Furman Lambright had strange eyes. Joe always thought so. As if they had no color at all.

"Jah, I've already put in the order," Joe replied, wiping the dampness from his forehead.

"Did you order some of those jitterbug bass things?" Furman asked. "Our neighbor says they are foolproof."

Talk quickly turned to summer fishing tales and which rod was the best for catfish. Joe would have put in his own thoughts if not for Leah and Beth joining them under the shelter house roof.

"I say we go fetch our poles," Furman suggested, adding excitement to the hour. "Komm, Michael, let's see if the bishop has poles in the shed."

"He's gone seeing over a few folks today," Michael Graber said. Beside him, Mary Elizabeth was working to improve batting her eyelashes.

"We'll need bait," Levi added, causing the women all to make faces. *Not Leah*, Joe noted. He liked knowing she didn't shy away from collecting her own bait.

"We should head back before they ask us to do something I'd rather not," Beth commented.

"I don't mind helping," Leah replied. Jah, fishing wasn't such a bad idea right now.

"You know Mamm will want us to help load the church wagon."

Hunting for a Husband

Beth gave her a confused look. "Why would you stay?"

"I. . .I. . ." It wasn't often Leah stuttered. Beth never was one for fishing, or worms. Suddenly all eyes were on her. Did she dare mention fetching worms sounded more exciting?

Joe spoke up. "She's helping me back up that hill."

Leah flinched, as did Beth. She appreciated Joe saving her a second time, though she had to admit, she was baffled why he did.

"That's kind of you, Leah, to help mei bruder, but don't be letting him tell you any tales about moonpies. It's all lies." Levi chuckled.

"That's not a story I plan on telling anyone," Joe responded.

"I'm sure one of the others will help with the chore," Beth whispered to her.

"It's not a chore." Leah shot Beth a look. "Besides, it can't be worse than mud."

"Nee." Joe grinned, his eyes smiling at her in a way that made her heart speed up. "It cannot."

Beth was none too happy to walk back without her, but Leah stood watching as everyone exited the shelter house and aimed up the hill. Michael had already talked Furman out of fishing, which only made the big man pout. "Guess Furman and Michael had a change of heart," Leah commented. "Ready to tackle that hill?" Leah placed both hands on Joe's chair.

"Or we can wait a little longer. I managed fine getting here, but you looked like you needed a minute to gather your thoughts."

"I hate that you saw that, which means others saw it too." Leah let out a frustrated breath. Beth was in the family way and fairly upset with Leah right now, but how much good news could one person take? "I'm verra happy for Beth and Daniel. I'm happy for Louise and Marcus, and I'm happy for Elizabeth and Levi too!"

"I see," Joe replied.

"What's that supposed to mean?" Leah glared down at him. Why did everyone think they understood more about her own thoughts than she did?

"That you're happy, just as I am seeing others marry and start families of their own. . .while we don't."

There it was. He did understand, but that didn't mean he needed to remind her she had selfish thoughts. "My, you're certainly plain speaking today. What about you? Just because you are in a wheelchair doesn't mean you can't marry or have kinner someday." Her finger wagged at him.

"Nee, and just because you're new to the community doesn't mean you won't be courting before Christmas," he returned.

Leah liked to think so and had been second-guessing her decision not to visit the local baker. She let out an exasperated breath. "I'm just terrible at it, I suppose."

"No one is terrible at that," Joe insisted. Clearly he hadn't courted much. "I see folks doing it all the time, yet none are terrible at it." He burst into sudden laughter. "Well, Leonard has no idea what he's doing. First time he asked to drive Mandy Schwartz to a gathering, he forgot to pick her up."

"Happens more often than you think," Leah mumbled and began pushing Joe toward the path. She tried not to stumble in the rocky earth circling the shelter house. "Jacob had no interest in me, and Abel. . ." Her eyes rolled.

"Jacob has much healing to do. He isn't interested in anyone, and Abel is a moron. Not sure they count."

Leah brought the chair to a halt. "I courted Conner Brinker for three years, and he jumped the fence!" She immediately regretted letting the name once more sting her tongue.

"I see." Joe studied her, his penetrating eyes reading parts of her she had yet to know herself. "I'm sorry to hear it, but Leah, you're not responsible for his decision." He looked down and added, "You still care for him?"

"Nee. I pray for him." Leah quickly started pushing his chair once more. "I pray for his soul and that he returns home to his family, but my family was right. We were not a good fit. We didn't like any of the same things, though I tried hard to be accepting of his interest."

"He hurt you."

That much was true, but if she'd been a better girlfriend, Conner might have stayed Amish and not broken more hearts than hers. "It was difficult, trying so hard, and all along, he never intended on marrying me."

"I imagine so. The heart is a fragile thing. Have you forgiven him?"

"What?" Leah stood before Joe once more. "He wasted my best years yet. He lied to me. He pretended to want a life with me. He. . .he. . ."

"Forgiveness is necessary, Leah. It is our way. You know this. How can you move on if you haven't. . .let go?"

Joe motioned with his hands how simple letting go sounded. What did he know of heartaches? Leah watched as he stared up at her, waiting. Forgiveness was their way, but she had already moved on. Hadn't she? "Have you ever forgiven what happened to you?"

"Don't be turning this on me. We're talking about you."

"That's not fair." Leah folded her arms and mimicked his judging stare.

"Life isn't always."

"It should be." Leah pressed her lips together. Life wasn't fair. Love was stupid. Conner was stupid, and Joe was. . .right.

"Leah, you need to let go of that time. We cannot go back. I know he broke your heart."

"He did." She lowered her head and sucked back a sob. "Little to worry with now, that's true, but. . ." Her head jerked up again. "I don't get it. I follow where Gott leads me. Accept His will in my life, and every time I think He's put someone in my path, it turns out he's courting, not interested, or married!"

Joe's laugh couldn't be contained. "Gott's will is not about us. It's about what we can do for others."

"Really?" She folded her arms once more. "So you've never prayed for more?"

"Of course I have, and if it comes to me, then I am blessed to receive it. If not, then I must accept it. Perhaps Gott put them in your path for a reason."

"To tell me I'm not worthy of having a family of my own. That I may have to live without holding my own boppli or burning pancakes in my own kitchen?"

"Nee. You will marry, Leah Wickey, and have a family of your own. We are all worthy of that, even me. My legs are weak, but my heart is strong, and I too want a fraa who burns pancakes in our kitchen."

The last thing Leah wanted to do was laugh, but Joe had a way of bringing laughter to even the worst conversation two possible friends could have. "I pray you have them, Joe. You really are a great guy. I hope you know that."

"And I hope you find a husband before I'm the last man standing. Well, sitting." He grinned.

Leah shook her head, but a sudden vision of Joe eating burnt pancakes came to mind. "So, you'll marry me if I'm thirty and no one wants me then?"

"I would, Leah." He held her gaze for a hundred heartbeats as the laughter went out of his eyes and something else replaced it, making her wonder if friendship was all he would ever accept.

"Danke, Joe."

On the way back to the Fenders', they spotted a killdeer hopping away from her nest, and bobwhites flew up in surprise.

"That Cooper's hawk is hoping for a quail supper." Joe pointed toward the clouds.

Leah shaded her eyes from the sun, noting the gray contrast over an auburn-spotted belly. "They're not friends to have around all those feeders of yours either. They eat mostly songbirds."

"Everything must eat," Joe remarked as they reached the Fenders' driveway.

"Says the man who had two plates today." Leah giggled. "It's really beautiful here." She paused to take a rest and admire the valley scenery below. No way would he have gotten his chair up the hill alone, but she knew Joe clung to his independence, so she'd not mention it.

"More today than most," Joe said, catching her off guard. "Um. . .I mean with the sky that shade of blue and meadow flowers blooming."

Leah said nothing, but offered him a smile. Of course he didn't mean it that way. She had done nothing but sound like a jealous child, undeserving of a kind remark. He, on the other hand, had given her a moment to collect herself after Beth's news. He was a good friend, and she did need a forgiving heart. Forgiving the one person she was upset with the most since Conner Brinker.

Herself.

"Are you as thirsty as me?" Joe nodded, a dot of perspiration on his forehead. He was more handsome today in his white shirt and black suspenders. "Wait here, and I'll fetch us something."

"No lemonade, please." Joe laughed and called out to her.

Pivoting around, Leah smiled his way. Joe Shetler was different. Not because he was in a chair or had the upper body strength of three men but because he didn't judge or hurl insults. He simply listened and spoke a plain truth.

"I like you too much to do that," she said before sprinting off toward the house.

Once Leah filled two plastic cups with water from the ice coolers, Beth and the newcomer who had stared at her came walking her way.

"Leah, this is Elam. He wanted to meet you."

"Hiya," Elam said. "I know this is forward, but if you haven't already agreed for someone to, I'd like to take you home today."

He looked nervous. Leah wondered if Beth had tried her hand at matchmaking and gave her sister a frown.

"I'm heading that way, and well. . ." Elam shrugged.

Up close, he was taller and skinnier too. Light tufts of hair under his hat sat touching the tops of his ears. When he smiled, she couldn't help but wonder if Gott sent her another chance. Hopefully she didn't mess this up. Hopefully he wasn't just another passerby.

"I promised Joe something to drink," Leah sputtered out.

"Of course Leah would love a ride home," Beth answered for her before taking a cup out of Leah's hands. "I'll see this delivered and let Mamm know," she said before hurrying off.

"If you're ready." Elam motioned Leah toward his buggy already hitched and tethered nearby. Lizzy shot her a wide grin from the front porch as Leah accepted his hand into the buggy. She'd long put away expecting sparks, and appreciated that he was a gentleman.

Elam was certainly no talker. After the first mile of silence, Leah guessed he was simply shy. "Do you often visit neighboring churches, or do you have family here?"

"Not often." His short reply added to the mystery of him. "I met Amos in town the other day," he added once they pulled onto the road to Cherry Grove. Sunday drives were always best. "He mentioned church here, and this is our free Sunday."

"What do you do for work?" Learning that Elam was a friend of Amos didn't earn him any marks on her list. If she still had lists, that was.

"My family owns a farm in Pine Valley, but I work seasonally as a guide."

"What's that?" Leah asked politely, noting a faint hint of stale cigarette smoke. Conner had tried smoking a handful of times, but Leah never understood why anyone would choose such a horrid habit.

"Folks pay good money to hunt on private land, and I take them to the best spots. They're just up the road from our farm." He shifted slightly. "Mr. Anderson gives me extra work when I need it."

Leah nodded but had no interest in talking about killing deer, especially after poachers had recently been on their farm.

"Are you making plenty of friends? I can't imagine moving. I've lived here all my life."

"I am." Her thoughts quickly shifted to Joe. "My eldest sister still lives in Pennsylvania, but she calls each week. My twin sister, Beth, whom you've met, is leaving soon as well."

"Family is important," he remarked. "I have four younger siblings."

The rest of the way Elam inquired about raising deer. How long did they live. What feeds her daed gave them, and so on. Leah understood the fascination, but was he interested in her or her family's farm? She was certain it was the latter.

"Danke for the ride home, Elam." His eyes looked everywhere but on her. It was clear that Elam was just another pebble in Gott's path.

"There's a gathering next week. Everyone goes, and I noticed you didn't attend the last one." His gaze focused on the ground, not her.

"Nee, we had things to tend to here." She'd not mention she hoped to avoid running into Barbara again.

"I see."

She waited.

"Would you like me to pick you up?"

It wasn't a proper invitation, and Leah was beginning to suspect Elam did many things she might not approve of. "I'm not sure I'll be attending the next one, but danke for asking and for the ride home, Elam." Jumping out of the buggy, Leah sprinted into the house and quickly shut the door. If he was the last man left to marry, she'd accept being an old maid.

CHAPTER TWELVE

It would be their last supper together until snow fell, returning Beth and Daniel home again. Leah tried not to think of the distance, the loneliness, and instead swam in the talk of bopplin, visiting new communities, and the excitement of traveling from one auction to another.

It had been a long week of canning strawberry pie filling and rhubarb jelly. Leah had helped Lena put up baked beans since the elder had scored a great deal on northern beans at the bulk foods store recently. There were peas and beets done up as well, as Daed insisted beets be included in every meal. Leah wasn't fond of either, but she had learned to make rose water from Dok Stella, and found she didn't mind at all walking around smelling of roses. Stella had also insisted Leah learn how to make plantain salve. They collected the young leaves straight from the bishop's yard, heated them in oil, added the proper amount of beeswax, and poured the concoction into tiny containers Dok Stella would add to her medicinal shelves. Leah wished they had the salve when foraging for stinging nettle.

Since deserting Joe on Sunday, Leah feared she had severed their blooming friendship, but Monday afternoon, he arrived at the herbal shop, and they shared another ride home. Neither spoke of Elam or Beth introducing them. If he wondered if Leah had an interest, he didn't ask. Instead, he peppered Leah with questions about roses, and in turn she mentioned all the benefits of nettle. Surely he already knew such remedies, but just in case, Leah was happy to share her newfound wisdoms with him. Then…Joe appeared at the herbal shop on Tuesday. She'd not ask if he was seeking more treatments. Deep down, she hoped his second visit had to do with her. Spending time with Joe was a blessing. One that she'd not expected.

With Beth's help, Leah put together a simple meal of skillet chicken using Mammi Iolene's treasured recipe notebook. The pages had been soiled over and the ink slightly faded over the course of many years. Leah had purchased a new notebook, and when she could without Mammi Iolene noticing it, she worked to rewrite each heirloom recipe, deciding it would be given to her as a Christmas present.

Leah had roasted and buttered fresh potatoes from the garden, added fresh rosemary Stella had given her. The green beans were purchased at the bulk foods store her cousins owned. In another week or so, they'd have enough to cook up themselves, she hoped. Store bought didn't taste as good, no matter who was cooking them.

Beside her, Beth stirred a spoonful of butter into a pot of skinny noodles that were swimming in chicken broth. Her dark kerchief always made her look younger, not the woman she was now. Her dusty gray apron and matching dress were smeared with dabs of cherry and blueberry pie filling they had worked up on Wednesday. Beth's previous job at the produce farm was the reason she sought out a local supplier just three miles up the road.

Beth wanted supper to be special this evening, as did Leah. They would soon be separated once more, and this time Leah could see her twin struggling equally with enormous joy and aching grief about leaving. Family was family, and it was not easy to start a life of your own after spending so many years with life as it was.

Leah's squirreling thought was interrupted when Mammi Iolene clattered down the stairs from her afternoon nap, her kapp askew and dress wrinkled. Leah smiled and added a few shakes of parsley to the potatoes and a healthy spoonful of fresh butter to the peas.

"I could smell a fine supper in my sleep." Mammi Iolene spared a rare compliment before peeking over Leah's shoulder. "The best way to catch a husband is a good recipe." Not all grins could be seen on the lips, but at times in the lilt of her voice or extra dose of pep in her waddle. "Told ya, Lilly, it's best to let them try things without you hovering."

"Perhaps I do hang over her shoulder more than I should." Mamm didn't like to admit she was wrong often, but she didn't deny it either. "Perhaps there's hope for her yet," Mamm jested. Her cheeks were flush from working in the garden, but a cozy light shined from her motherly eyes. Lilly Wickey was not one who practiced playfulness. Her focus was solely on what needs had to be addressed. Leah liked that she tried despite how unnatural it looked on her.

"Hey, I made the noodles," Beth put in. Her skinny noodles would be the highlight of the meal.

"Ei. Ei. Ei. You are already married and will soon be adding to your blessings." Mammi added another spoonful of butter to Beth's noodles. "Yet you tend to do life in a hurry. Slow is the way, and an extra wallop of butter." Mammi Iolene winked.

"Wallop?" Beth questioned but received no reply. Leah wasn't sure what a wallop was either.

"Admit it, Mammi, you're gonna miss having me around to pester," Beth said, shaking a spoon in her grandmother's direction.

"True, but Amos has been making these old knees sore praying for him. It's best I put my attention on that, now that you've come to your senses. His troubles may be far worse than yours."

"Amos is a gut sohn," Mamm declared.

"He is too full of pride, that one." Mammi Iolene spoke her mind without a care. Sometimes Leah appreciated that about her, unless she became her grandmother's target.

"No woman wants to marry one with such big talk or who tosses hard-earned money on a horse that's only nice to look at."

Mamm's lips formed a firm line. Leah admired her willingness to remain quiet when it was obvious she had a waiting response. Instead, she turned her attention back to Beth. "First Louise, and now you," she said, looking longingly at Beth. "We all fall short, and I should be ashamed to want to keep my kinner near, but I'll miss you so much."

Leah felt a tingle of emotions. She too would miss Beth terribly. She'd packed two of her own dresses into Beth's suitcase for her sister to use as she grew.

"Be happy knowing Daniel wants to return and make a home here once we've saved enough." Beth's cheeks warmed a pretty rosy shade. It had nothing to do with the rising temperatures of the kitchen and long day's chores, but in speaking of her husband.

"We'll be home by Thanksgiving. Dok Stella says that's plenty of time for me to get settled."

The prospect of a grandchild outweighed Mamm's initial grief of seeing another of her kinner leave the nest.

"My blessings continue." Mammi sucked back happy tears.

"Perhaps we best stop jabber-jawing and get the table laid out. The menner will be coming soon enough," Mammi Iolene remarked.

"Jabber-jawing?" Beth lifted an amused brow. "I know naet what that is either."

"I'm learning the native language," Mammi Iolene said as she quickly dispensed plates around the table.

"She's been chatting with Betty Marie again this week," Leah informed everyone. Not only did Betty Marie have a love for sour things, but her accent stood out among others from being raised in Tennessee. She also had Englisch neighbors who spent more time at Betty Marie's supper table than their own.

"No matter. It's good to know you'll be making a home here soon enough. I'll just have to practice my patience." Mamm was the epitome of patience.

"That reminds me." Beth turned to Leah. "Will you be speaking with Elam again soon?"

"I'm not certain I want to." Leah carried the bowl of store-bought green beans to the table. "He only asked about the farm. I'm not sure he's even interested in me." Suddenly the thought hit her. "Did you ask him to talk to me?"

"I did not," Beth defended. "He asked if I was Leah."

"So he didn't even know who I was?" How embarrassing. Leah turned to her grandmother.

"A handsome man asked to get to know you. Is that not what you want?" Mamm questioned.

Was it? Leah thought it was, but now she wasn't so sure. As much as she wanted a family of her own, she also wanted to be loved. She wanted a life with someone who understood her. A sudden vision of Joe entered her mind again.

"I heard he supports his mamm and siblings. The daed left not long after the littlest was born."

Leah hadn't known that.

"You're not interested in him, are you?" Beth continued to prod.

"I'd rather spend time with someone who wants to talk about more than this farm. I should have asked about his family, but he never even asked what I like to do or anything. He's just like..." Leah bit her tongue.

"Conner Brinker," Mamm clicked her tongue. "Your heart has not yet healed. There is no hurry in matters of the heart," Mammi spouted for the nineteenth time since Leah was old enough to attend her first youth gathering.

"I have forgotten Conner as quickly as he has forgotten me. I just don't think Elam and I are a good fit." She placed the chicken dish on the table and went to retrieve the potatoes.

"Perhaps it's another who holds her interest," Mammi Iolene muttered not so quietly. "I saw you with Joe Shetler at last church."

"We're just *freinden*." Though Leah had to admit that when he looked to her with those rich brown eyes, her heart did flutter.

"Friends, huh?" Beth questioned with a half grin. "He didn't look very friendly when I took him a cup of water."

"See, I'm even a terrible friend. I told him I'd fetch us something to drink." And although Joe had said nothing about that day, she knew it was wrong on her part.

"He comes from fine kinfolk," Mammi told the room as if Leah weren't standing right there. "Doesn't hurt that each of them has a fine look to them either," Mammi added.

"Mammi!" Leah wondered if the room had grown a hundred degrees, as hot as her face felt. Such talk was not proper. Need she remind them of that? Instead, Leah pictured a set of dark eyes, strong shoulders, and perpetual smile that could make a woman forget her heart had ever been broken at all.

Mamm placed a hand on Leah's shoulder. "Trust Gott with your heart. He won't let you give it away to the wrong person."

"Not a second time, at least," Mammi Iolene muttered, not so quietly.

"It's hard to know what is best for me," Leah admitted. "It feels like every time I think Gott is leading me down one path, it suddenly gets rocky and veers in another direction."

"If the path wasn't so rocky, then you wouldn't feel a thing," Mammi Iolene said with certainty. "Love is not easy, and one must go the distance for it."

"I just wish I knew what to do next in my life."

"You should offer to become the new teacher," Amos replied as he stepped inside the house ahead of the rest of the family. "You're terribly bossy, and I reckon it won't be long before a teacher position opens." He stared at the table. "Please tell me Beth did most of the cooking."

"Leah doesn't need my help, but you soon will if you keep making jokes," Beth threatened. Leah loved all her family, but there were times when their ease of testing one's ability to overlook such comments was beyond her capabilities.

"All right, kinner, no meal or time together shall be wasted," Mamm called to them.

Once the silent prayer was prayed, Leah took a fair helping for herself.

"The sheriff left us a message," Daed informed them before spooning out two large servings of noodles on his plate. "He has yet to learn anything new." Daed's frustration was warranted. He'd invested a lot to have well-bred stock, and that had been threatened.

"We can take turns standing watch," Mitchel said with a mouthful of chicken. Leah wasn't a terrible cook, at least to starving *buwe*.

"I'll not allow for that." Daed quickly shut that idea down, though everyone knew he strolled over the property each night after they had all gone to bed.

"I can call my cousin to fill in for me for a week or so. Stay a spell longer until this is all resolved," Daniel offered. His inclusion in the family was instant, and his concern for all of them was appreciated.

"Nee, you have work to see to, and so do we. The sheriff will sort this out." Daed sounded like he lacked his normal confidence. "He doesn't feel they will return. Everyone has heard of it by now, so folks know to be vigilant."

Leah set her fork down and swallowed her mouthful. All this talk of poachers spoiled her appetite. She hoped the sheriff was right and that the poachers wouldn't return. "Let's not spoil our time with Beth and Daniel talking about such things."

With that, Beth got to her feet. "I'm going to miss all of you," Beth remarked, glancing around the table. "Leah and I made something special for dessert."

Leah followed her twin to the ice cooler. The large Styrofoam shelter was nothing like their icehouse back home and held less than half the food. They even had to buy ice to fill it, which was unheard of considering that for as long as Leah could remember, ice was cut on Ronks Pond each winter to supply all the families with enough to last through the warmer seasons.

Setting aside another difference in communities, Leah carried the cherry delight while Beth carried a similar pan made with a graham cracker crust, cream cheese and powdered sugar middle, and freshly made blueberry glaze on top that had Daniel Fisher's eyes twinkling. Joe's eyes twinkled, Leah recalled. She did owe him for his kindness. Perhaps she could have Caleb deliver him a pie, since according to Mammi, muffins weren't acceptable.

"Is that blueberry?"

"Only your favorite." Beth smiled. Love looked so easy for them.

CHAPTER THIRTEEN

Joe signed his name to the delivery slip as Levi and the bulk truck driver unloaded the new fishing stock. It had been a costly investment, but Levi was right. What was an outdoors shop without fishing gear?

Joe smiled as he recalled the last time he and Levi dropped a line into the water. The look on Mamm's face when they returned with five large catfish and a dozen bluegill was still ingrained in his mind, but they had eaten like kings that night.

That was then.

Joe sighed heavily. There was a time he would have jumped at the idea of snagging a few poles, a cup of fresh-dug worms, and challenged Levi or Matt to a sport of it. Not since the accident. His love for anything water related had gone rancid. Land, smooth enough for his wheels to maneuver, was his preference now. Wasn't it? He was no longer sure.

You asked Leah to go fishing.

What was he thinking? What woman wanted to spend a day on a pond bank with a man in a wheelchair? He gave his toes a wiggle. Levi had done most of the work to make room for the new displays, but Joe did his part. He hoped the soreness would diminish soon. Most of his discomfort resonated in his hips. The shattered sockets and pelvis always reminded him not to overdo it. At least he still had control of his feet, he thought, but he wished his legs could bear his weight enough to stand. Shifting in his chair only shifted where it hurt.

"Folks are gonna like this," Levi said, standing with his hands on his hips and staring over a room filled with boxes, a smug grin sitting lopsided on his face.

"Bonnie said she'd come over and take a few photos once we got everything up." With a pocketknife, Joe lifted the lid on the nearest box and began sifting through a selection of fishing lures. Bonnie Lewis sold Avon, and for a small price, she kept internet users up on the details of Shetler Outdoors and Archery.

"Lizzy and I are going to the Lengachers' this evening. Wanna komm?"

Joe wasn't interested in attending the youth gathering. "You know I'd rather be in here than crowding your buggy." Joe studied the Arbogast Jitterbug. He'd done his research, and these would hook a lot of bass. Furman would definitely be interested in these. Jah, he'd rather go through the inventory, price the new stock, and avoid attending another basketball game where he'd have to sit and watch others enjoy themselves.

"Leah might be there." Levi inspected a casting reel, giving Joe a sidelong glance.

Joe set the lure down and reached for another, pretending as well that the mention of Leah's name didn't strike a certain chord in his chest. "She might."

"Bruder, I know something is going on between the two of you." Levi crossed his arms in stubborn brotherly fashion. They had always been two peas of the same pod. Levi sought out Joe's advice on a great many things, and Levi had helped dress and bathe him each day after the accident until Joe learned to do it for himself. They had no secrets between them.

"It's none of your business." Joe pointed him a look. Some thoughts were best kept to yourself. Joe wasn't about to admit he had feelings for Leah. Levi would only become more insistent that he go.

"I saw how you helped her. Lizzy says her family has been trying to match her up after her intended let her go. I know she's a newcomer, and some think she's hurt because he called it off, but I like her." Levi shrugged.

Hunting for a Husband

"He wasn't right for her, and did Lizzy tell you that he is no longer Amish?" Joe quickly replied. It was unbelievable how any man would choose being Englisch over being a part of Leah's world. "He never planned on marrying her and didn't care what damage it did to her." Because Leah was heartbroken. Anyone could see that behind the smile on her face. Her family shouldn't be pushing her to marry so quickly.

"EE kaw sell nit glauba." Levi's face scrunched. "But she will heal. Time can do much for the heart."

Joe wondered if that was true.

"I saw her talking with Elam Zehr." Levi stacked two boxes together and went to open a third box.

Joe grunted. "Leah and I are just friends." He didn't want to talk about this any longer. Not with Levi, who could read so well between the lines of Joe's thinking.

"Freinden, huh? You and Jacob are freinden, and you don't look at him like that." Levi laughed.

"She's free to talk to whoever she wants." Though he didn't like the idea of Leah chatting with Elam or anyone, for that matter. It had taken a lot out of him to see them leave the Fenders' together. If he hadn't been in sore need of another session with the dok, he would have pushed aside his growing feelings and let it go as he did many things that had disappointed him over the years. But one ride home and Joe wasn't so sure Leah was interested in Elam at all. When he insisted on seeing Leah to the door, he couldn't ignore the way she looked at him. That's when Joe saw something in her eyes that told him she might feel something too.

"And she will with that attitude, bruder. *Es ish ke fershtant!* Why are you being stubborn? I know you like her. Lizzy thinks she likes you too. If you don't tell her you like her soon, then Elam will."

Joe wanted to, but reality was, Leah didn't deserve another heartbreak. A relationship with her could only end in hurt for one of them. "What of you and Lizzy?" Joe quickly changed the subject. "Set a date yet?"

"Oh, we've set a date," Levi said, sliding another box across the floor. "At least I think we have. Lizzy's mamm has thoughts." Levi rolled his eyes.

"Not surprising, and you know she'll just keep having them." Everyone knew Verna Wickey had a habit of pushing her thoughts ahead of others.

"Which is why Daed and Matt agreed to help start our house the next day." Levi chuckled. It was customary for a newly married couple to live with the bride's family until a home was ready, and Levi clearly wanted that stay to be short-lived.

"Joe, I want you with me. I need you with me."

Levi was asking him to be his sidesitter. "I'm always with you, but wouldn't you rather have. . ." Joe glanced down at his chair. "James, Jacob, or even Mahlone would serve best."

"I want you." Levi's tone didn't waver in his decision. They had done everything together their whole lives. Of course Levi wanted Joe to be part of his very special day.

"Then you have me."

After Levi left, Joe considered Levi's words as he added the small white pricing labels to the new merchandise. With a fine point pen, he wrote down the price and logged everything in his books. Bonnie had insisted, for a small price, she'd do his books, but Joe had always been good with numbers and saw no reason to change what worked well as it was.

He did like Leah. She stirred thoughts in him that he'd set aside long ago, reminding him how much he wanted a family of his own. *What would it be like to kiss her?* he wondered. There was a time when kissing sat heavy on his boyish thoughts. He'd gone to gatherings, but the maedels he'd grown up with had always had eyes for someone else. It only took a few years to realize that no woman wanted to marry a cripple.

At least, that had been his way of thinking until now. Leah had uncovered old wants and thoughts. Those couldn't be good for a person when so much work was to be done. Nee, it was best he not kindle that fire and start something he couldn't finish. He had his home, his family, and his shop. He had archery classes and Sunday church. He was blessed with an abundant life, and that was that.

Once all the fishing rods were priced and set neatly on the racks, Joe reached for a box of artificial worms and baits. With a grunt, he heaved to bring the heavier box to his lap, but he hadn't calculated the angle of his chair and the awkwardness of the extra weight. His lower body began to slide. Once he started, there was no stopping gravity from working, and Joe was helpless to prevent his full body from falling onto the hard floor.

The impact sent a flood of pain radiating through him. He had shouldered pain since he was young, but when it hurt, it hurt, and he cried out.

Sitting there for a good five minutes, waiting for the pain to ease, Joe peered at the shop door, the window revealing that evening had quickly shifted to night. If not for the new supplies, he wouldn't have thought to work so late. Tomorrow was a workday, and the shop would be open.

Now I've done it.

This far away from anyone, no one would hear him call out. There would be no customers to find him. He knew then he would have to depend on his own strength to get off the floor. He had maneuvered himself from bed to chair many times but never from the ground.

"Might need a hand up, Lord," Joe said and drew in a deep breath. He didn't like bothering God so often. He needed to rely on his own strength. Wasn't he the one who convinced Levi he was capable of taking care of himself?

Pushing aside the pain in his hip, Joe maneuvered to lock his chair in place. Noting his surroundings, his gaze rested on the nearby sales counter. It was sturdy and would provide the extra leverage needed to get himself back into the chair from this position.

With one hand latched firmly on the countertop and his other hand spread out firmly on the seat of his chair, Joe attempted to lift himself. The uneven support put too much strain on his arms, and he quickly let himself back down before he caused any further damage.

He couldn't stay like this all night. With fresh determination, Joe gripped the counter with both hands, raising himself high enough off the floor to shift his body onto a nearby box. Thankfully, the top remained solid under his weight.

"Halfway there, Lord," he said before taking another long breath. It was times like this he wished Levi was near. Grasping the chair handle with one hand and a palm on the first shelf of the counter, Joe worked his way upward. The pain in his right hip grew. His balance, awkward.

It soon became apparent that he again had put himself in an uneven situation. Joe grabbed the counter. In the slightly bent standing position, he took another deep breath and leaned his body on the counter and rested.

Suddenly, the reality of his present situation hit him. Joe was. . .standing.

It had been too long since viewing life at this altitude. Bravely he lifted up, adding slightly more weight onto his legs, and for a moment, despite the burning of his arm muscles or thoughts that falling from this height would send him to the hospital, Joe held tight, drinking in the lost memory.

Dok Stella's words visited in that moment. Was it possible that doktors did get it wrong? He suddenly wasn't so sure. His legs weren't as weak as the doctors insisted, but with the slightest added pressure, he knew it best not to test that theory right now and risk falling even harder. He turned and, with a more controlled fall, sat back in his chair.

Soaked from all the work and fighting the pain still radiating through his hips, a grin slowly bloomed over his lips. For the time of a half minute, he'd stood as tall as Levi again. And it felt wonderful.

CHAPTER FOURTEEN

On Monday, breakfast had been subdued. With two empty chairs at the table, Leah's family had little to chat about. They all missed Beth and Daniel already. Her family had heaped their plates with crispy bacon, biscuits, fried eggs, thick sausage gravy, and coffee soup. Leah had poured glasses of orange juice made from frozen concentrate. But she ate so little that Mamm floated her a worried brow. Beth was gone again. Half of her was now traveling north. Leah truly felt it was her better half.

Once Daed and her bruders went to work on the barn, replacing old boards and putting on a fresh coat of paint, Leah slipped her black bonnet over the crisp, heavier white kapp and climbed into Driver Dan's van with a melancholy surrounding her.

"Good morning, sunshine."

The warm greeting forced Leah to smile. She suspected he welcomed everyone that way. "*Gut mariye*," Leah offered politely and fastened her seat belt. It was, after all, Driver Dan's number two rule, and Leah believed in obeying the rules. "Do you have a busy driving day planned?" Driver Dan often spoke of his Monday schedule as if it was a grueling task.

"Got to drop you off at the doc's, then head over to Sadie Schwartz's. It's a shopping day for that bunch." He let out a sigh. The life of an Amish driver wasn't for everyone. A shopping trip for one family more than not meant many stops along the way and could last all day. This was one way to keep the miles down. Many drivers were paid by the mile, though Leah was learning that some also charged waiting time as well. Although some had a quarrel with that arrangement, Leah believed everyone's time was of value, and that it was best to squeeze in all your running errands in one trip.

At the Grabers', Leah finally smiled listening to Bishop Graber and his son Michael. "I don't care how many times she tries to talk it up, I'm not drinking that." Michael stared untrustingly at a tall glass of something green on the counter before turning his gaze on the silver hund standing nearby with an equally confused stare.

"Ellie won't drink it either, and Stella will know you tried giving her your share again," the bishop said.

Leah snickered behind one hand. She'd been a witness to Michael offering Stella's hund his leftovers. "What's in it?" Leah leaned in to inspect the contents of the glass.

"I don't know! Grass and herbs," Michael replied. "I don't mind having a salad or a tea before bed, but Daed, a man has to draw a line somewhere. I'm not a cow, and this looks to be nothing more than silage."

"Get on to work. I'll take care of it," the bishop said, lifting the concoction and pouring the contents down the sink before turning to Leah.

"Mum's the word. I'm only here to play with Viola, and I'm not a fan of drinking grass either." Leah smiled.

"Now I know why Stella hired you," he said with a chuckle before heading off to the smithy just next door.

After tidying up the haus and seeing Viola fed and put down for a nap, Leah was regretting having missed breakfast. It was no surprise when Lena came into the house. Instead of her normal knitting bag, she carried a bag containing all the ingredients for her special chili soup. Leah wasn't accustomed to eating the midday meal before noon or having chili soup in summer, but Lena had gone through so much trouble preparing it, and Leah couldn't very well decline. It was only one hour later when Leah wished that she had.

"This is the best for settling one's stomach after Lena's chili," Dok Stella offered after all was eaten and dishes had been washed up. She handed Leah a warm cup of tea from her fancy wooden shelf. Leah had never seen such a beautiful display of teacups in an Amish home before.

"I should have never had that second bowl." Leah took a sip. Peppermint, ginger, and honey made for an unusual yet pleasing combination. Viola stirred as she lay on a soft quilt nearby, her eyes taking in the room as a breeze had kicked up, gifting the overly warm home a respite from the heat.

"Lena tends to go heavy on the spices, but she would say I go heavy on the herbs. I reckon between us we will keep them all healthy yet."

Leah sipped her cup, keeping this morning's incident to herself. The bishop and Michael adored her and would never let her know liquid grass was best poured down the drain. Leah suspected that had happened plenty. Dok cared for others, and her intentions, though a little strange, were well intended.

"You are ever so good to them. I know Lena enjoys your company, and Viola hasn't shared a complaint yet." Stella smiled, a glimmer of joy flickering in her eyes.

Leah adored the child and elder. Viola stirred and her mother went to her, so Leah finished her tea while Viola ate.

"It's the biggest blessing I have been given." Viola let out a healthy burp. "She has Michael's appetite," Stella added, shifting her from her shoulder into the bend of her arm. Leah took her cup to the sink and gave it a quick washing.

"Some think me selfish, keeping the shop open after Viola came along."

"We cannot judge others," Leah quickly replied. "You do much to help so many, and. . ."

"I want to close the shop some days," Dok Stella revealed to Leah's surprise. "I want to enjoy our dochter. I've longed my whole life for her." The sentiment was raw and real. "Yet she is here with me, and aside from a few hours spent with you, I'm available to help others. I always knew that was my calling. Gott never gives us more than we can handle, so I pray He continues to bless me with the ability to be both."

"How did you know that healing was your calling?" Leah didn't feel she had a calling.

"My grandmother was a healer, and my *dawdi* loved to hike and collect herbs for her. Gott provides everything we need within reach, and even *you* have a purpose."

Leah doubted that. There were so few things that she did well enough to be considered. . .a calling.

"Are you homesick?"

"Nee," Leah replied, hoping Dok Stella didn't insist on another cup of tea that might contain grass to cure homesickness. Leah didn't mind fetching fresh flowers and herbs and weeds when needed, and learning their purpose, but she wasn't of the mind to try them all.

"I miss my sister, my freinden. I knew my way before, even if it wasn't so good. Now I don't know. . . ." Leah wrangled her lip, not sure how to finish that sentence. Something about hills and valleys brought a strange comfort to her. Like protective arms keeping out what could harm you. "I'm just uncertain of my future."

"I know what it is like, being here and being there." Dok nodded. "But, if you want both ends to meet, best be taking out some of the middle." Dok Stella winked. "My mammi used to say that to me many times."

"You're saying worrying over anything is a waste of time." Leah had heard that plenty in her life.

"Jah, I do. *Alles vell racht ousa choa.* All will come out right. Life comes no matter what we do. You will be looking one way, and something good will come from another way." The dok lifted her eyes from her daughter to give Leah a full study. "Does worry keep you from finding an interest in another?"

Suddenly Leah felt as if she was one of Dok's customers. "Nee. I don't worry overly much. I've courted. I had someone." Her thoughts went to Conner. "He found the world a better choice than a life with me."

"I see."

Why did everyone respond that way? How could they see what she was clearly missing? "You are a healer, not a doktor, so why does everyone call you Dok Stella?" As Dok Stella lifted her child into her arms, Leah ached for such a love between her and her own boppli. "I mean, we don't seek such schooling."

"Folks prefer Dok as there is only one true healer."

The sound of a vehicle pulling up the drive said the mother again was being called upon. Leah had a fresh respect for all the good Dok Stella was doing. "I'll take her and see if Lena's awake from her nap."

"Lena needs all the rest she can get. I have only one appointment left, but it may take a while longer than usual. I'm determined to get one very stubborn young man to see that sometimes Gott's will involves listening—or, better yet, trusting others."

"Oh." Leah slipped onto the porch behind Dok Stella and noted her driver in the familiar van. When Driver Dan opened the door and let down the ramp, Leah felt her heart suddenly speed up.

"Joe," Leah whispered.

On his stomach, Joe lay facing the floor through the hole in the chiropractic table. Dok Stella worked his legs firmly, incorporating more of her special oils. Though they did offer some relief, he'd smell like a meadow if she added anymore.

He worked to relax, per Dok's instructions. Not easy after seeing Leah on the bishop's front porch, all smiles and delight. With a boppli in her arms, she looked like the future he craved.

"It's gut the fall was not a hard one," Dok Stella said, yanking him back to the present torment. Joe had given her a not-so-detailed account of his fall. No man wanted to admit to every mistake.

"Newer joints would serve you well," she added. "They can do all kinds of things to a body these days. Mayhap they can have you standing by Christmas."

"Trying to stand on my own two feet is what got me hurting in the first place."

"Just think about it, Joe. I cannot say for certain all will be well for you, but you cannot know if you don't try." She said nothing more as she helped him back into his chair. He had no interest in talking about surgeries any longer. Had he not put his body through plenty already?

"I heard you hired help," Dok said as she rounded her desk to fill out a receipt for his treatment. Her metal desk was heaped with vitamin bottles; stacks of old copies of *The Communicator*, an Amish paper where friends kept up on the happenings in different districts; and a vast collection of pens.

"Jah, and I'm not sure leaving him alone on his first real day was a wise thought. I should get back." He pulled two bills from his wallet and offered them to her.

"It's good you hired help," Dok Stella said, taking her pay before opening the front door. "Now you may want to consider setting up an appointment with a real doktor."

Outside, the sun shone brightest at this end of the herbal shop. Blinking to adjust his vision, Joe noticed Leah standing next to the van, chatting with Dan. "Jah, I will do that," he replied absentmindedly, his gaze solely on the most beautiful woman he'd ever seen. Just seeing her again made the last half hour of stretching and massaging worth it. She wore a dark blue dress. Her eyes brightened above the contrasting shade. Her narrow shoulders shrugged under the straps of her backpack purse. "Need a lift?" Joe said with a grin.

"This is becoming a habit," Leah said.

"Some habits aren't so bad." Nee, how could spending time with her ever be considered bad? "Ladies first." Joe urged her into the van and tried not to wince as he tackled the ramp and backed his chair into the spot set aside for him.

"It's good to see you again, but who is watching over your outdoors shop?"

"Caleb." Joe could see it pleased her that he had hired her brother. "I sure hope he can manage well enough. Mondays aren't so busy, but folks are still signing up for classes."

"Of course. He left so early this morning and didn't mention it, but no worries. Caleb's good with people and pretty good at math too. What kind of classes?"

She tilted her head his way, the perplexed look on her face adorably scrunched. "Inside my shop is a small archery range, as well as targets behind the shop. Folks pay to come practice shooting, and I teach first-timers. The town holds a couple of competitions each year. It's kind of a big deal in these parts."

"I don't see why anyone would want to learn to shoot things." Leah shook her head.

Joe understood her misunderstanding. "Not everyone shoots to hunt. Like volleyball, there's no real purpose in it. Folks play the game because it's fun. They run bases and dunk balls because they can. Archery is no different. Jah, some come to get better because they do like hunting, and some to get ready for competitions, but many of us like controlling where the arrow lands."

"Guess I never thought of it that way." She looked at him. "Did you go to gatherings and games. . .you know. . .before the accident?"

"I didn't. I was too young, though I did sneak in a time or three." He held up three fingers and grinned. "I reckon by now you know what an unruly bu I was," he said as he nudged her shoulder and laughed.

"I know you fell, but I don't go about asking such personal things about others."

Her face turned a pretty shade of pink. "I jumped." Joe had never said the words aloud before and strangely felt a twinge of chastisement with them.

"I'm sorry, Joe."

"It was my own doing. Levi and I and a few friends went to the creek bank. It had rained a few days before, but the current wasn't much. When the water is high, the swimming hole there is usually pretty deep."

"Usually?" Leah clutched the fabric of her dress as she learned just what an idiot he was.

"I wanted to jump first." Joe glanced out the window. The day had been equally warm, and the sky was the same chicory blue. "I always wanted to be first. Matt was eldest. I guess I just didn't like him being first at things. That day was no different. Just a different outcome."

He felt the soft touch on his arm. The tenderness and compassion were a gift. Joe turned to catch the look of pity once more on her face.

"We all make mistakes, hurrying into things without a thought. You are not alone in that."

Nee, he could see that, but it didn't change the truth of his own mistake. "I hit a rock. A large rock. The fast-moving water pushed a lot of rock into the spot too. We hadn't a thought that it was so shallow. I broke both legs and shattered everything from my knees up."

"I heard you and Dok Stella that day." Leah lowered her head. "She says you can have replacement surgery. My grandfather had a hip replacement, and he was as good as new afterward."

"But it may not even work." He wasn't an old man, but one who had been completely broken. "I've taken treatments, had a few rods and screws put in to hold things together, yet they said I'd never walk again. I'd rather not do that all again. Maybe *Gott* wants this for me."

"Maybe He wants more for you, Joe Shetler." Her chin lifted slightly, and her eyes bore into his as if a plea awaited there. "What do you want?"

Joe held her gaze a moment longer as the van pulled into the uneven drive of the Wickey farm. He wanted her. A chance to be someone who could erase her heartbreak and restore her hopes for a future. He wanted to kiss her.

"Peanut butter pie." It was the safest choice. Joe didn't dare share his most private thoughts.

"I'll see what I can do about that," she said as she exited the van from the left. "Pray on it, Joe. Sometimes trying on something new can be scary, but it can also be worth it."

She had given him a lot to think about, and none had to do with being disabled.

CHAPTER FIFTEEN

On Friday, Joe swiped his brow with his rolled-up sleeve and gave his straw hat a tug back over his head. Heat and humidity had twisted together, making everyone hard pressed to find relief. Even inside his outdoors shop with open windows, dim lighting, and cool concrete floors, the heat seeped in.

The indoor target range had been built for cold weather days, but Joe found it safer for teaching young and first-time archers. He angled young Chasen's nine-year-old body to line up with his target. "Now pull back and pause like we practiced. You've gotta see the arrow striking red. Take in a breath, and when yer ready to let it out, let loose yer arrow."

It took patience to teach, but watching confidence bloom in another as a target is hit always reminded him he had a purpose. Joe celebrated each victory. Whether it be for a bull's-eye or for arrows that found themselves buried into the foam board wall, it was the doing and not giving up he encouraged.

Now if only you could take your own advice.

Was he giving up by accepting he'd never walk again, or was Dok Stella right that there was possibly a way he might stand on his own two feet once more?

Joe tried not to let himself dwell on his last visit with Leah or the delicious pie Caleb delivered this morning. Instead, he and his appetite regained their focus on the class he was currently teaching.

The local boys' club consisted of five young boys, Chasen's younger sister, and their daed, Brad Tackett. They were frequent archers at the indoor shooting range. Joe enjoyed working with the kinner, watching them improve each visit, and he hoped they found joy in archery, not simply competing against others. Brad had competed a few times in the archery tournaments and was eager to see the children ready to compete in their age groups. He always paid in advance and never forgot to book the indoor range ahead of coming. He was a dedicated customer.

"When can we shoot deer targets like Dad does?" Raylen asked. Now that she had hit red twice, she was determined to move to the next level.

"It's hotter out there than in here," Joe replied, but he could see it had no effect on the eager girl.

"Raylen, stop pestering Joe while he's helping your brother," Brad scolded.

"I'm not pestering. I'm asking. Mom says you have to ask questions if you want any answers."

Joe chuckled at the levelheaded advice as Brad shook his head.

"I heard Barry is looking for a new trophy soon," Brad added. The upcoming tournament started tomorrow and ended on Monday with archers from nearby and faraway counties hoping to be awarded the One Target win. It was all Joe's customers rambled on about these days.

"He might get him one too," Joe replied. Barry Anderson competed professionally and had won the last three local events.

"I don't care much about competing anymore." Brad kicked a sneaker over the floor, making it squeak. "Too costly, but I'd sure like a shot at a good buck this year. We put cameras out near the neighbor's soybean fields, and I've got my eye on a nice ten-pointer."

That was most men's aim—a talk-worthy buck. After the archery session with the boys' club, Joe discovered Levi's idea of fishing gear was a profitable one. Two older gentlemen bought new casting baits, while a few others purchased two rods, Ugly Sticks, and reels in hopes of snagging a few catfish. All in all, it had been a good day.

Joe locked the doors of his shop. He took time to note how the red-streaked sky darted sharply over the horizon. Instead of going to the haus and putting together supper for himself, he lingered to admire the beauty above him. He thought of Leah, wondering if she too noticed how beautifully put together the heavens were this evening.

A lonely shiver ran through him. If only he had someone to share his day with. Someone to laugh about little Raylen's shooting or share supper with. All Joe had awaiting him was a quiet home and an image of a woman he'd gladly share it with.

Since Dok Stella had closed the herbal shop for a few days to visit relatives in Ohio, Leah had the next few days off. That gave her ample time to weed the garden while admiring her newest feathered friends. Indigo buntings and robins seemed to have taken up residence here. A small flock of sparrows were trying out new wings as they dived from the barn and back again. Bluebirds found safe perches to watch her work, singing stuttering whistling notes.

Once the weeding was done, Leah picked the first of the beans and helped put up twenty-six quarts before Barbara Bontrager arrived to say her hellos, delivering two bushels of peaches from what she referred to as her meager orchard. Leah knew from passing by the Bontragers' that their orchard and flower gardens were anything but meager.

By evening, Leah was eager to read Alma's newest letter. She helped ready supper while Mamm poured fresh peach slices covered in sugar and just a smidgen of flour over pressed dough. Thinking of Joe, Leah wondered if he enjoyed her gift. Perhaps she could make peach pie. Using Mamm's recipe, of course.

The Glicks, Betty Marie, and her family, came for an unexpected visit. Since Leah's family was the next family in line for hosting the biweekly service, Betty Marie wanted to ensure that Mamm would have plenty of help readying for it.

Leah cradled young Fiona as everyone sat on the front porch, watching a fire-bloomed sky cascade over the nearest hill. Stroking the sleeping child, Leah wondered if Joe was visiting family tonight or if he was alone. It didn't seem right that anyone be alone on such a wonderful evening as this one. A nesting wren began to sing, capturing her attention while talk of weather and paint filled the comfortable night air.

It was past nine before the Glicks' buggy rolled out of the drive and Leah could finally get ready for bed and read what her dearest friend had sent her.

> Leah,
> I'm glad you are making friends. Just don't forget about your best friend. Mamm always says that a friend who can make you laugh will give you happy wrinkles. Isaac is so serious. I fear I will have sad old woman wrinkles that may scare my grosskinner.
> We are putting up strawberry filling all week. Louise had a bumper crop and was kind enough to share the last of her harvest.
> Isaac missed home church, and his bruder says they never hear from him while he is working away with the work crew. Now you and I are the only two in all our friends to not yet marry. Mamm says to be grateful in all things, and patience is a virtue. I'm trying to do so. Blinkers is not so bad, and he does kill mice!
> Widow Lapp from Ebby Road went to heaven this week. I know Iolene was a dear friend to her. Word is her niece will take over the milking barns, and the house will be put up for sale. Your cousin Irene broke off her engagement to Willis Lapp, but rumors are that he ended it because he knows she wears her hair down when all the youngies go to Ronks Pond. She didn't join the baptismal classes either.
> Daed had to put our horse Mattie down. I cried all night. I know you can remember the day he brought her home, and we took turns driving her up and down the driveway in the pony cart.
> So many changes around me. Please write back fast. I miss you so much.
>
> *Alma*

Leah missed Alma too, and quickly gathered pen and paper to respond. If only she were closer and able to help Alma through these difficult times.

> *Alma,*
>
> *I'm sorry about Mattie. She was a good horse indeed. Don't lose faith or think hard on it. Isaac will come around. Men who want to plan a future must do many things beforehand. Perhaps he is saving up so you can have a six-bedroom haus. One cannot know the thoughts of his heart until he shares them.*
>
> *Mammi Iolene still thinks I should be more like Irene, but thankfully her match-meddling days are over. I do hope she doesn't insist on me visiting the local matchmaker for a hurry-up husband. I'm eager to marry, but not so to a stranger.*
>
> *We canned beans and peaches today. My job as a mother's helper is only a few days each week, and I feel it will not be long before I will be looking for work elsewhere. I miss you too and am thankful Gott watches over you. Mamm has made close freinden with the Glick family. Betty Marie is a kind sort with two girls my age.*
>
> *I've been sharing a ride every Monday with Joe. We have been getting to know each other. Only I do think he isn't interested in more than friendship. A person can always use a friend, can they not?*

Joe's brown eyes filled Leah's mind. If only he didn't feel himself not worthy of taking a fraa. Leah smiled and leaned back on her pillow. His disability didn't define him. He was strong yet, and he lived alone. The pen slowly slipped from her weary fingers as her thoughts shifted to dreams.

CHAPTER SIXTEEN

Waking early, Leah stepped into the kitchen and sought out Mammi's recipes. She had every intention of working on Mammi Iolene's Christmas recipe book this morning, but once she reached a recipe for peanut butter pie, Leah was gathering up the ingredients. Joe had mentioned one, and he didn't mind at all that she burned pancakes.

Once that was done, Leah sat the pie to cool on a cooling rack. She'd ask Caleb to see it delivered, and she stepped outside to greet a brand-new day. Bright yellow rays of light burst through the tree line. With a warm cup of kaffi in hand, Leah looked over the slant of earth that formed the backyard as morning dawned. Just beyond the gravel drive that made a wide circle, the newly painted barn took on new life. No longer stood a forgotten structure but a vast new barn.

Mourning doves cooed while a red-winged blackbird chased away a few sparrows and cardinals feeding at the bird feeders. Its trilling song of victory reminded Leah that each new day delivered a fresh hope of a better tomorrow.

There were three holding pens near the back of the barn where her father secured all four bucks. Timber King, Brax, Beast, and Legend, their horns were still velvety, but the massive growth over the last few weeks made her wonder how they managed to walk around on skinny toothpick legs and hold their long necks up without breaking them.

She thought of Joe and smiled as she took another sip. Looks were deceiving, as even in nature, everything found a way to do what it needed to.

Below the barn and holding pens lay the swath of woodland that always urged her onto the porch at sunrise. Light penetrated through any open gaps and empty spaces as if nature were penetrating a plain world. It was behind those tall fences, among the parade of trees and foliage that the does wandered about freely, munching on leaves and acorns within reach. When the sun reached high, they would find solace under the shade of the trees. Leah always enjoyed watching their graceful steps and their poised movements.

An hour later, Leah filled the small bucket with warm water, a cup of vinegar, and a heaping spoonful of baking soda and started in the upper bedrooms. It would be another week before they would be the hosting family for church, but no Amish woman in this state or the next hosted her home in less than perfect order and cleanliness.

Living under the same roof as her mother and grandmother meant Leah would be scrubbing until her fingers were raw. She missed her sisters terribly lately, even more so with added chores falling to her now.

In Mammi Iolene's room, Leah crinkled her nose at the strong scent of vapor rub, Mammi's supposed protection against southern allergies. A clock over her five-drawer dresser struck twice. Mammi Iolene claimed she paid a man in Lancaster two arms and a kidney so it no longer lost time.

In the corner, Leah noticed the new quilt top. A double wedding ring was traditional for any new couple, and this one had blurry shades of blue and gray against a soft creamy backdrop. Had not Mammi Iolene already gifted Beth with a quilt? Whoever this was for would certainly be given a gift.

As she cleaned, Leah thought of her most recent letter to Alma. She shouldn't have revealed that she shared a ride with Joe each Monday or how much she looked forward to the next time. Surely Joe would have an opinion on the peanut butter pie. She was careful to follow Mammi's recipe closely and felt the crust was thin enough not to overwhelm as Mammi Iolene often accused her of.

No matter. Leah felt certain that even if she was the worst baker in all of Kentucky, Joe Shetler would not mention it. He was too kind to do so. He was also handsome, making her heart flutter in her chest anytime he was near. Better yet, Joe had not once showed any signs of a man wavering in his faith and even gave Caleb a job he truly enjoyed. Joe was...

Leah clutched her chest and sucked in a breath. He was her kind of wonderful, and she cared for him. Somehow over these last few weeks, she'd given Joe pieces of herself. He knew she struggled in the kitchen, with love, and with watching both her sisters live happily without her. He didn't judge her. Instead, he shared his own weaknesses. He was conscious of the fact she was aching for a life of her own, yet refused to address that he was too.

Two peas in a pod—that's what they were.

With a smile, she lifted up the bucket of now brown water and headed back down the squeaky stairs. There was no time for daydreaming today.

A tangy steam of air met her. Canning pickles was Leah's least favorite chore. She had no druthers canning tomatoes or beans or even winter soups and stews. Before she stepped into the kitchen, the sound of buggy wheels urged her toward the front of the house.

"We've got visitors," Mamm announced from the kitchen where she and Mammi Iolene worked up two full buckets of cucumbers.

At the window, Leah watched the cousins emerge from the buggy. Cousin Verna, along with her daughters, Lizzy and Laura. They were ten years apart and as far in nature as a cardinal and a cat.

Lizzy would soon marry Joe's brother, and on that thought, Leah thought of the man plaguing her daydreams as well as her sleep. If Leah wasn't careful, she might simply give her heart away again without counting the cost, and if she had learned anything from her past mistake, it was counting the cost of her heart.

"It's Cousin Verna, Lizzy, and Laura." Leah leaned closer to the open window, her nose nearly touching the screen, to see who rode in the second buggy, and quickly stumbled back.

"Well, who is here?" Mamm asked, coming to her side and taking a look for herself.

"Betty Marie, her *dochtern*, and. . ." Leah felt a sudden onslaught of nausea. "And Linda Shetler."

"Linda Shetler, the minister's fraa?" Mamm said with as much surprise as Leah. Though Linda was wonderfully kind, she was also Joe Shetler's mamm.

"Perhaps she hopes to spend more time with Lizzy. I'm sure Verna simply asked her to be a part of our sister's day so they could better know each other. They will move in with her after the wedding while getting their haus built," Mammi Iolene added, her hands held up before her, dripping onto the freshly polished floors.

There was a time Conner spoke of her and him doing much the same. He had been eager to move out of his family's home, but clearly not out of love for her. He'd led her on, promising he was saving for their home. She quickly shook off the despairing reminder and opened the front door.

"What a vunderbaar blessing. Folks just stopping their busy day to see ours goes better. Leah," Mammi Iolene said sharply. "Go change that apron before someone sees you in it."

Leah looked down at her chore apron. A worn, faded brown length of fabric dotted with time and labor.

"She's choring, and I'll not have her ruining a fresh apron," Mamm said over her shoulder before plastering on her best smile as Cousin Verna stepped into the house.

Verna was family, but no doubt it was Betty Marie that Leah's mamm most especially enjoyed seeing. The two had become fast friends over the wintry months as Betty Marie helped get them settled. Mamm looked pleased as pudding to have visitors. Since Beth's leaving, her moods had been rather solemn and more quiet than usual. Mamm also had fewer neighbors now. Miles separated families, where once they were just next door. It was a blessing Mamm had made such a close friend.

"Betty Marie said you were behind on your canning and hoping to start readying for church," Verna said, carrying a plate of what looked like chocolate chip cookies. "Instead of sister's day at my Lydianne's, we decided to come lend a hand and make it a day here too. I seldom get to leave the house or store, but Joel and Rachel were happy to step in and let us come calling."

Brown-eyed Laura entered next, followed by Lizzy and Betty's two dochtern, Delilah and Mary Elizabeth.

"Where are Susie and the kinner?" Mamm sounded disappointed. She had been taken with Betty's youngest kinner, more so with fourteen-year-old Susie.

"She's keep'n Fiona and Levi. Stephen's hund had pups, and now that they are old enough to move about, they wanted to play with them. I wasn't about to load up four more children and six pups. I couldn't even drag them away knowing Verna here had kichlin." Betty Marie wiped her perspiring brow, but her bubbly smile was signature to the woman.

"Komm ena. Let's get you all something cold to drink."

"It only gets hotter and hotter. Cold anything sounds good." Verna replied to Leah's mamm as she stepped inside.

Leah watched as Verna's eyes took in any changes made since visiting just two weeks ago. Mamm wasn't settled on if the Hoosier cabinet needed to go here or there, if the couch was best facing the window of the sitting room or with its back to it, or if purchasing a new propane refrigerator would be necessary. After all, they had spent plenty on ice. Best to use it, Daed said.

"I thought you were ordering a new refrigerator." Verna's nose wrinkled.

"Nee, we're doing well with the icehouse for now," Mamm said, clearly making an enormous effort at cheeriness at the remark. Verna meant well, but she often left others feeling lacking in spirit.

"Use it up before fretting over another expense, I always say,"

Mammi Iolene put in, earning her an agreeing nod from Betty Marie.

"I'm sure I can order one for you if you haven't the time," Verna continued. Verna had been blessed with a smart husband who worked hard, and they had more than their needed share. She also clung to a thought like a cocklebur.

"Mamm, not everyone can afford such fanciful things." That was Laura, defender of rudeness and handicapped at whispering. Leah watched Mamm's face turn a violent shade of red. She didn't say anything. Mamm was not one for stirring an empty pot, but her expression was plenty.

"I'll see to fetching us something to drink." Laura ducked her head and scurried out the side kitchen door.

"How is Beth?" Linda asked. "I saw Amos in town the other day speaking with those Englisch buwe who like riding their four-wheelers up the road late into the night. He said she was skipping across the map, happy as a jaybird."

Mamm chuckled. "She is happy indeed. She and Daniel are on their way to Michigan. They will be staying with my cousins, Esther and John, while Daniel works the auction houses nearby. It does my heart good to know Esther will get to spend time with them."

"You must be ready to be a grandmother. I'll never forget that joy," Linda said, looking at Lizzy with hope in her eyes.

"In due time." Verna smiled. "Let us have a quick break," she told everyone as she uncovered a plate of cookies. "I reckon me, Betty, and Linda can help you with the canning while the maeds see over what's to be done with this house. A house this size might take weeks to ready with so few upkeeps finished."

Leah wanted to ask her if she had seen the barn, but she thought better of it.

"You must be terribly overwhelmed. Why, your new windows have not arrived either," Verna said, looking at the old wooden frames with flaking paint still intact.

"Leah and I aren't overwhelmed, but we will never turn down a charitable heart and time with freinden."

With cold water and two dozen chocolate chip cookies, everyone sat. Talk of Lizzy and Levi's wedding took up much of the conversation, giving Mamm a rest from Verna's left-handed compliments.

"I'm partial to green, but Levi likes silver and blue," Lizzy revealed.

"I'm sure Levi will be fine with green napkins," Linda offered. Under her kapp, dark strands of hair haloed her face. Leah suspected Linda was of the same age as her own mother, but her wrinkles did show lines of laughter that Mamm didn't possess.

"Have you set a date yet? Levi tells me nothing." Linda sat eagerly waiting on Lizzy's reply. Her smile couldn't be contained. The joining of two families spurred hope.

"Levi wants sooner. Not later." Laughter filled the table.

"Such is the way of men, but a wedding takes much planning, and she's yet to make invitations or decide on decorations. I wonder if Hazel would make the wedding rings." Verna asked and reached for a cookie. Wedding rings weren't rings at all but small cakes in the shape of circles and covered in confectioners' sugar.

"Mamm," Lizzy said, "I have to decide on the colors first, and Anna Mary said her cousin in Locust Creek makes wedding rings."

"I don't see why we can't make them and save a few bucks," Verna scoffed.

"I'll help anyway I can," Leah quickly offered.

"I'm glad to hear it. I want you and Delilah to be my sidesitters."

"How gut. Levi has already asked Joe and James Graber to witness for him." Linda turned to Leah. "Joe says you help Dok Stella."

Leah tried not to choke on her cookie when all eyes landed on her. Weddings were more than just a celebration of two becoming one; they were also a way a young couple tried their hand at matchmaking, pairing up others to what they saw fit.

"I see over Viola if the dok has someone who needs her help. Sometimes I help in the shop or with Lena if she's of a mind to tackle a big chore."

"I'm sure Lena enjoys the company," Betty Marie added. "She is still in a fuss over the Lambrights and those blackberries."

"Can't blame them for making a go of it, though," Verna added. "Lena is much too old to start a blackberry business. Little Viola reminds me much of Lizzy," Verna said, offering her daughter a sweet smile. "Viola has certainly got her mamm's eyes."

"And her daed's quietness. None of my kinner were ever so content," Betty Marie said with a chuckle.

"Working for the Grabers must make it hard to spend time with...those your own age." Linda gave Leah another questioning look.

"Most young maedels find work at home to keep them plenty busy," Verna added.

"She used to wait tables, so our Leah is gut with folks." Mammi Iolene surprised Leah with the unnecessary compliment. Mammi got to her feet and walked stiffly to the sink. "She's learning to bake too. Baked a pie for your kin just this morning. I do hope his health is good."

Leah was going to die. Now Linda Shetler might be under the impression she'd have two upcoming weddings to look forward to.

Linda turned to Leah, and a smile bloomed over her lips. "That was kind of you, baking for my sohn."

CHAPTER SEVENTEEN

Joe mouthed the words. "*Die Glocke schlagt und zeigt damit.*" The bell strikes with it. Time has decreased. He didn't want to simply be waiting for a final sleep. He wanted what every man in the room hoped for. Gott surely understood that a man could be faithful and ready to walk in the kingdom, but that he had to live in this world too.

In Joe's world, it was a lonely journey filled with moments of family and community, but when the sun set, the quiet formed aches that only fed his loneliness.

"*Soll diese nun die letzte sein. Von meinen Lebensstunden. So schliesse mich durch den Glauben ein.*" This should now be the last one of my life's hours. So enclose me by faith.

Faith had been the cornerstone in facing his terrible prognosis. Faith had pushed him to seek independence and create a livelihood of his very own. *For a man who doesn't labor didn't eat.* Jah, his faith was strong, but dare he think to God for more?

His gaze found its way toward the far side of the room where the baptized women sat, and he immediately spotted Leah. Her blond hair was lighter today, the sun bleaching the strands. He wondered what it looked like down, then shook off such notions. He was at church no less, but Leah had been consuming him since the fretful spring rain.

He'd missed those running-around years. His time had been spent on learning new ways to adapt and carving out his place among his community. Now those boyish fancies were all-consuming.

After church the men set up tables and moved benches for seating. He hated not helping and, at times, wished he could. He'd certainly have fewer sorrowful looks.

After two seatings of the fellowship meal, Joe watched Elam Zehr approach Leah. The man was becoming a regular. Joe frowned. However, to his delight, no smile was offered by Leah to Elam, and she hurried off into the house to help the rest of the women tidy up.

Joe found a place next to friends on the long front porch but had stopped hearing talk of late summer storms and a bottleworm that had somehow infested a few neighboring farms' cattle of late when Leah emerged from the house again.

He wheeled himself to a solitary corner. Levi quickly took notice, and with the help of Matthias, both set his chair on the ground. Joe shot both men a "danke" over one shoulder before rounding the house to a fine view of Leah as she chatted with cousins visiting since it was a free Sunday for his former district. Her royal-blue dress swished as she fetched a small hat for a rambunctious boy.

Seemingly sensing him, Leah turned and offered another brilliant smile. Joe's heart lifted each time she did so. She said something to Lizzy and began to walk his way. He had hoped she would.

"Beautiful day, is it not?"

She eyed the sky, the sun kissing her freshly tanned cheeks as her lips curved into a cunning grin. If she had qualms about his noticing her, she surely wasn't acting like it. "It is," Joe replied, believing she was more beautiful today than she was yesterday.

"I saw two buntings fly off just before I noticed you," Leah said, pointing.

He tore his gaze away, noting the many bird feeders between the house and the newly painted barn. "I see. I reckon they earned that smile, then. I'm a little angry at them now," he teased and warmed when her cheeks flamed a bolder red.

With that, Joe expected her to say her so longs and return to her cousin's side, but Leah remained, lingering, with eyes watching the comings and goings about them. A few birds caught both of their attention. Darting in and out, hoping to grab a quick meal before someone scared them off again. They watched and admired them in silence, and she remained. She stayed despite knowing eyes were on them. Jah, he wasn't imagining the attraction between them.

There *were* many eyes on them. Joe's own mamm included. He hated to further disappoint her, knowing Leah might only accept his friendship despite his willingness to give her his heart.

"I feel eyes on us just now," Leah replied to his unspoken thought.

"My ears are on fire. No worries, freinden can visit, and we have plenty of chaperones, have we not?" Joe winked. Inside he was thrilled she chose to talk to him over Elam, who was currently looking mighty disturbed.

"I see your father's livestock is faring well." Joe looked at one deer with sizable horns lazing behind some of the surrounding fencing. "I'm told they have grown much since I last saw them." Her gaze turned to him. "Most of my customers hunt, so it's much of what I hear gossiped."

"I didn't think you were one for gossip."

"I listen if it gives a man time to decide on what to purchase. Folks are just fascinated with your family's farm."

"It's not a common way to make a living. Much can go wrong with domestic livestock. Disease and all sorts of unnatural habits, but Daed is wonderfully vigilant and does well, I suppose." Leah's gaze traveled to the barn before flashing him another shy smile. "It's terribly hot, and I do believe it is cooler by the barn."

"Jah. We can talk there, but we best hurry before one of the elders think better of it," Joe teased and gave his chair wheels a hard, dramatic push.

A laugh bubbled out of her before gripping his chair and pushing. "Don't try outrunning me, Joe Shetler."

With that, Joe melted again. Leah didn't mind his odd humor, finding laughter in spite of his limitations. In fact, she turned it on him and made his heart smile. It no longer mattered if she pushed or hurried beside him. He was content with simply knowing Leah was with him. That Leah didn't mind. . .being with him.

Goodness, thought Leah, feeling a fresh flutter. She'd only wanted to keep from having another conversation with Elam. The poor fella. He'd be hard pressed to find a special friend with that horrid smoking habit of his. She hadn't expected Joe to flirt with her. . .or that she wished he would keep flirting with her.

"It isn't bumpy down this way." Leah put both hands on his chair, though Joe didn't need any assistance, not with arms like those, but it felt proper to be helpful. Leah simply hoped to give him rest. Pushing that chair everywhere had to be a chore.

"Ach, well, if it gets rough, we'll manage," he said with a chuckle.

His laugh was one of the best parts of him. The memory brought a genuine smile to her face. "We did manage it. I thank Gott I saw you out there during that storm. I was a bit worried I might be alone there all night."

"I'm thankful you came out to help me, and neither of us were stuck all night." He reached over his shoulder, giving her hand a pat much like Mamm gave Daed after a long day's work.

Leah's heart fluttered again with the noticeable affection, igniting a surprisingly different awareness of him. Outside of family, Joe was her dearest friend in Kentucky and made her feel as if she were the only woman in the world. What a silly thought. Her grip on the chair's hand bars tightened. Conner once made her feel special too. She best remember that.

But he's not Conner.

Leah pushed out the dark memory, not letting yesterday rain on her today.

Beyond a dried path and clumps of purple wild thistle, they spotted two of the bucks. Brax had grown, and his massive horns looked painful. Leah found them ugly, despite how her bruders described them.

"Nice fella. I thought there were four. Caleb gets *a talk on* about them, and it can last for a spell." Joe chuckled.

"It's all mei bruders ever talk about." Leah rolled her eyes. The men of her family lived, breathed, and dreamed of deer. She latched onto the wire fencing and looked for the other males along the stretch of fencing nearest the south side of the barn. "Each male is marked with a red ear tag. My favorite is Legend," she said, pointing to a young buck. "He's easy to feed. I never minded feeding him right out of my hand, but Timber"—she pointed to the older buck—"that's the one Daed dotes on because he came from a buck up north worth a lot of money. He's not tempered until colder weather."

"The rut," Joe added.

"Jah. I'm not allowed to help feed then. While growing up, none of us girls were allowed to feed them either, though Beth did anytime Daed wasn't around to see it."

"Glad to hear it. Nothing is more unpredictable than a buck in rut." Joe gave the deer a full scrutiny. "I know little of it, but I remember when Mamm set her heart on goats."

"Goats are easier, for sure and certain." Leah could see Linda happy with a lot of playful goats.

"We had Pan Pan, because Levi had difficulty saying Roman. He weighed about 180 pounds. A Nubian buck who gave Mamm plenty of reasons to regret wanting goats." Joe laughed again. She could sit and listen to him talk all day.

"That first fall we had him was short-lived."

"Why?"

"Because after three weeks with a buck in rut, she sold him for half the price and nursed bruised ribs and a sore backside all through winter."

Leah hid a laugh behind her hand. "That's why I don't want animals, with the exception of a good horse. I love seeing them, but it looks painful having to carry around all that extra weight. One day, when I have a place of my own, I look forward to watching young does and fawns race over a meadow, but I'll not be keeping animals penned. It isn't...natural."

Leah appreciated his nod, seeing they were both of the same mindset. Another check on her imaginary list. "Will you be visiting Dok Stella tomorrow?" she asked, hoping he was.

"I've yet to decide, though," his dark gaze traveled to hers once more, "seeing you is reason enough."

Leah ducked her head, hoping her cheeks did not reveal too much.

"I told the dok I'd keep up with the exercises, but I'm not so sure they do more than just keep things aching."

"Perhaps you should consider the surgery she spoke of." Leah wished she had kept the mention of surgery to herself. Joe might think her nosey. "I confess that while Viola and Lena nap during the day and little is left to be done, I read. I read about joint replacement and know Stella spoke of learning more about it herself." Leah shrugged one shoulder. "She left a booklet on the table. They use ceramic, plastic, and poly for those."

"I'm not certain I want any of those inside of me," Joe said, shaking his head.

"I can understand that. It would be odd to know it's not flesh and bone."

"I doubt it would help anyway. The doctors said I'd never walk again, but..." His dark eyes landed on her once more. "I wish I could. Things would be...different for my life, but trusting Gott is what we are called to do."

"Jah, but Gott offers opportunities, does He not?" How could he not see the possibility in such a surgery? Giving him back so many freedoms he'd been left without. "It's your choice, Joe. No one can choose for you." Just like Mammi Iolene couldn't choose for her. Some mistakes had to be made without help, but she wished he would at least consider what the surgery would do for him.

"Mamm wants me to give it a try. Levi too. They fret over me more than they should. That's why I hired Caleb, so Levi could spend more time thinking about his own future."

"That was verra kind of you, Joe, but what of your needs?"

"I have none. I'll not have what my bruder will have, nor will I burden him."

Leah didn't like hearing this. "Why not? Don't you want a family of your own someday?" Leah quickly slapped a hand over her mouth. What a question. Joe lifted a brow and grinned.

"I didn't mean..." But she did. Leah could just fall over now from embarrassment.

"I do pray for kinner of my own someday, but I'm not one to wait for miracles. No one wants to start a life with a cripple." She watched the misery of his perceived future on his face.

"Everyone falls short somewhere, Joe, and Gott has a plan for you even if you don't see it." Had she not fallen short plenty, especially in matters of the heart? Leah's heart ached for his lack of confidence. Joe was a fine catch. Even Mammi Iolene thought so, and Leah was convinced she had a secret list of her own for selecting proper husbands for all her family. "But..." She smiled at him. "If you are thirty and I'm the last woman left in the community, then I'll marry you."

Joe once promised her the same, but something in her words sent an unexpected hope within her. Joe couldn't see what she saw. Nee, Leah didn't believe being married to a man like Joe a burden as he felt he was. In fact, a life with Joe wouldn't be difficult at all. It would be an adventure filled with long talks, birdsongs, and friendship.

"So..." His lips curved mischievously. "Whoever turns thirty first?"

"Sure. Whoever turns thirty first." Leah knew he was only joking, but for that moment, she had never before felt more sure of a promise.

"I might hold you to that, Leah Wickey."

That evening, Leah settled on the couch as their father read from the Bible. Caleb and Mitchel lay sprawled out on the newly sanded and polished plank floor. The house was coming along wonderfully. The breeze moved through the open windows and screen doors. Amos had chosen to join all the youth for an evening of singing at the Fenders' barn, but seeing Joe ride away with Levi and Lizzy, Leah had lost any interest in attending herself. Besides, what if Elam was there? Leah wasn't sure why he acted interested in her when he spoke only of the deer or how busy her bruders had been lately.

Looking at her family, Leah felt blessed. Today was another wonderful day. Good days were collecting and growing, she thought with a smile. Renewed hope and contentment as warm as Louise's spiced apple cider at Christmas filled her. Currently pleased with the turn of events in her life, Leah couldn't wait until Monday to see Joe once more.

CHAPTER EIGHTEEN

Leah opened the window with a broken balance string and set a coffee can filled with loose coins on the windowsill to hold it up. Daed had ordered new windows back in May, but they had yet to arrive, and here it was, the final days of July. His daily grumbles displayed that he was just as disappointed as Cousin Verna with the worn-out, ugly frames.

Golden rays of a summer morning greeted her. Songbirds sang, sounding like a choir of heaven. It was already warm in the house, but the occasional ripple of a breeze made it more bearable than in passing weeks.

With a Wednesday washday waiting for her, Leah pulled her most recent letter from Alma out of her apron pocket and read her dearest friend's words again.

> Leah,
> I hope this finds you well. I've missed you terribly. It's a free Sunday here, and I'm sitting home listening to Mamm and Daed talk of weather and common things. The gray catbirds are so many this year, stealing from Mamm's cherry bushes. I fear the blackberries don't stand a chance.
> Isaac came for a visit, if spending an hour with me can be called a visit. He used to enjoy watching the birds with me and striking up talk about them. The cowbirds are pestering, but after hearing its song, I found a Kentucky warbler among them.

> *I missed you all the more thinking about that time we found one hiding under the bushes near Ronks Pond. They will soon head your way, and I pray you hear their song too.*
>
> *I find that while things here are not so bright, your letters have given me hope that Gott still knows our hearts. I miss Isaac and find this time apart has not served either of us well. He feels like a stranger to me now when he comes calling, not the man I was ready to give my future to.*
>
> *Mamm thinks time will reveal Gott's plan. I just want time to stop so I can have the love I've felt for longer.*

Leah's heart went out to her best friend. How well she too remembered those first trappings of love. How easily it blinded and captured your every thought, masking those little telltale signs that God was trying to show you.

Isaac never showed as much interest in birds as she and Alma did, but Leah never dared share that observation with her best friend. She wished she had. If someone had told Leah what Conner's plans for his future, for her future, were, who knows where she'd be right now? Happily married? Holding bopplin of her own?

Leah took some comfort in knowing at least she wasn't the only naive girl. Choosing a forever partner was like the husk on corn. You didn't know what truly lay inside until you peeled away each papery thin layer.

> *Your friend sounds like a kind man. You are right that one cannot be judged by appearances. Just remember that when you feel as if you too have flaws beyond looking past. You know I can be a little bossy and that I love birds even more than you do. Mamm thinks I'm obsessed and that obsession is a sin. I don't see why everyone doesn't love Gott's winged creatures as I do, but I do know even I deserve someone who doesn't see my flaws as flaws at all but just what makes my heart happy. Your new special friend sounds like someone who understands that well.*

Leah felt her cheeks warm. Joe was her friend but not really her special friend. For a moment, she wondered what it would be like if they were "special friends," and the thought brought a smile to her lips.

Leah cupped the letter to her chest and considered her next reply. She hadn't planned on letting her heart open too widely after the heartbreak that had taken up much of the space, yet every door and chamber sat ajar. More so after reading Alma's letter for the third time. Would Alma still offer the same encouragement if she knew of Joe's disability? Likely so. Alma wasn't conceited. It felt terrible that while Alma's life was not going as it should, Leah was slowly finding her footing again. No longer were her days dark and merely something to endure, but she woke each morning to misty, sun-kissed days that sang in her soul.

She and Joe were getting to know each other, and the more husk she pulled away, the more she was discovering that inside were rows and rows of golden kernels. He teased but never insulted, and not once had he mentioned what a terrible cook she was. One didn't need to be anything more than themselves around him.

Tucking the letter in her apron pocket, Leah continued to unpin the last towel on the line. The sound of a distant blow, what most deer did when signaling a warning, caught her ears. The last few days the herd had seemed unusually unsettled. So much so that Amos and Daed walked the fences more regularly, but Daed had assured them all that the threat of an early winter was the cause. As the sun grew higher in the sky, the temperature rose along with it. Leah wondered who he was getting his weather reports from. If it wasn't ninety, it was ninety-five.

On the porch, Mammi Iolene sat in one of the new chairs Daed purchased from a local furniture maker, shucking the first-picked corn. The garden would produce a bounty of white-and-gold Serendipity ears in the coming days, and Leah anticipated fresh corn with supper tonight. Especially when Mamm left a few silks behind. They would turn to candy under butter and sugar and fried on a high heat, making the plainest meal all that much sweeter.

Canning sweet corn required many steps—all worth all the time invested. It wasn't like cooking with various ingredients, all needing to be added, beaten, whisked, or folded at the appropriate time. Canning just took patience. A trait Leah and her twin didn't share. Leah never failed at canning, whereas Beth often rushed through the chore, leaving many jars to become feed for livestock.

A lowly howl from over a hill sent a shiver up her spine as the breeze picked up. A rustling sound, followed by two more snorts, alerted Leah once more. Hopefully nothing was upsetting the herd. Setting down the full basket of freshly dried laundry on the porch steps, Leah aimed to investigate. With the men all making hay, it fell on her tender shoulders to see all was well.

"Where are you going?" Mammi Iolene clucked as if Leah were a child sneaking away from choring. For the last few days, Mammi had been crankier than usual. A summer earache brought on by allergies, she claimed.

"The does sound upset. I can see two only of them from here."

"You've never had a care for them before." Mammi Iolene's lips pinched. "Well, don't waste the day. Corn needs to be shucked and jars washed and ready for the morning."

Leah knew Mamm had every jar washed already. And from the scent of hot pork wafting outside, she was working on supper, but she reassured Mammi Iolene with a smile. "I'll be but a minute."

Along the path leading to the barn, Leah's thoughts drifted to Joe once more. Overhead, the sky grumbled. Freshly baled hay stacked to the rafters on one side smelled sweet and warm. Noting two bucks safe under the enclosure, nodding off under the warming day, she veered toward the slant of earth and gravel drive that met pavement. Perhaps the other two were simply lingering out back, just out of view. She never understood their nocturnal habits.

In the distance, gray clouds puffed up, but it would be a while yet before rain reached them. If it made it this far at all. It had been a dry summer, but hills and valleys were hard to measure for, turning clouds in a blink. Hopefully rain would come but not before all the hay bales from the upper field were stacked safely in the barn. Daed would be a bear if the hay was ruined, growling and such as he often did to express himself without words. He was two hands short today with Mitchel at school and Caleb working at the outdoors shop.

High fencing ran parallel to the ditch lines alongside the narrow country road, but freshly mowed grass and a well-traveled path left her plenty of safety without worry of cars coming too close around the curves and bends. The fences protected the deer from predators and disease. Rare diseases such as hemorrhagic disease, tuberculosis, and cutaneous fibromas, which could be found in elk and deer, to black tongue, had been a problem in many states, affecting the deer population, as well as CWD, chronic wasting disease. Kentucky currently had no reported cases, but Daed had been keeping himself well informed how close it was coming to the central states. Then there were concerns with things such as Lyme disease, which didn't affect the deer at all but was terrible for people. Leah had all but run out of reading material recently and had read up on Daed's magazine subscriptions, though now she wished she hadn't.

Over the grade, she admired a small patch of chicory blooms. The bright blue weed was eye catching. Dok Stella spoke of it so often that Leah would have never considered its potential, though she had no interest in tasting the bitter coffee Stella insisted tasted just like nature.

A mullein plant sat at the corner where the fences veered downhill toward a creek bed. In the center, standing erect, the tall flowering spike caught her attention. Dok Stella revealed that the tight-five-petal blooms were best plucked and added to oil for earaches. Leah found working for the local healer to be an extended gift and began plucking the blooms and dropping them into her apron pocket. Mammi Iolene would be happy to know a remedy grew nearby.

Once picking all the blooms available, Leah brushed her fingers over the velvety tobacco-shaped leaves and collected three wide leaves as well. When dried, they could be made into a tea to fight congestion.

They also reminded her of the many tobacco farms back home. *Conner hated working in the tobacco fields owned by his family.* There were many things Conner wasn't fond of. How had she not seen the forest for the trees?

Farther down the hill, the brambles grew denser. So did the tall timbering trees. Pausing, she looked up, marveling at how sunlight filtered through limbs and leaves. God's work was everywhere.

Since poachers had been there to walk the perimeter of the property, making a well-marked path, the trail was easy enough to follow without getting lost. So Amos and Daed had not let a day go by without walking it.

Only now did she realize she'd reached the far eastern corner of the property line. She had no intention of taking on such a hike; she just simply wanted to see that all the precious does were safe. Perhaps she shouldn't have been so foolish to come by herself. What if it was something she couldn't outrun? She knew not what animals lurked in these hills. Stray dogs might be nearby. That lonely howl earlier now felt disconcerting, and she gripped the mullein leaves in her hand much tighter. What if it was something bigger? Her breath quickened. A bear perhaps. Had she not heard mention of bears moving into the area? Susan Keim mentioned something about a nearby sighting not so long ago.

Nerves taut, she turned to leave when movement caught the corner of her eye. She was not alone in these woods. Fear unlike any Leah had ever known sent hot, acidy bile to rise in her throat.

Why would anyone be here on their property? Forcing her breaths to quiet, Leah noted the man wore a dark hood over his head, despite the smoldering hot weather. He hadn't seen her among the thick of trees and foliage. Her eyes curiously tracked to see he was crouched down on one knee facing the fence. In his hand were blue-handled wire cutters—the heavy-duty kind her father used when constructing the new chicken run.

Leah clutched her middle as her thoughts raced through various scenarios. None making her feel any safer. Taking a slow step back in hopes of not being discovered, she failed miserably when the sound of footsteps behind her spawned a gasp out of her.

There are two.

One to her right, one behind her, and the air suddenly smelled of smoke and...Mammi Iolene's vapor rub. Surely her heightened senses were confused. Just then, the hooded man's dark gaze landed on her, narrowing faster than the wings of a hummingbird.

Run! her head screamed. She could go over the hill, hope to reach the road before they did. She wasn't as fast as Louise, but Leah could sprout wings when fearing for her life. And she was fearful right now.

"Poachers!" She hoped her scream reached the porch, where Mammi Iolene sat shucking corn. But before her feet could retreat over the hill, blackness enveloped her.

CHAPTER NINETEEN

The smell of fresh-cut grass filled Joe's nostrils with a distant memory. It had been over a decade since he'd held the reins and ridden on the hard inclined seat. This morning Caleb had taken great care, seeing him secured to the seat with a wide strap, and Old Nell, Caleb's mare, did in fact seem to enjoy the chore even more than Joe.

"All you gotta do is turn her. She's seasoned," Caleb had assured.

Caleb had even thought to add a short-cut two-by-four bolted to the tongue, serving as an extra measure of safety for Joe's feet to perch upon. In reality, if the dok, or worse yet, his mamm, saw Joe right now, they would certainly disapprove of their boyish devices. Thankfully, Joe's outdoor target range was free of stumps and stones, leaving no need to operate the foot lever.

When the chore was done, Joe pulled back on the lifting arm with one hand, reins with the other, and brought Old Nell to a halt. "Danke, Caleb." He was soaked from the humidity and work but had never felt so good.

"All I did was let you mow your own yard." Caleb shrugged and fetched Joe's wheelchair, which was a reminder that this too was only temporary.

No matter. Caleb had taken time to consider him. He'd given Joe a chance to do something for himself that he hadn't been able to for a long time. Levi would be impressed. It was a gift, and the young man didn't even know what a precious one it was. Like Leah, Caleb truly considered others.

"I guess I just assumed it was out of my reach," Joe remarked as he unstrapped himself from the seat while Caleb freed his feet. The young man was strong for his age, helping Joe maneuver his way over the mower's tongue and single tree bracket, attaching the mower to the horse. Caleb helped him lean against the wheel while he tugged Joe's wheelchair closer. Standing, even if for a moment, he grew taller in mind and spirit.

"I guess there are many things out of reach if you let them be," Caleb said with a wry grin.

"You are much too wise for a youngie," Joe jested as he settled in his wheelchair. "I wish we'd been freinden years ago. I would have never been so foolish with you at my side." Joe meant the words. If he and Caleb had been friends all those years ago, no doubt jumping into a raging river would have never crossed his mind.

"We're freinden now," Caleb said with some certainty. "You know, Joe, I met a man last week in Walnut Ridge. Daed is looking into purchasing a new buggy."

No doubt the Wickey family was in need of a new one, considering the ones they currently used, Joe noticed, had all the bells and whistles that didn't follow the Ordnung. Even the kapps the women wore were different, but each new family had a full year to amend to the change. However, it was proof that Pennsylvania Amish and Kentucky were two very different districts.

"He can do fine things," Caleb continued. "I reckon he could take a chop buggy, install a platform, and add a small ramp that lowers as Driver Dan's van does."

Joe sat and stared at the young man in newfound astonishment. Now why hadn't he considered such an idea? *Because you believed life was as it is,* he silently told himself.

Such a custom-made buggy would be costly, but Joe had no fraa. He had no kinner. He owned his own shop. He had the funds. But there was a hurdle in Caleb's thought process, was there not?

"If you're thinking keeping a horse would be a hardship, don't. I hear Matthias Martin is looking to sell a mare that is well seasoned. Few folks are willing to even consider her, being small as she is, but with some practice, and maybe"—Caleb looked beyond Joe's house—"a little fencing for grazing..."

"You are giving me much to think over." Joe glanced about. He had plenty of land for a horse. In fact, the idea of owning a horse after all this time appealed to him.

"With a buggy, you could komm for supper sometime. Maybe ask a special friend to ride to a gathering with you." Caleb's bashful smile warmed his cheeks.

"I don't have any special friends," Joe told him, but the fella wasn't just a thinker. Joe suspected his new friend was wonderfully observant too.

"I know you got eyes for mei schwester. I see you looking at her and her looking at you."

"Leah is a fine woman, but she need not be burdened with a fella like me."

"She's seen hardships plenty enough." Caleb looped his thumbs in his suspenders. "She still smiles and hums, not letting it dull her happiness." Caleb turned back to the horse. "Leah is different. She's not like Louise." He unhooked Old Nell from the mower and began guiding her toward his buggy sitting under the shade of the only real tree in Joe's yard. Hopefully those skinny maples would start growing soon.

"Louise was much like Mamm, seeing over us all plenty. Beth liked beating us at everything." Caleb chuckled. "I pray for Daniel every day."

Joe watched the young man shake his head before growing serious again. "Beth and Leah were close, being twins and all. They even share many of the same thoughts, but Leah is her own person. At least she tries to be. I see her. I reckon with Louise and Beth both starting families, she might feel a bit left behind."

Joe knew what that felt like. "I know she had a bad breakup."

"I could have told her he was a bad catch. He was a fool, as sure as one ever was."

"He had to be that to leave her for anything out there."

"We are of the same mind, then." Caleb held his gaze. "All I'm saying is if you ask her, she'd be happy to ride along with you anytime."

Joe warmed at Caleb's awkward blessing to court his schwester. It wasn't as if Joe hadn't been thinking on it. "Danke, Caleb, for today, and the blessing, but I'll have to think about it."

"Don't think too long. Time has a way of making us wish we did things a little quicker." He eyed the sky, the dark clouds on the horizon. "I should head on home. I can't be late for supper." Caleb quirked a brow as he worked to harness his buggy. "I'll fetch the mower later. Daed won't need it for at least a few days."

The sound of distant thunder rolled over the valley and floated through the hilltops, followed by an all-too-familiar sound of a siren as it split the air between valleys. The hairs on Joe's neck lifted in warning. Ever since his accident, the memory of those rescuers and the struggle to safely remove Joe from the water and steep terrain... He always lifted an immediate prayer for whoever was now in need of emergency help.

"That sounds to be getting close," Caleb said, and even the mare remained still as the sirens grew louder.

Joe agreed. It was getting closer. Something didn't feel right. Both men waited for what felt like minutes, but soon it was apparent that the emergency vehicle had turned just short of Joe's drive.

"That's heading our way," Caleb spouted and worked frantically to harness Old Nell to the buggy cart. There were only two houses on Robin's Nest Road. Driver Dan's small farm and Caleb's family's.

"I'm going with you." Joe was already working his way from his chair.

"Hold on, let me help." Despite concerns for his family, Caleb saw Joe safely onto the seat and Joe's wheelchair quickly folded and secured under the seat on the welded framing before slapping the reins and aiming for the Wickey farm.

As soon as they reached Leah's, Joe knew his gut had been right.

Hunting for a Husband

The first responders had been called here. He hoped Leah's parents were all right. Not one but three sheriff's cars sat in front of the house, their lights flashing in blue and white, but the earlier sirens had been quieted with the exception of those in the distance also responding and making their way down the narrow road.

Caleb bounded out of the buggy and rushed to Rueben and Lilly's side. Joe shot up a quick prayer for Leah's grandmother. One never knew when his time was over, but when Iolene emerged from the house, Joe felt the sudden jolt of unease prickle his spine.

Apparently sensing his predicament, one of the deputies assisted Joe into his chair.

"What happened?" he asked.

"Young woman went for a walk and never returned." And just like that, gooseflesh ran up his arms as he hurried toward Leah's parents.

"She said she was going for a walk. Our Leah likes her walks and watching the birds," Lilly was informing the sheriff and his deputies. "That was two hours ago! Leah would never be gone so long without telling someone." Lilly hid her face in the palms of her hands as Rueben Wickey held a long arm around her.

Joe's heart plummeted.

"We have plenty of volunteers coming, but the deputies and I can start looking right away. Which direction did she take off to again?" Sheriff Mitchell was over six feet and broad in the shoulders. His hello had a calming tone but could command the most unwilling participant into doing as instructed. Within the Amish community, he was well respected and even liked.

"Toward the barn," Iolene pointed. "She has bird feeders around there, but we already checked." Iolene wrung her apron in her hands. "She mentioned checking the herd. Ach, I should have paid more mind."

"It's all right, ma'am," a deputy said. "We'll check the area again and look a bit farther in case she simply wandered out and just lost her bearings."

"These hills and valleys can be confusing," the sheriff said in a reassuring tone. "You folks haven't lived here that long, and it took me a couple years to know my way about." He turned to Leah's mamm, grief and worry etched on her face. Joe felt just as helpless. "I'm sure she is fine, Mrs. Wickey. Most likely she just got twisted around."

"Fraa, see to putting on coffee and readying something for the men," Rueben ordered to his wife. The chore would do her well, keeping her mind off fearful scenarios for Leah's well-being.

More volunteers arrived. Some by car. Some by buggy. Joe shook hands with Matthias Martin, Will Lapp, and about two dozen Amish men. A woman living on the other end of the county drove into the yard. She quickly leashed two redbone hounds. Word traveled fast from one community to another, but the more folks who came to help, the more Joe feared the worst.

After the sheriff divided folks into various groups, it was clear the main focus was near the barn and hills leading in various directions and hard terrain. In his chair, Joe felt even more helpless than before. He couldn't just sit there, waiting. Leah was alone. She didn't like storms, and it was easy to see it wouldn't be long before the one circling the valley reached them. His heart tripped. He had to find her, chair or not.

"Caleb, I can't just sit here. Let's go check that way, in case she walked the fence lines. If my ears heard right, they mentioned her seeing about the deer."

"They did," Caleb said with a wide-eyed expression. "Could be she was seeing to the does and not the bucks at the barn. Mammi Iolene wasn't certain. Let's go."

The roadside fencing would be easy to travel in a wheelchair. He had to find her. Despite his limitations, Joe managed the ditch lines and dry brambles as they made their way to the end of the property.

"Look." Caleb pointed at a set of tire tracks leading out of the ditch and onto the road. "Could be someone ran off the road or just pulled over here."

"Jah," Joe agreed. The black lines on the asphalt could mean anything, but it did seem that whoever left them sure left in a hurry. His fears couldn't be silenced. "What if someone stopped and picked her up?"

"Leah would never leave without telling Mamm. She's not like that." Caleb pushed forward.

Nee, Joe didn't suspect she would, but fear rose in his throat knowing she might not have had a choice in that. What if a stranger picked her up against her will? Though such things he'd read about didn't happen often within their Amish communities, it did happen. Had not a young child been stolen right out of his mamm's arms just a year ago in Ohio?

"Wait here, and I'll walk down to the creek and take a look before we head back."

"I can manage." Joe ground his teeth and pushed himself deeper into the woods. He'd not stand by, waiting. Just the thought of Leah out there somewhere, afraid and alone, was all the encouragement his body needed to tackle harder terrain.

They had barely gone a hundred feet when Joe spotted Leah's bare feet, attached to her limp body on the ground near a tall pin oak. Caleb must have seen her just as quick, and rushed to her side.

"She's hit her head"—Caleb touched her hair and lifted his hand to reveal the crimson proof, quickly looking about—"on something. Leah, it's Caleb. I'm here, schwester. *EE glech dee*, Leah. We've come to take you home."

"Nee! Be careful! She could have a neck injury," Joe instructed, watching helplessly as Caleb examined her. Her kapp was missing, revealing long strands of pale blond hair over her face.

"We can't move her without knowing for sure. You can run for help. Let them know we found her, and have them send the paramedics," Joe ordered. Thankfully Caleb didn't need to be told twice as he touched Leah's still shoulder before disappearing straight uphill through the woods, his feet digging for purchase as he quickly disappeared in a sea of tall timber.

Joe worked his chair over dead limbs until he was right at her side. Looking down, he could tell her breathing was shallow, but with each rise and fall of her chest, he was thankful that she was breathing at all.

Her dress was smeared with dirt. Her arm was bloody from a long scratch that looked as if she had tangled with the briars. Three furry, oblong leaves lay just inches from her right hand. She was picking herbs, Joe told himself. Leah had been learning about many local remedies from the dok, as well as herbs she could add to make dishes taste better, but aside from a few twigs scattered about that could have caused her to lose her footing, not a stone or stump was nearby. He noted the rough bark of the nearby trees that could have been the culprit until...

It was less than twenty yards out where he saw the gap. At least ten feet of fencing rolled up. It didn't take a genius to realize that the fence had been cut, considering the deliberate breaks in the wire.

Joe quickly looked down at Leah and then back to the fence. She hadn't fallen. Something more sinister had happened here.

With deeper suspicion, he studied the area more closely. To his left, Joe could see the dirt around the area had been stirred up with boot prints and a wide area down the center as if someone had been dragging something.

"Poachers!" White-hot anger filled him with such force that Joe hadn't realized the tight hold he had on his chair wheels. It was a temper he'd long ago buried under other emotions, like pride, doubt, and vulnerability.

How could he even fathom what Leah had gone through? Sliding from his chair, Joe brought himself to her side on the ground. He wished desperately to pull her onto his lap and wrap two protective arms around her until help arrived, but he knew not to cause her more harm. Instead, Joe placed her hand into his and started to pray.

"Lord, don't take her," he prayed in earnest. Then Joe prayed for understanding. Leah had quickly become one of the most important people in his life, yet he could not protect her. At least, not the way he was right now.

CHAPTER TWENTY

Her head was pounding. Her eyes hurt. As a wide door opened, revealing more light, she squinted. It was already as bright as a summer morning, and the smells of a hospital were enough to make anyone sick.

Mamm touched her arm. "Stay awake just a little longer, my dear," she would whisper each time she caught Leah nodding off.

The last time Leah was in a hospital, Beth had broken her arm, and Leah did all the crying. Leah's sympathies had been so deep that even her arm ached as she watched Beth endure X-rays, straightening, and a cast. Mamm said such things weren't possible since Leah hadn't even tried climbing the oak tree on the Kings' neighboring property, but Leah's right arm disagreed, though Leah never dared tell Mamm that.

"*Vort a klee.*" Daed's voice, telling Mamm to give her a few more minutes to rest, forced Leah to open her eyes once more. Oh, she was incredibly tired, but as the room began shrinking under the accumulating bodies coming in, it was a wonder she dared try to sleep at all.

Caleb stood behind Mamm, who sat at Leah's side. Leah wasn't sure, but if her mind wasn't playing tricks, Caleb's jaw sported a dark shadow. The sheriff began speaking, but Leah wasn't sure what he was saying exactly. *Trespassers. Stolen. Attack.* She turned, hoping to make out the conversation going about. Was dizziness one of the symptoms?

Daed stood to her right, his hat in his hand. He wore a frown, but that was common, telling her nothing. In a far corner sat Amos, and

Mammi Iolene was at his side. Everyone looked as if she might have an acute case of appendicitis. Leah knew she had none of the symptoms, since Jeralyn Miller visited the dok at least once every two weeks with some sort of ailment. Jeralyn's latest was acute appendicitis. Only, Dok Stella insisted if her pains were under the ribs and she was still fostering a diet soda habit, then she likely had gas. Jeralyn, of course, disagreed with the dok's prognosis even after learning symptoms.

One thing Leah was very aware of was that Beth never had to lie in a hospital bed barely dressed with a room full of folks. Pulling the covers up to her neck, she gave Mamm a fretful look as another deputy entered the room. What were they all doing here?

"Leah, the sheriff needs to know what happened to you," Daed said.

The tall sheriff nodded at her and moved a little closer. His light hair and pale eyes looked kind enough, but his massive frame had her wishing to stay hidden under the covers.

"Did you see anyone while you were bird-watching?" the sheriff asked. "Was someone there, in the woods, perhaps? Did you hear a vehicle or four-wheeler?"

Leah had little recollection of what happened, but she was sure she hadn't been bird-watching. Closing her eyes, Leah tried to remember the last thought in her head. "Daed was cutting wire for the coop." Her voice sounded light, even soft to her own ears, but she was trying to collect the visions and thoughts in her head.

"Leah." Daed bent and looked at her. "That was a month ago. The sheriff wants to know, while you were bird-watching at the fence lines, did you see any strange Englischers?"

"I was fetching the laundry," she informed him, recalling just how sweet a robin sang nearby as she unpinned each dress from the line. "I wasn't birding. I heard the does." Talking made the throbbing harder, but she understood how important it was to tell the sheriff what she knew.

"Perhaps her mind is addled," Mammi Iolene said. "Noah Petersheim lost his mind when a horse kicked his head."

"Mammi," Daed scolded. "The nurse said she would be confused for a time. What Leah needs is rest. If she recalls anything that may help you in your investigation, I will see to share it with you."

"I do understand, Mr. Wickey, but now that one of your bucks is missing and your daughter is hurt, I think it's more serious than someone trespassing or trying to poach a deer."

"One of the deer is missing?" Leah started to rise. Her family depended on the herd, and even the loss of one could set them back. Daed had invested much of the sale of their home in Lancaster on the move and improvements.

"Jah, Legend is missing," Amos said gruffly and got to his feet. Clearly he was as upset as Leah by the news. "He was our tamest yet. We never even got to breed him this year!"

"I understand, young man. We've checked the whole area. I still have a few men out there turning up stones for something, but other than the cut fencing and the tracks your friend pointed out, I've little to go on." The sheriff pointed his hat toward Leah. "She's the only clue we have, and these things require fast attention. Meaning the longer it takes to learn what she knows. . ."

"The less likely you find them," Caleb replied. "Leah, we found you near the fence. Someone was there with you. Do you remember who it was?"

Leah remembered the does and wild chicory blooms. She remembered the faint smell of vapor rub and quickly realized her head must be addled, confusing too many recollections into one. But. . .the man. A dark shadow slowly filled her mind's eye.

"This man is dangerous if he'd go to such measures as to hurt a woman and steal livestock."

"I saw a man." Leah closed her eyes and tried to concentrate. "I thought a dog was scaring them, or a bear."

"You should have never gone so far alone," Mamm told her, squeezing her hand much too tight.

Leah agreed. She hadn't meant to go so far. Never would she have imagined the dangers that lurked just beyond their home.

"You saw a man," the sheriff repeated. It was easy to see desperation in his eyes. "Did you see what he looked like?"

A young deputy stood behind him, notebook in hand. She had to stay awake and focus. A buck was missing, a man willing to do anything to get him. Jah, she was remembering now. Slowly the smells and sounds were returning.

"He was cutting the fence. Blue handles like Daed's." Leah winced again and swallowed. Mamm quickly tilted a straw to her mouth.

"Drink, Leah. The doctor says you're allowed to have as much as you want."

Leah drank and let the ice-cold water tame her dry throat. "He wore a hood. A hood over his head. It was black. There was smoke." And vapor rub, but Leah couldn't imagine such a scent in the forest and assumed her mind was tricking her from one memory to another. The sheriff might not trust what recollections she did have if she went on spouting about Mammi Iolene's vapor rub.

"He didn't know I was there. I saw him cut the fence, and the wire rolled back. I tried to sneak away before he could see me, but. . .I heard something." Fear of the moment revisited, and she closed her eyes tight. No doubt it was Mamm's hand on her shoulder right now.

"What did you hear, Leah?" That was Caleb again, pulling her forward.

Leah opened her eyes and stared at her brother as she finished sharing what she could remember. "Someone moved behind me. I was gonna run to the road. I yelled." Leah clutched the blanket up to her chin, but it did nothing to keep the fear from returning. It did nothing to hide her away from the vision of that exact moment when everything turned to nothing.

The sheriff didn't need to know she was a fraidy-cat. He only needed to know who the men were. But Leah hadn't a clue.

"So you saw two men."

"Jah, but I only saw one cutting the fence. He had dark eyes and. . .denim pants with holes in the knees. He didn't hit me. It was the other one. I never saw him, but he said, '*Don't turn around*,' right before I stopped knowing anything at all."

"*Ach, der Lord.* What kind of man would do such a thing?" Mamm squeezed Leah's hand so tight she was sure it might be bruised by morning.

"I cannot know the thoughts of men, but I have never felt our family in danger before coming here. I fear what these men will do to steal from us. Legend is young yet but worth much. I have two worth much more, but none worth the safety of my family. I will sell the whole lot to end this nonsense."

With that, Amos stormed out of the room. Surely he had to know Daed wouldn't sell the herd, Amos' future livelihood. Leah suspected that as shaken up as she was, she wasn't the only one suffering from what others tried to do to their family.

"Don't worry, Mr. Wickey. I'll have my deputies pay regular trips to your farm day and night. I've called the next county too, and they are sending a detective to help us out. We will find these two men." The sheriff turned to Leah. "Miss Wickey, my thoughts and prayers are with your healing. You get some rest, and let your family take care of you. Don't worry. We will find these men who hurt you, but if you remember anything more, even something you don't think is important at all, like the sound of a motor or the color of shoes, please let me know."

As Daed and Caleb saw the sheriff out of her room, Leah couldn't help but catch a glimpse of a chair. Beside the wheelchair, her cousin Lizzy. It only lasted a second, but when Joe's eyes met Leah's, she knew all would be well.

"He's been here the whole time. His driver picked your daed and bruders up to be here with you. I rode in the ambulance."

"It's kind of him to come, but I'm not sure why. I hope I didn't worry him."

"Leah, he and Caleb found you. Caleb ran straight up the mountain yelling they found you. My heart was ever so happy. Joe Shetler stayed at your side until we got there. He's been here all night. He refuses to leave until he knows you are well."

Leah slowly turned to her mother and met her tender smile with one of her own. "I guess I did worry him a little."

Mamm laughed. "A man who worries over you has a care in his heart."

Leah hoped Mamm was right about that.

Joe shivered against the cold air of the hospital, his clothes damp from the rain pouring outside. When Driver Dan had arrived at the Wickeys', Joe immediately knew Leah's family needed him more than Joe needed to follow the ambulance. Waiting for Levi and Lizzy to arrive felt like hours, but Leah was all right now. He kept repeating the nurse's assurances over and over in his head as he waited outside room 425.

"I can get you some coffee or something warmer to drink," Levi said, offering Joe bottled water as another deputy slipped into Leah's room. By his count, ten folks were crammed in that room. Joe wanted to be one of them, but not being family, he was assigned to wait in a small room down the hall. He couldn't wait like that for word of Leah's condition. So he'd set the brake to his chair near her door.

"I'm fine," he replied to Levi. Over an hour went by before the sheriff and his men left. Joe watched the door close but not before catching a glimpse of Leah. He let out a breath, thankful she was all right.

"Thank you, Joe, for helping today. If you remember anything else, please call us." The sheriff handed Joe a card with his number on it. Joe couldn't tell him more than what he'd seen. The torn-up ground, cut fencing, and drag marks.

"Who would do such a thing to another?" Lizzy said under a tight breath as the men turned the corner and disappeared.

Joe could not believe it either. Evil was part of this world, but to see it firsthand had everyone concerned. "Levi"—Joe turned to his bruder—"I'm ready."

"Jah, they said she will need to rest tonight but should be let go by morning. We should get you back."

Joe did need to get home now that he knew Leah's wounds weren't as severe as he first believed, but the whole ordeal had left him...changed. Sitting next to Leah while she lay there, motionless, had taken more from him than he expected. He couldn't keep on the same path he was traveling and expect anything to change. "Nee, I'm ready for something else. Can we talk, bruder?" Joe motioned Levi to follow him.

"I'll go call our driver while you two talk," Lizzy said before strolling to the end of the hall where the nurses' station was.

"What's wrong, bruder?" Levi stared down at him with concern. His straw hat looked to have seen better days, as did his dusty trousers.

"I could do nothing." Joe inclined his head. He rarely admitted to his vulnerabilities. There were times when he felt helpless, unable to do simple tasks or things expected from a man. But Levi had been there with him through each disappointment.

"No one could. Don't be blaming yourself for Leah's attack. No one would have expected such to happen."

"I'm not blaming myself. I'm angry I couldn't do more. I'm ready. It's time to try on something new, even if it scares me to death." Joe peered up at Levi with fresh determination.

"I don't understand."

"I'm considering adding to my life, and I trust your thoughts, bruder. I've never really done anything without you being part of it."

"We're bruders. I'm here for you as long as you need me."

"Then tell me if I'm being foolish now, because I think it's time to take another jump." Joe couldn't be the man Leah needed as he was. But if he considered agreeing to the surgery Dok Stella thought might help him, then he might be.

Leah needed him, and he wanted her.

CHAPTER TWENTY- ONE

A rooster crowed, startling Leah from a deep sleep. Instantly she reached over to the other side of the bed. However, Beth hadn't shared a bed with her since last Christmas. Oh, how she missed her twin, more so since talking with her last night. Beth struggled with being so far away and unable to be at Leah's side, but Leah assured Beth she was fine and that after two days of rest, all was well.

But all wasn't.

A warm August breeze stirred the window curtain, and she closed her eyes once more. If only she could bury deeper within the pillows and summer quilt, pretending morning was yet to arrive, but the aromas of a hearty breakfast wafted up the stairs, reminding her of the hour. Mamm would make a fuss if any of her kinner missed a meal. Then again, it had been Mamm who insisted she drink the tea concoction Dok Stella insisted upon, knowing how weary it made her.

The house was oddly quiet for a family still counting seven. More than likely, Leah missed breakfast.

A clack of jars forced Leah's eyes open once more. Tomatoes would need to be put up today. There were buckets and buckets of perfectly ripe Oxhearts, Brandywines, and Romas that sat waiting on the washroom floor.

Picking the garden was usually Leah's chore, yet Mitchel said nothing to seeing to the chore himself. Mitchel more often than not needed prodding to do what he referred to as "women's work," but somewhere inside her mischievous youngest bruder lay a man waiting to fill bigger shoes.

Aside from canning, there would be washing to do as well today. Nee, Leah couldn't lie in bed all day. Beth would call her "lazy bones" if she did. Her family had given her space since returning home from the hospital. Mamm insisted rest was a great healer. Amos had not even once teased her, as he was prone to doing, and Mammi Iolene hadn't meddled or forced Leah to visit the local baker.

Rolling onto her back, she rubbed her tired eyes with her knuckles. Sleep had been hard sought after tossing and turning at every sound. Nocturnal nature had suddenly grown eerie, as whippoorwills, owls, and a hund that howled relentlessly from over the next hill sent shivers over her. She wasn't a fraidy-cat. Everyone knew a dangerous person lurked just beyond the safety of old walls and new windows.

When sleep did come, it was filled with visions of running deer, roaring creeks, and Joe. She wasn't at all surprised to learn he'd been there. Joe was the kind of man who didn't tend to lose things important to him, and Leah was starting to believe that she might be important to him. Not in the way Conner made her believe, or how family came to your side when needed. Why else would he have sat all night in a hospital waiting room while she was being looked over by doctors, nurses, and her family?

On that thought, she smiled and peered at the daisies sitting on her windowsill. They were such pretty, simple flowers. Like goldfinches on fields of winter wheat. Caleb didn't make a joke when delivering them. He too had grown fond of Joe and found joy in working at the outdoors shop. Caleb also never failed to mention how Joe asked over her. Surely these flutters were shared. If only Leah knew for sure.

One thing Leah was certain of was that her feelings for Joe had certainly grown since that spring rainstorm at the Amish auction when they both found themselves stranded and alone. Feelings that were beyond appreciation and respect. Like blooming daisies on a windowsill, love had bloomed in Leah's heart.

But can I trust my heart? She'd been wrong before, mistaking hope for a future that Conner never shared. But she could see not all men were the same. As Caleb, Amos, and Mitchel all were born under the same roof, no three bruders had ever been more different.

Joe was not Conner. He was plainly and simply...Joe. Steady and strong. Thoughtful and informative. He listened with both ears and didn't hide the thoughts of his heart. Nee, Leah could never again let herself care for a man who kept secrets. Joe also did not allow for his limitations to define him. He trusted God, even with the life handed to him.

"All this time..." She laughed into her pillow like a dreamy schoolgirl. How closely she almost missed what God was telling her, where He was leading her. What had been right there all these months.

Upon that thought, Leah watched a thick slice of light enter her room. Outside, the sound of buggy wheels crunching over small pebbles of rock told her the menner were heading out to chop wood to store up for winter. The rooster crowed again, followed by the sound of the gas-powered washing machine downstairs.

It was time to come out of hiding, sleepy or not. Daed was right. Fear of what may happen would shorten your days. Leah didn't want to miss any more days given to her. She'd trust God and accept what the day delivered. Doing it without fear in her belly was probably not very trustworthy, so she shot up another prayer that the sheriff would find her attackers soon.

Once dressed in her everyday pale blue dress and dark blue kerchief, Leah went downstairs. "It's a fine morning for canning," she greeted her mother.

"Leah. Well, how nice to see you are up and going. You look rested and ready for a new day." Mamm's eyes twinkled with optimism.

"I was tempted to sleep the whole day, but then I remembered all those tomatoes needing put up."

"The doktor said you needed plenty of rest. I can manage a few tomatoes. Want me to make you another cup of tea?"

"Nee," Leah said quickly. "And there's like a hundred tomatoes." If Mamm only knew how tired she looked, she might think to drink the sleepy tea herself. "Besides, Mammi Iolene will be fussing over her back for days if I don't." That was a given. Leah went to the stove in hopes there was kaffi left. She wasn't a fan of the bitter stuff, but with a healthy amount of cream and sugar, it was sure to combat weariness.

"If you are certain," Mamm replied softly.

The day required four hands instead of two. Leah had just finished washing the last tomato when the sound of a vehicle pulling into the drive stopped them both. No one mentioned visitors today.

"Who could that be?" Leah reached for a towel to dry her hands and felt a sudden chill run over her. Surely the men hadn't returned. Dangerous sorts didn't drive straight to your door. Leah shook off the troublesome thought. She was being ridiculous. What if it was the sheriff or one of his deputies? They could be checking up on her. Hopefully not to ask more questions for which she had no answers. What if they were coming to share news the men had been found?

"I reckon that would be your schwester," Mamm said with bright eyes and a fast-blooming smile.

"Beth's coming back so soon?" Leah couldn't believe it. Beth had been on her mind so much lately, and here she was, returning home two months early. Leah trailed her mother out the front door.

The red van looked as aged as Mammi Iolene's favorite quilt. It too was worn and ragged, but it kept out an early morning chill. The sliding door opened on the van, revealing a much larger Louise than the one Leah had hugged months ago at Beth and Daniel's wedding. In her current condition, Louise and her husband hadn't come for the first visit yet. Leah felt her heart explode with immense joy. Louise, the second mother to all her siblings, was soon to be a mamm herself.

"Louise!" Leah called out as Mamm quickly pulled her firstborn into a lingering hug. No doubt their mother had longed for this moment. Leah stood smiling, waiting her turn patiently.

"I see Louise has been missed, for sure, but is there not one fine welcome for me?" That mousy voice had Leah pivoting.

Alma! Dressed in bold blue and a heart-shaped bonnet, Leah's best friend rounded the front of the van with the same crooked smile she'd worn since their first day of school. She'd barely set down her gray-and-blue overnight bag before Leah tackled her with two wide arms.

"Alma Fender! What are you doing. . .in Kentucky?" Leah's voice squeaked. And to think she almost considered not leaving her room today.

Alma's laugh was deep and hearty as she gave her apron a straighten. "You don't think I'd put off coming to see for myself you're not dead. You've been my best friend since we were bopplin."

"Oh, Leah, my poor schwester." Louise served up a warm embrace of her own. "Beth called days ago saying something was wrong. I didn't believe her. Oh, I should have known. You two have a way of ya."

It was true. Leah and Beth might be separate in size and interest, but they always knew if the other was troubled.

"She called yesterday while Leah was resting. She shouldn't have worried you. Not in your condition." Mamm clucked her tongue.

"She shouldn't worry herself either," Louise added before turning to Leah once more. "When Mamm called about what happened and that you were in the hospital, Alma had just stopped by. Of course we both knew we had to come fast away to see you were all right."

"Where's Marcus?" Leah peered toward the van, but her brother-in-law was not there. Leah had been blessed with two fine brothers-in-law, yet Marcus had been their neighbor all their lives. Leah already thought of him as family. If Louise hadn't married Marcus when she did, Leah was mighty tempted to trade him for one of her own bruders. Amos most likely.

"He wanted to come and see for himself you were well, but the harvest is ready for market." Louise shrugged.

"I'm surprised he let you come alone," Mamm said, her forehead wrinkled in disapproval.

"He was none too happy for me traveling so near my time, but once Alma agreed to come with me, he had no fuss left in him."

"Louise didn't give him much time for fussing." Alma snickered. "She was packed and had a driver waiting before I could gather a bag. Thankfully, I won't need socks." Alma lifted a hand to the sun, marking the warm weather.

"Well, I'm glad that you are here," Leah said. "I'm glad you both are. Tell me what I've missed. How is the jam business?" Leah lifted Louise's suitcase and trailed behind her schwester as they made their way inside.

Work went a lot faster with two extra sets of hands helping. By noon, they had fifty-six jars of tomato juice cooling on the summer kitchen table. Laundry flapped in the hot August wind just outside. Leah listened as Louise described the space Marcus created for her jam business. Louise was being modest, but Louise had ached for a place for making jams since she had finished school. Sharing a kitchen with Mamm and Mammi meant she had to make her jams and jellies late into the night.

Marcus also insisted his schwester, Clara, help out a couple of days a week. Leah was glad to hear of it. Clara and Louise were dearest friends, and Louise's jam business was growing. Three new stores now wanted Louise's Fresh Homemade Jams.

"We changed the labels," Louise went on. "Now they say King Farms."

Louise had never been one to paint buggies or the like on her signs or labels to attract more customers, and Leah admired her for not doing so. At noon, Daed, Amos, and Mitchel returned from chopping wood blocks from logs hauled out of the tree lines.

They weren't nearly as hungry as they claimed when Louise appeared in the kitchen. Daed had been so surprised to see his eldest that he never thought to question Mamm about her secret-keeping. Wood stacking was set aside for another day as he insisted today was a special time for each of them. A time for family.

Mamm gave Louise a tour of the house, while Daed showed her

more than once each new window he finally had installed. Leah helped prepare a fine supper of baked chicken, mashed potatoes, gravy, coleslaw, stewed tomatoes, and chocolate cake. Mammi Iolene too seemed lighter in spirit in the presence of Louise. Leah always admired the way her eldest schwester could bring a smile to anyone's face simply by being in the room.

"Will you stay on for a few days?" Daed asked, taking his place at the head of the table.

"Our driver needs to return. She has a family event to get to," Louise replied with a sorrowful expression.

"Well, we will just have to be thankful for the time we have," Mamm said.

"Well, that is no time at all," Mammi Iolene put in before turning her gaze on Alma. "You cannot think of returning home before seeing your family first. What would I say to Erma if she asked me why I didn't share you with her? They are getting older. It does them good to see their grosskinner."

"I'd love to see them," Alma put in. "I just don't want to make Louise late with her driver. Mammi and Dawdi will understand."

"After supper, we can see you over there," Leah put in. "Mammi Iolene is right. You are right here. They live only four miles up the road." Leah set the coleslaw on the table and found a seat next to Alma.

Just then the side kitchen door opened. Caleb removed his hat, hanging it on the last peg farthest from the door.

"You made it just in time," Mamm announced. Since when had he grown so tall? Leah wondered.

"Louise." Caleb went to her immediately. There was the little boy Leah remembered. Even Louise seemed to notice the fast changes Caleb had taken on in the passing months as she studied him affectionately.

"When did you come?"

"We came this morning, and Mamm's trying hard to get us to stay the night. I'm just so glad to see the farm. It truly looks just like Mamm described in her letters. And Daed finally got those windows,"

Louise jested, looking at her father with affection.

"Took long enough," Daed grumbled, while Mamm poured water into his glass.

"I hope you don't mind." Caleb looked to Mamm and then Daed. "I invited a friend to supper. I didn't know Louise was coming, or I wouldn't have."

"The more, the merrier," Daed replied, always happy to add another seat to the table. Mitchel shot to his feet to fetch a spare chair from the closet. Mamm insisted on keeping at least six spares after having so many unexpected visits around suppertime since they'd moved in.

That's when Leah peered behind Caleb and in the doorway saw their newest visitor. "Joe." Leah spoke out loud, and suddenly, all eyes were on her.

"Komm ena, Joseph. We are glad to have you," Mammi Iolene welcomed.

CHAPTER TWENTY-TWO

A yeasty scent caught Joe's attention as he made his way into the Wickey kitchen. He didn't like intruding or being late, considering Caleb's family was just sitting down to supper. However, he was desperate to lay eyes on Leah for himself. Caleb said she was well, but Joe couldn't get the image out of his head of the last time he saw her. The bright smile greeting him now would surely scare away those previous visions. Caleb had mentioned Leah's reluctance to get out of bed. That's why he didn't hesitate to come.

On a nearby counter sat a large chocolate cake with thick buttercream frosting. His mouth watered. When was the last time he'd had chocolate cake? In two blinks, Joe was introduced to Leah's eldest sister and Alma Fender. Joe knew Alma to be Leah's close friend, and her mousy features and a voice that hiked more than rusted was just as Leah described.

"So you're kin to Minister Fender?"

"Jah, he's my dawdi. I'm hoping to see them before we have to leave," Alma replied. She looked to be no older than fifteen. Leah had mentioned that she too was an avid bird-watcher.

"I'm Louise. Caleb's schwester."

Joe nodded a hello.

"Let us give thanks," Rueben announced, encouraging everyone to a seat. Caleb motioned Joe next to Leah. His chair was wider than the chair Caleb removed from the spot, but sitting closer to Leah was no hardship at all.

After the silent prayer, Joe turned to Leah. "I see you are well," he said as she poured water into a glass.

"She is well, for sure," Lilly replied before Leah could. "Though I think she should have rested more. She helped with the canning and washing today."

"Irene Yutzy once canned two hundred quarts in a day, and she had just had her gallbladder removed," Iolene said as she spooned coleslaw onto Joe's plate. "Irene too is a mother's helper."

"Mammi, Leah will find other work," Lilly said. "Dok Stella is hoping to take more days to be a mamm and not a dok."

"I heard Nancy Lengacher was there today seeing over Viola," Iolene added.

"Leah cannot see over a little one until she is healed."

"Another maed who'd rather spend her days alone," Iolene scoffed. "No matter, Leah is needed here and will soon be ready to make a fine fraa for any man, for sure and certain." Iolene pointed Joe a look. He wanted to laugh but managed to ignore the unease she was trying to bring between him and Leah. Joe was no stranger to meddling family members.

"If he doesn't mind eating sandwiches at every meal, that is," Amos teased. "Remember the time she made that strawberry cake for Widow Hostetler?"

"The widow thought it was the kindest thing, but no sooner had Leah set it on her kitchen table than the center sank." Mitchel burst into laughter.

Joe gave Leah a sidelong glance. Under her thin smile, he could see she didn't like being poked at by others.

"Leah has many good qualities," Louise scolded. "Better for keeping naughty buwe from swinging from the barn rafters."

"It's true," Leah told him. "If I hadn't suspected them to be up to something that day, no doubt all three would have broken limbs."

"I heard you planted cat food on Marcus King's porch." Alma's eyes glinted with playfulness.

"And I'm thankful she did. Who knows if Marcus would have ever gotten around to asking to marry me if she hadn't kept sending Blinkers his way." Louise laughed.

"She can match her schwestern but has yet to find a husband for herself."

"And why would she when our Leah has you to do it for her?" Lilly said. "Enough talk of Leah's shortcomings unless we are all ready to confess ours as well."

Joe curved his hand around the glass, but he didn't drink. Hearing all about Leah's shortcomings didn't trouble him nearly as much as seeing the results in Leah's downcast posture. Beside him, Leah picked at her food, saying nothing. Joe didn't like seeing her so submissive. Leah had just been in the hospital. She was the only witness to whoever had stolen the family's breeding buck, and now she was being compared to another. Joe hadn't remembered a time his own parents compared him to another. They of course encouraged each of their children to follow a plain path, dress the same, and follow their faith, but they supported their differences too. Leah had many great qualities.

"I've learned, by Gott's grace alone, that not everyone can do everything. I mean, I can't shoot hoops anymore, but I can harness a horse and..." Joe swallowed, knowing it wasn't his place to speak out. "I can cook a fine meal. Laundry still stumps me, but we all have our vices."

"Jah, we all fall short somewhere." Leah's appreciation sent his heart racing.

Joe felt a hefty addition of renewed hope fill him, and he finally took a drink.

After supper, the women set to cleaning up. "We should see Alma over to the Fenders' now," Leah said solemnly.

"Amos can see to that," Daed put in. "Louise is only home for the evening."

"You must be exhausted after riding so long." Leah looked to her sister. She looked worn, her eyes not nearly as bright as when she arrived.

"I'm sure we can find you another driver so you can stay on tonight." Amos too seemed to notice how weary their sister was.

"I'd love to, but Marcus paid our driver already."

"No worries." Rueben held up his hand. "Amos will see to a driver and call Marcus. It will do my heart good to have you under my roof again, even if just for the night."

"Leah and I will take Alma to see her family. I need to see Joe home anyhow," Caleb put in, giving Joe a passing glance. Any time he could have with her was a gift.

Still red from all the attention given her over supper, Leah climbed into the family buggy next to Alma. She didn't mean to be difficult. Leah had been open to each man Mammi Iolene set before her.

While her brother and Joe talked of the shortening of days, Leah stared at the back of Joe's head as he rode in the front of the buggy. Days were shortening as leaves were beginning to sport more yellows. Wild plums were going crimson, but this far south, Leah had hoped for an extended summer. Talk of an early winter loomed over everyone's conversations lately.

"I'm excited to see the bed-and-breakfast. Mammi writes about all the folks who stay there." Alma squirmed in the seat, no doubt eager to reunite with her grandparents once more. *She wouldn't be so eager if Erma Fender had any of the same tendencies as Mammi Iolene,* Leah thought to herself.

"The bishops are all meeting here in a couple of weeks for their yearly talks," Caleb commented from the front seat. There was no wind, but the evening did include the sounds of the first crickets of the season.

"Then I'm glad I'm visiting tonight instead," Alma jested. Twice a year all the local bishops met up to talk over rules and changes within communities. Dok Stella's husband would be there, standing in for his district as well as their own. Daed hoped the lot would take place in September, as it did back home. A community needed its bishop to run well.

The Fenders' property was dotted with trees aligning both sides of the short drive. A small barn, used for keeping their only horse, sat to the left, and many times, one would see a car or van parked inside when all the rooms were full.

"I'll see Alma to the door. You two wait here." Caleb helped Alma down just as the front door opened, revealing Erma Fender. Whereas Gabriel made one think of an Englisch Santa, Erma made one think of sunshine for how bright her smile was. At sixty-six, she had sparkling brown eyes that always made one feel welcome.

"Alma? Is that you, child?"

Leah watched the sweet reunion. Alma hadn't visited her grandparents in over four years. "It's good to see how much they missed her. I know how Erma feels."

"I'm sure there are many you miss back in Lancaster."

"Not so many. Alma is my dearest friend, next to Beth, of course." In truth, Leah didn't miss life as it was as much as she feared she would.

"I see you're not sleeping well," Joe remarked.

"Is that your way of saying I look bad?" Leah teased. "You do know we canned tomatoes all day, put up laundry, and made supper." She folded her arms over her chest, enjoying the way his ears warmed under her teasing.

"Are you not sleeping? Caleb says you walk the floors all night. I'm only concerned."

"Don't be. I sleep." He didn't look convinced. "I sleep so well, Joe Shetler, I can do it with my eyes closed." His laughter sent her heart aflutter. Oh how much she missed him.

Alma waved before slipping into the house.

Once reaching Joe's home, Leah felt as if the last few days had been but a bad dream as life returned to normal. Joe had a way about him to make everything around her disappear.

"Hold here while I help Joe out," Caleb instructed. Leah climbed into the front seat and took up the reins.

"I enjoyed supper tonight," Joe offered.

"I'm glad you came and hope you will again soon," Leah said.

"I'd like that." With both hands, Joe lifted one leg and then another over the side. Caleb made the transition look effortless, and Leah couldn't help but wonder if she too could help him in and out with such ease.

"We have a free Sunday coming. . ." Joe said, looking up to her with that mischievous glint in his eyes that she adored.

"I hope I can call on you then."

Leah worked to contain the joy bubbling to the surface at his request. She hadn't mistaken it. Joe Shetler was. . .interested in. . .her.

"You can, Joe."

CHAPTER TWENTY-THREE

Alma trudged into the kitchen as Leah started clearing away the breakfast table. It had been wonderful having her friend and Louise visit. If only it wasn't so short-lived.

"I almost forgot how blessed I am to have Mammi and Dawdi. They stayed up until ten, drinking tea and eating cookies while I told them all the comings and goings they've missed."

Alma had talked nonstop since she and her dawdi, Minister Gabriel Fender, arrived this morning. "Family is important. You should tell your daed you'd like to visit them again. I'd be happy if you visited them next week!" Leah filled the sink with sudsy water and gave her friend a wink. How wonderful it would be if Alma came to Kentucky more often.

"I might do just that," Alma said, setting water on the stove for a fresh kaffi. "The bed-and-breakfast keeps them busy. I don't know how Mammi gets up and down those stairs all day. Just this morning a family from Michigan called and booked all nine rooms for Christmas. I'm certain they could use a break every now and then," Alma continued.

Leah recalled the weeks her parents came to Kentucky to visit the community and purchase the farm, staying at Fender's Bed-and-Breakfast. She also recalled how Mamm insisted on helping Alma's elderly grandmother with small tasks, but Erma Fender had fine-tuned common organizational household chores down to the minute of each day and never went to bed with a chore unfinished.

Hunting for a Husband

"Joe seems kind, and he certainly has eyes for you, but...you failed to mention everything about him in your letters."

Leah washed all the glasses first before dropping forks and spoons into the dishwater. Alma, like her grandmother, never left a stone unturned. "I shared the important parts." Joe's disability didn't change her opinion of him or how her heart was taken by him. It need not matter to Alma either.

"Has he asked to court you yet?"

"He asked to call upon me," Leah replied and smiled, remembering the thrill of excitement that raced through her when he did. In the next room, her family sifted through remnants of material. Mammi Iolene was no doubt having Louise choose fabrics for a boppli quilt.

With her voice low, Leah added, "I know you, Alma, and our friendship has lasted nearly as long as we have lived. Please don't worry for me. You have you and Isaac to worry about."

Alma rolled her eyes and groaned. "Isaac," she said in a raspy voice. "One day he forgets he has a girlfriend. The next, he wants me to visit his cousins with him."

"That's good." Leah smiled. "You worried for nothing. He clearly was just busy saving up."

"I guess that's true. I'm not sure yet, but we're not talking about Isaac right now. We are talking about you. I don't want to see you get involved too quickly with another person."

Leah understood that, but did Alma not see that she wasn't the same naive girl from Lancaster that she once was? In the eight months of living in Kentucky, Leah had learned three valuable lessons. One was never to trust Mammi Iolene outside of the kitchen. Two was never to walk alone past the view of her own yard, and three, when you think you've failed to find what is truly important in life, it finds you. Leah felt terrible for her previous envies of her sisters. For allowing herself to feel left behind when, in fact, love came at the appropriate time.

"Alma, you've helped me to see that even though Conner left a deep mark behind, my life still has to go on. Joe has been an unexpected gift to me. We met under. . .stormy skies and strange circumstances, and yet the more we talk, the more my feelings grow. I'm blessed he even asked, though I will admit, I did have hopes that he would."

"Leah, I know since Conner, you've been. . . Well, I'm your best friend, so I will just say it."

"You look like you might faint. Maybe it's best you don't say anything." A word given could not always be taken back, and Leah feared whatever Alma was about to say might sting.

"You've been hunting for a husband ever since Beth and Louise got married and Conner left you for whatever is out there." Alma waved her arm.

"Mammi Iolene has been hunting for a husband for me. Did you not read my letters? I'm not very good at doing so myself." It was true. Leah had walked out with a few nice fellows, but none of them suited. Even when she thought things were looking up, it was clear they weren't.

"I'm worried about you and fear you may be making another mistake."

"A mistake? How so?" Leah planted two hands on her hips and cut her eyes to her longest and closest friend. She didn't like where this talk was going. Alma had always been blunt to a fault, but kindness never escaped her. Right now, Leah was not sure.

"Well, Joe seems verra kind. He's funny and, well, he does get your jokes. Sometimes I don't even get them, but if you let your feelings grow for him, you will be asking for a life of hardship. Leah, his life is a hard one."

"Isn't all life hard if we see only the stones in the path and not the road ahead?"

"Sounds like something Iolene would say. Well, what of kinner? You want seven. You said so when we were barely old enough to watch the older kids play basketball."

"I'm no longer a child. I don't wish on stars anymore, either." Nee, Leah found that each day brought forth its own gifts. "Who's to say I'll never have kinner?" Of all the people in her life, it galled her to think

Alma was being so judgmental of someone with a disability.

"What if he can't give you kinner?"

"Alma!" Leah quickly lowered her tone. "I love you, but that's up to Gott. I cannot ignore a good man for fear of not getting what I want. I don't feel afraid, or worried, or even alone when we are together. I find myself wishing I could help him from a buggy or hem his trousers. I worry if he's eaten or if he's willing to go through surgery. I've read all about it." Leah waved an arm, slinging water over the floor. "I worry for him and with him, and you know what is most important?" She was too upset to give Alma a chance to answer her question. "He sees me. He doesn't forget he has a friend or run off instead of talking to me." Joe went out of his way to talk to her, even with others watching.

"Good answer. I guess you have my blessing, then." Alma gave an approving nod.

"Your blessing?"

"Well, I had to be sure, you know, that you weren't making a mistake and being like Irene."

"Ach, of all the stuff, Alma Fender. You nearly got my dander boiling. Cousin Irene is a flirt. I never understood why Mammi Iolene always said I should be more like her."

"Me either. She's courted every available man in all of Lancaster County, yet none have asked to marry her." Alma's brows hiked.

Leah wanted time to slow as she carried Louise's bag to the van. In the last twenty-four hours, she'd reunited with her best friend, spent time with her beloved sister, and discovered her feelings for Joe were returned. With conflicting emotions, she watched Louise say her so longs to their parents while Alma gave her dawdi a lasting embrace.

"Leah," Louise called to her. "I do hope you'll consider coming for a visit soon."

"You know we will. I have to meet my new niece." Leah placed her schwester's suitcase in the back of the van.

"Or nephew." Louise smiled and looked down to her middle. "I wish we could stay longer, but I do miss my husband. He'll be happy to know you're courting a fine man."

"Or he may think me foolish like Alma did." Leah blew out a breath.

"Alma has her own growing yet to do," Louise whispered. "What matters is how you feel."

"Joe." Just saying the simple name brought a smile to her face. "He makes my heart sing." Leah blushed. "That's silly, is it not?"

"Nee, schwester." Louise touched her cheek. "My heart still sings every time Marcus looks at me. Especially since I've grown so big to crowd the buggy." Louise chuckled. "We've been truly blessed, have we not, to be loved by good men? I'm proud of you," Louise whispered again. Pride and compliments were often frowned upon, but Leah couldn't help but lift her head higher at her schwester's words.

"I've made enough mistakes and hope I'm not making another one." Leah hated to sound so doubtful—her feelings for Joe were unlike those she'd ever had before—but she had been wrong in trusting someone with her heart before, had she not?

"You've been through much. It does my heart good to leave knowing Joe has eyes for you. Mammi Iolene says he comes from a good family and has a kind heart."

"He does," Leah confirmed. Joe would never make a promise he didn't intend on keeping, as Conner had. "I just hope after he's learned what a terrible cook I am, he doesn't change his mind."

CHAPTER TWENTY-FOUR

To onlookers, he looked mighty silly leaving Minister Fender's house on a Saturday morning in his new custom-made buggy. But with both reins in his hands and a stack of fluffy clouds overhead blotting out the sun, Joe was the king of the hill.

The buggy maker in Walnut Ridge had not been the most pleasant man to deal with these last few days, but it had taken Freeman and his father only a short time to consider Caleb's idea and create a buggy that would support his chair, giving him freedoms he had been neglecting for years.

The chop buggy, or spring wagon as some called it, had been shortened, with a custom-made ramp for his wheelchair. Joe could manage all the parts from his chair. A power drill, Caleb's idea, allowed for Joe to raise the ramp once inside or lower it when he needed to wheel up the ramp and take his place behind the reins and footboard.

Curved black sidewalls gave it a more appealing look than the slat sides that were signature to the community. Freeman even installed a track on the floor for his wheels to sit in, locking him in place. It was brilliant!

Caleb did all the wiring, installing the blinking lights required for their district, and all three standing ministers were not only impressed by the custom-built buggy but also felt that Joe and Caleb did well keeping it within their community buggy guidelines. Of course every community didn't mind bending a rule under special circumstances, and Joe was thankful for permission to keep the brake Freeman installed for extra safety. Freeman was right to go ahead and put it in at Joe's right side. The extended armrest doubled for a brake when pressed with the use of his elbow.

Of course, the mare Caleb talked Joe into purchasing wasn't at all content with pulling the awkward-looking cart, but her size had made it easier to tackle the long process of harnessing her. Joe practiced for three days until they both understood their new roles in each other's lives.

Joe let the new horse pick up her pace in the short stretch of road. He knew they both had a lot to get used to yet, but progress had been made.

Glancing right to the shortened seat, he couldn't help but grin. *Room enough for another person.* The newness was expected, but nerves still riddled his insides. He was making lots of big decisions lately, and today he would know for sure if Leah was part of the future he was eager to chase.

Veering onto Hickory Hill Road, Joe felt his grin widening into a smile. There was just one more stop to make before calling upon Leah. Betty Marie was certain she had just the right match for the Wickey farmstead.

"Ei, ya look put together, but stop fussing over your kapp. Best put on shoes. I don't care if it's summer—it isn't proper to go courting barefoot!"

Leah fetched her shoes and tried not to laugh at her grandmother. As nervous as Leah was, Mammi Iolene appeared to be equally nervous. It was to be expected, Leah thought, considering Mammi Iolene had spent so much of her time invested in Leah's future. Of all the Wickey sisters, Leah never imagined she would be the one to cause Mammi such pains.

"And don't go on talking about yourself. Gott says we are to be gut listeners, for talkers have poor ears."

Leah was a good listener. In fact, she could sit for hours listening to Joe talk of his day. Her face heated in the very idea that the one man she hadn't even considered was the one who won her heart.

"I know how to be quiet, Mammi. It's Amos and Mitchel who should concern you. Joe wouldn't have asked me to go fishing with him if he thought me too chatty."

"He's being kind," Mammi Iolene said bluntly. "You maedels can talk the ear off a goat these days. It wonders me who thought to go fishing instead of taking a nice ride through the valley like a sensible couple."

"He did, which is why I'm looking forward to today even more," Leah replied. Mammi was just being difficult today. Joe enjoyed talking about birds. In fact, there were few subjects he shied away from. "He's here," Leah said, not trying to hide the eagerness in her voice.

"Don't you go running outside. That boy must prove he has some patience," Mammi Iolene continued to badger.

"Ach, leave Leah to her visit. If memory serves me, you didn't worry Beth to slow down when Daniel came calling." Mamm gave her mother a calculated look.

"Of course not. Beth was bound to never marry with her foolish thoughts. It was best she ran and grabbed hold of that fine man while she could."

"Such talk." Mamm shook her head. "Leah knows what is expected and how to be. She always has known." Mamm smiled sweetly and patted Leah's arm. "Enjoy yourself, dochter. I'm sure you and Joe will catch plenty of fish to eat."

"I can't believe I'm nervous. I mean, we were already friends, but now..." Leah wrangled her lower lip in nervous excitement. She couldn't remember a time she was this nervous to ride with another before.

"That's the best kind of feeling...isn't it?" Mamm asked her in a soft voice. "I remember when Rueben used to talk to me during recess. Your daed could go on and on about growing hay. I never knew such could be interesting."

"That's because you were too busy enjoying the look of him. Hay's not interesting," Mammi Iolene clucked. "Now don't make her late.

Joseph will think her lollygagging." Mammi Iolene waved Leah toward the door.

"If Beth calls..."

"We will tell her you will call her back this evening." Mamm handed Leah the small red lunch cooler filled with sandwiches, soda, and sweets.

Leah wanted to run to the buggy but remembered her grandmother's words and took her time down the steps. How many times she had ridden with a young man she couldn't count, but this was the first time she could ever remember being so excited. What had started as a simple friendship had bloomed into more than she could have ever imagined.

Joe sat smiling, a handsome twinkle in his eyes as he held both reins in his hand. He wore his black hat and matching vest as he did during church Sundays. Her heart fluttered.

"I see you have bigger wheels today," Leah remarked. Caleb had given her a full account on the progress of the custom-made buggy. It made her heart glad to see him sitting there as if he had always done so.

"The only six-wheeler around," Joe returned in common playfulness. "I hope you don't mind." He patted the smallish seat beside him.

"Of course not. Seeing you here in your own buggy means more than where I am to sit. To be honest"—she ducked her head—"I feared you might change your mind."

"Some changes are good, but I would never let a chance to spend time with you be more important than anything." Holding out a strong hand, Joe helped her into the buggy.

Sparks and lightning filled her in his words and his touch. Was that even normal?

Leah sat on the cushioned seat feeling rather special. Amish buggies never had cushions, and there was plenty of room for Joe's wheelchair. Leah took in all the details of a one-of-a-kind buggy. It resembled a spring wagon. Only shorter. "Is this a ramp for getting in and out?"

Joe nodded. It wasn't so different from some of the special buggies she'd seen in Lancaster, but one thing stood out right away: Joe's buggy allowed for him to sit in his chair and drive the horse instead of room in the back for him to ride. He wasn't a passenger any longer. Joe was a man in charge of his destination. Leah knew what an achievement that was, and her heart swelled with joy for him. Surely he felt wonderful accepting one more change in his life.

"I truly like it," she further complimented, meeting his gaze.

"I'm glad to hear it," Joe replied.

He was the most handsome man she'd ever known, with a grin that made her knees wobble. If he was nervous, Leah hadn't noticed. She could sit here in her family's driveway all day and still be perfectly content to be looked at in such a way.

"Did you bring fishing poles?"

"Jah, and bait. Figured we'd try out some from the shop. If they prove good, I can talk them up." He chuckled.

Leah was about to comment when a soft whine drew her to a large box in the back of the buggy. "What's that?"

"Just something I thought to add to our day," Joe replied, but the grin on his lips made her even more curious. Coming to her feet, Leah reached for the box and opened the flap. She was immediately met with a pair of pointy ears, a snubby nose, and eyes as happy to see her as Leah was to see them.

"That's your newest friend. He's quite the protector."

His chuckle was deep and teasing. Unhesitant, Leah lifted the furry ball of cuteness out of the box and brought him straight to her chest. "You got me a puppy!"

What a surprise. The pup had four white paws and white around his neck and down the center of his head. The rest of him was covered with a rich auburn-red color that stole her heart immediately. He pressed his tiny wet nose to her chin, spurring a laugh out of her.

Joe pointed to the puppy. "He's a fierce guard dog. Don't be fooled. He can chew through a barn door, according to ten-year-old Stephen Glick." Joe reached out and gave the small bundle a head rub. "I know neither of us are taken with pets, but I felt you could use a good ankle biter to keep those bruders of yers in order."

Leah suspected the reason behind the gift, and it had nothing to do with her bruders. "Joe, it's..." It was thoughtful and sweet and the kindest thing anyone had ever done for her.

"He's small now, but he'll grow." Joe put the buggy in motion.

"Danke, Joe. He's perfect." The small creature would require some training and care, but this was more than flowers and flirty winks. This was an extra sense of security she had been struggling to find since her attack. This was a commitment.

"His name is Moses," Joe went on to further add.

Joe didn't do things without intent, and she was curious how he came to name such a small pup after Moses. "Like Moses who protected so many from slavery?"

"We can all be a slave to something." Joe shrugged. "But, nee. I named him Moses because he was all alone. Betty sold all the other pups but this one. When I went to him, he wasn't afraid, though he was alone without his bruders or schwestern with him. I offered him some dog food Betty insisted he didn't like."

"Let me guess. He took it."

"He did. Better yet, when I turned to follow Betty out of the barn, he growled."

"Oh, he did not." Leah held Moses up. "Growling at folks is not allowed if you think to be mine. Once you meet Daed, you'll understand." Leah chuckled.

"Nee, it shows he knows who feeds him, and he didn't like me so close to her. Remember when Moses sent shepherds on their way for troubling the women at the well?"

"So, he will watch over me?"

"Gott will watch over you. He just might use Moses to do it."

If hearts could overflutter, Leah's was. Joe had given her more than a gift. He had shown Leah that she was important. That she meant something special to him.

It was a short drive to Joe's place. Leah held Moses as if he were a fragile thing. A hund wasn't so terrible, she was coming to realize.

Once Joe lowered the ramp using a battery-operated drill, Leah handed over Moses, an appropriate name for such a small critter. "I'll tie us off." She quickly tethered the older mare to the nearest tree and collected her lunch cooler before taking Moses into her arms again.

Joe had said it was a small pond, but Leah marveled at the clear blue water, low banks, and the fact it was larger than Ronks Pond back home, where she'd spent countless hours skating over the frozen winter ice.

After they'd tied on new baits and cast their lines out onto the water, Moses found a spot at Joe's feet to nap. Apparently he'd warmed up to Joe since that first visit in Betty Marie's barn.

"Do your folks like fish?" Joe asked, reeling in a large bluegill.

"If it comes from the diner we used to eat at, then the answer is yes. Mamm can't stomach the smell, but our neighbors, the Kings..."

"The one who married your schwester, Louise?"

"Jah, Marcus." Leah loved how Joe absorbed her every word. Conner had seldom listened to a thing she shared. "His family would have fish on Saturdays. Each of us siblings would take turns finding a reason to go, and if Mamm knew what we were up to, she never mentioned it."

"Do you know how to clean one?" Joe cocked his head as he dropped another bluegill in a bucket nearby.

"I do. Marcus taught each of us how," Leah said with a lift of her chin. She was no delicate woman but liked to consider herself capable of a great many things.

"I should like to meet him one day."

"I hope you do." Leah smiled his way. Just before the sun rose straight above them, Leah opened the cooler she and Mamm had packed. Mammi Iolene insisted on all kinds of fanciful foods, but Leah wanted something simple and less difficult to mess up.

"I reckon they've stopped biting anyhow." Joe beamed, seeing her removing food from the cooler.

"I did catch almost a dozen," Leah jested as she handed him over a sandwich. She held up two soda cans and allowed him to pick which he preferred. Taking a seat close to Joe, Leah sat on the ground, using the cooler top as a makeshift table. She pulled out a bag of plain potato chips and two chewy chocolate chip granola bars she'd wrapped up just this morning.

"My family will eat fish at every meal if they can. Mamm will appreciate them."

"Then I say we clean them for your mamm. Danke again for Moses." Leah offered her new friend a piece of ham. The pup was already a good listener. "I know you got him to make me feel safer."

"A gut hund is worth his supper." Joe set down his soda can. "Has the sheriff found out anymore?"

"Nee. He or one of the deputies comes about, hoping I'll remember more. I'm glad I have little memory of it at all. They are looking into a lead, the deputy said, but that was three days ago." Leah gave Moses another bite. "I just wish it was over. I don't like looking over my shoulder all the time. I don't even fetch eggs in the evening. I feel foolish being afraid of going to a henhouse."

Joe leaned forward, placing a hand on hers. "Someone hurt you. There is nothing wrong with being aware of your surroundings, but do not be afraid."

She was trying, but when shadows danced at dawn and dusk, she failed miserably.

"I've been selling a lot of game cameras lately, and it got me thinking." Joe took a drink of his soda.

"What's a game camera?"

"It's a camera that takes pictures. Most use them to hang on trees in the woods to see what's hanging around. Hunters find them helpful in tracking game."

"Doesn't sound like a fair advantage to the animals." Leah pulled Moses onto her lap and dipped her hand into the potato chip bag for two more chips.

"It wouldn't hurt to add a couple around your family's farm."

Leah jerked her head up and stared at him. "You think they might return?" She clutched Moses tightly to her chest.

"I don't, but I cannot know what men like that think at all. If they don't, I'm only out a few batteries, but if they do. . ."

He was thinking of her well-being again. "You will catch who they are." Though Leah didn't want to think of the men returning, it was a good idea. Men were unpredictable, that was for sure and certain. "Can we put one up today?"

"I pulled four off the shelf before I left. When I see you home, I'll have Caleb help hang them, as long as Rueben isn't against it."

Leah's father was not opposed to some newer ways of thinking. Having lived in Lancaster most of his life, he had grown accustomed to change. So much so that he stopped building houses for a living and started breeding deer for an income. "Daed will appreciate your concerns, I assure you. He cares about his deer, and knowing one is still missing has been pressing hard on him."

The matter was settled, and as the day strung along, they talked of better things, like Levi and Lizzy's upcoming wedding. They had yet to be published at church, but Joe was certain Lizzy and Levi had plans for a late September wedding. They watched a flock of geese take flight and disappear into the sun. Leah blinked, and when she retained her focus, Joe was staring at her.

"Leah, there's something else I want to share with you."

He sounded so serious that her stomach tightened in knots. It had only been their first official date, and Joe was already ready to share that he had no interest in a second. It was Abel Lambright all over again. Either it was "not the right time" or "perhaps we're best with other people." Leah had heard every excuse, but this time she feared facing tomorrow without a man who considered her so completely. One whom she looked forward to seeing every single day.

"All right."

"I've been trying on new things and ideas lately."

"Like the buggy."

"Jah. You deserve to be courted properly." Joe lowered his head and smiled.

"You didn't have to purchase a new buggy to do that."

"Good to hear, but your bruder was right. There are so many things I thought were just beyond my reach." He leaned closer, taking one of the strings of her kapp into his fingers.

Leah sucked in a breath at his nearness.

"I'm learning differently."

She felt her blood warm to an unhealthy heat. He wasn't pushing her aside after all. "Caleb does know much for one his age."

"When I found you, it tore me up inside. Knowing someone could do that to you and that I couldn't do anything about it."

"Joe." This time it was Leah's turn to offer support, and she placed a hand on his forearm. "There was nothing anyone could do about it. Let's just pray these cameras of yours help find who is responsible."

"I care for you, Leah."

And there it was. Affirmation in words from a man who didn't spin yarns or make false promises. Nee, she would not cry. "I care for you too, Joe." She loved him. No man had ever given her such a plain vision of her future as the one beside her right now.

"I don't want to ever feel like that again. That's why I will be leaving next week. I'm not sure for how long."

"I don't understand. Are you going to visit family?" Was his condition getting worse? Had he kept something more serious from her? Louise's words found new wings, and she worked to calm her racing breaths. She cared for him and would, no matter what he revealed to her now. "It doesn't matter," she assured him. "I'll miss you, but I'll be here when you return."

"I'm counting on that, Leah. You were right that day, when you said I could try something new. I'm traveling with Dok and my mamm up north. The surgeries alone will take a few days, and then there is the rehab."

Leah's mouth opened at his news, but the words there were stuck.

She could see worry on his brow and hear fear in his words. He'd already been through so much, but Dok Stella insisted the surgery would be good.

"I cannot pretend to say that I'm not happy you have made this decision, but I know it comes at a great cost. No matter, I'll be here, and if you're gone too long..." She locked eyes with him. "I'll just have to come visit and give Dok a rest."

"I would like that." Joe brushed a hand over her cheek. Slowly he leaned down closer, his eyes falling on her lips. "I want to stand at your side. I want to..." His words fell short as his hand slipped from her.

Leah quickly mimicked his affections by putting a hand on his cheek. His beard tickled her palm as warmth radiated up her arm. "But even if you don't, I'll be beside you no matter what," Leah promised before rising up on her knees and placing her lips on his.

CHAPTER TWENTY-FIVE

Today felt a week long. At least this particular Tuesday felt seven days long as Leah rushed between chores. Those first days after Joe left for Ohio, it was all Leah could do to concentrate on the tasks at hand. His open confession of his feelings for her and that first kiss, mingled with concern for his well-being as he faced an uncertain future... It had been all-consuming. Leah prayed all went well and for the doctors to have steady hands.

Delilah and Lizzy had paid a visit on Thursday past. Now that Lizzy and Levi had been published, it was easy to see how much work was yet to be done before the wedding. Leah also suspected Lizzy needed a break from Cousin Verna, who thought Lizzy's choice in wedding colors—royal blue and silver—were poor choices.

"Levi says Joe is faring well. There are plans of releasing him soon," Lizzy told her. Now a fresh week had come, and Leah continued to worry. Dok Stella had been kind enough to leave daily messages on the answering machine, updating Leah on Joe's progress. The first surgery repairing his knee had gone well, but it was the second that left room for concern.

"He may walk on a tilt, but Joe will walk again," she said with absolute certainty. All the nearby communities had been praying, and those prayers were being answered. Leah didn't care if he never walked at all, but she knew how important it was to him.

Thoughts of Joe had consumed Leah's days so heavily that she had little time to entertain further fears of the thief who had attacked her. As summer blended into an early and wet fall, Moses had become the center of attention. Even Mammi Iolene, who had qualms about animals indoors, didn't mind Moses napping at the foot of her bed in the early afternoons. His rounded belly made his head look too small. Both red ears stood at attention anytime he felt someone was taking a step in the wrong direction. Joe said his breed was raised as cattle dogs, keeping every animal in its proper place. Leah wondered if that worked the same for bruders, knowing there were three nights in a row now that Amos had sneaked out of the house to meet friends.

Removing towels from a makeshift line just under the porch roof, Leah peeked through the front sitting room window. She could see the clock in the kitchen from there, and she let out a frustrated breath, noting it was a whole seventeen minutes past four. Caleb promised he'd be home at four to check on the battery-operated cameras.

With no new leads according to the sheriff, Leah wondered if it was at all possible the men still lurked about in hopes of stealing another buck from the upper lot. A chill ran over her spine, hoping they wouldn't just as she heard the sound of Caleb's buggy on the blacktop just beyond their drive. Setting the basket inside, Leah went to meet him.

"You're late," Leah scolded with arms folded over her chest.

"I tried closing up, but that big-time Englischer fella was spending his money. I know Joe will need every dime. New hips and joints are costly."

"I'm just eager to see what's on the cameras. Joe did right by hiring you," Leah told her brother. It was true, even if he didn't pay mind to clocks as well as he should.

"Not sure about that." Caleb shrugged and tethered his mare to a hitching ring on the side of the barn.

"Well, late or not, you're home now. Let's go," Leah urged him.

"You sound as bossy as Beth anymore." Caleb gave her kapp a flick of the finger, sending it rolling off Leah's head and tumbling into the soft dirt.

"Vunderbaar! Now you'll give Mamm something else to fuss over." Leah quickly snatched it from the ground and ran after her lanky bruder as he worked his way beyond the barn.

"So, do you know where each camera is?" Recent rain made the lower parts of the hill more damp. Leah minded her footing, careful not to slip.

"I helped him hang them, so. . .jah. Are you gonna keep up?"

"Now who's bossy?" Leah muttered under a breath. Caleb had been watching over Joe's outdoors shop for the last two weeks, along with keeping up his everyday chores. He was entitled to a little grumpiness, she figured.

"There's the first one," Caleb announced as he moved to a tall oak. A strap held the camera in place. The lens aimed along a stretch of fencing marking the family boundary lines. Caleb opened the camera and flipped a switch. "Joe said to always turn it off before removing the little card inside, or else all the pictures stored will be erased."

"So when we collect all four of them, how will we see the pictures? I mean, that is verra small," Leah said, staring at the small card in Caleb's hand.

"His neighbor has a computer. Joe said all she has to do is insert the card, and it pulls up the picture right on her television screen."

Leah had no clue such devices even existed, and once all four cards were retrieved and replaced with new picture memory cards, she did everything she could not to bite all her nails off instead of eating supper.

"I know you're eager to see what those cameras have found. I am too, but you best eat up. Caleb isn't going to leave you," Mamm instructed. Leah finished off the meat loaf, wishing Caleb wasn't so hungry this evening as he filled his plate a second time. If she wasn't mistaken, her bruder was doing it on purpose.

After supper, they rode to the home of Bonnie Lewis. The quaint little haus resembled a cottage from a children's picture book with vines scaling a small picket fence that surrounded a small yard. Leah immediately noted three hummingbird feeders, all busy with visitors. Sunflowers towered along one side of the house, and shading hostas, hibiscus, and early blooming chrysanthemums flanked the other.

Caleb knocked and took a step back, placing both hands in his pockets. Leah knew from Joe's account that Bonnie was in her fifties, sold Avon products out of her home, and charged a small fee to run internet sites for local Amish businesses. When the door opened, Leah was surprised to see a woman nearly as tall as Caleb. Dressed in a long gray skirt and black button-up blouse, Leah wondered if she dressed up in hopes customers would come to buy her Avon products on any given day. Her red hair was shorter than any woman's Leah had seen before, and she was almost certain the color was unnatural.

"You must be Caleb. Joe said you'd be stopping by." Bonnie smiled before peering around Caleb to notice he wasn't alone. "Oh, you sure are a pretty thing. I bet you would look even more beautiful with some Bashful Blush lip gloss."

"I. . ." Leah didn't know what to say. She certainly didn't know what Bashful Blush was, but she was certain it was a tinted lip gloss she wasn't permitted to wear anyway.

Bonnie didn't look fifty, not with all that makeup. Her lashes, like her red hair, looked unnatural. Did folks really have lashes long enough to kiss their cheeks?

"We've just come to see if you could find any pictures on these." Caleb opened his palm to reveal the four small picture memory cards. Leah was still curious how photos could fit on such a small device that looked capable of breaking under pressure.

"Of course I will, but you've caught me at a bad time. I have a party to get off to." Bonnie swiped all four cards from Caleb's palm and disappeared inside.

"Oh." Leah's disappointment showed.

"No worries," Bonnie hollered out behind her. A few seconds later, she appeared again, this time pushing a large purple suitcase with a handle and a large black bag over one shoulder.

Setting down her bag, Bonnie went to fetch a pink box. Opening it, she gave Leah a more intense scrutiny. "I bet red would make you look like a supermodel."

"I'm not in the market for such," Leah replied kindly.

"Oh well." Bonnie rushed to close the case of lipsticks and creams and reached for her bag once more. "I'm really going to be late, and even though Avon nearly sells itself, I'm on a tight budget and can't lose any potential customers. Once you buy Avon, you never buy anything else," she jingled. "No worries. I promised Joe I would help any way I can. I'll check the cards when I get home, and if I see anything out of the ordinary, I will call immediately."

"Danke," Caleb offered as he helped load the purple suitcase in the back of Bonnie's car. With nothing more, they watched her hurry out the drive before climbing back into their buggy.

"I wish she wasn't in such a hurry. I was eager to see if there was anything on the cards."

"Jah." Caleb took up the reins before shooting her an intense look. "Don't even think of wearing red lipstick," he said under his breath as he veered the buggy back to Robin's Nest Road.

"Like I would." She gave Caleb a playful punch.

He was a walking bag of parts. Rods, screws, plastic, and metal. Titanium, to be precise. He and Mamm were equally surprised how he had been pieced back together. For sure and certain, if Joe was ever foolish enough to jump at any height, he'd not break so easily.

It would take some time getting used to trusting man-made parts in a God-gifted body, but Joe pushed through his first therapy sessions with his assigned therapist, Melissa. She was a forty-something mother of two who insisted that her enthusiasm for Joe's expected prognosis was on account of being a former cheerleader who couldn't help but believe that positive encouragement promoted better healing.

Joe didn't know about all of that, but the daily exercises that were supposed to help him regain the use of his joints and muscles that had been dormant for over a decade were anything but encouraging. He'd agreed to strength training. It was much the same as the exercises Dok Stella had already convinced him to do, and despite the pain, Joe remained steadfast in healing. Even with Melissa's help, he'd yet to bear weight on both legs. The walker made for some work, but it was trustier than crutches.

As days lingered, his determination and strength grew, along with Melissa's "you've got this" attitude. Today, he bore the weight of his body long enough to see a silver lining. "Baby steps," Melissa called them. Joe never remembered such awkward pains learning to walk the first time.

"You have to keep on schedule but never overdo it." Melissa repeated his recovery instructions so often that Joe had them memorized. "I know it hurts and feels wonderful at the same time, but don't think because you've got strong parts in ya that you're superman. When you bend the rules, you pay the consequences."

How well he knew that wisdom.

"It's best to keep anything of importance at waist level. No racing or basketball. Keep it low impact. Three months at least, you have to be good to your body, or you could damage something and be back here. Keep stretching. You don't want those muscles to stay tight, or you'll walk funny. Dr. Shylm said you are his best work yet!"

He did walk strangely, but to stand on his own feet was an answered prayer.

Joe stared at the ceiling of the bedroom Aenti Meg put him in. It was a small downstairs room, and his younger cousin Jamie was none too happy to give it up to a distant family member he had been too young to recall ever meeting.

He wished to be home, seeing over his shop and spending more time with Leah. Baby steps were holding him back. Dok Stella returned home after that first week, seeing Joe out of recovery. She had been right there, next to Mamm, praying and offering words of encouragement.

In the next room, Mamm and Aenti Meg chatted over chicken dishes and who could quilt tighter stitches. How many times had he and Levi had similar chats? Closing his eyes, he considered how tomorrow would be another grueling day and then thought about the sweetest kiss he'd ever been given. That was all the encouragement Joe needed.

Caleb had said he'd watch over things and see the camera cards delivered to Bonnie. His Englisch neighbor promised to call the sheriff if she found anything, but Joe wished to be there. More than likely, she'd spot a few pictures of birds in flight, the occasional squirrel being nosy, but he wanted to know for sure. He couldn't do that three hundred miles away. Plus his feelings for Leah had grown to a strange protectiveness. But he was here, and all he could do was pray for her well-being.

"Gott, if it be Your will, let me heal quickly and get back to her. If not, keep her safe."

CHAPTER TWENTY-SIX

He was coming home. From the moment Lizzy came rushing through the front door, Leah hadn't thought of anything else but the welcome-home supper Joe's family was planning.

"Levi told me to hurry and tell you. You must come. Joe will be verra happy to see you."

"I wouldn't want to miss it," Leah replied, then quickly sought out Mammi Iolene's recipe collection. She had yet to handwrite the desserts into the new recipe book. Leah knew Joe liked pie, and she was getting better at making a fine crust. Flipping through cards and folded sheets of paper, she came across a recipe for cherry pie. *Daed's favorite.* There was chocolate and peanut butter, which were always a welcome sweet at any table. A tiny pencil drawing in the lower right-hand corner of berries caught her attention. Leah read all the ingredients for a blackberry pie filling, which invoked a lovely memory.

Since her grandfather's passing, Leah hadn't recalled Mammi Iolene making blackberry pie. Louise had always made sure the family never ran short of blackberry jam. She stared at the card with its worn and thin corners. They had the ingredients on hand. Three gallons of blackberries fresh from Lambright's Berry Farm. There was plenty of sugar and ThermFlo to thicken the mixture.

It looked easy enough, and with an oatmeal granola topping, it would make Joe's welcome home a fine one.

Collecting everything, Leah went to the summer kitchen to put together a recipe of her very own. With a pencil, she quickly did the math to cut the recipe down to only a fourth, considering Mammi Iolene's recipe was for storing up pie filling.

In a pot she added two cups of freshly washed blackberries and four cups of water. Turning up the stove, she measured out a cup and a half of sugar in a separate bowl while the water heated. Waiting for that to boil, Leah put together the topping. Brown sugar, oatmeal, and butter. A crumbly top just like the one Mamm always put on her apple crisps. Jah, in the solace of a lonely kitchen, she felt more in control and confident.

It took some convincing for the doctor and his therapy nurse to say that Joe was plenty able to return home. He suspected they would keep him for months if he said nothing, so he promised Melissa he would keep to her rules and therapeutic exercises. He didn't need to be watched over, and the longer he was there, the more costly it would be. Joe didn't want to think about the total he had already handed over.

But he couldn't convince his mother that there was no reason he had to stay in his old room. Joe had been gone for three weeks. He preferred his own bed, not the one he'd outgrown by the time he was fourteen. He needed to see the mare had been tended over well in his absence and his shop was just as he left it.

He needed to see Leah.

What kind of man confesses his intentions, kisses a woman, and vanishes for three long weeks?

I'm like the man who left for firewood in summer and returned in winter with a walking stick. He rolled his eyes.

"I see Levi is home. He's been helping your bruder, Matt, with the add-on. I do hope he remembered to invite Lizzy for supper," Mamm said as the van pulled into the circle drive.

"You know he did." Joe noticed the three buggies in front of the long, rectangular barn. Surely, in time, he too could take part in helping his bruders for all the years they had helped him.

"You're glad to gain another dochter." It wasn't a question but more an observation.

Mamm's face bloomed into a wide smile. Dark circles under her eyes showed just how hard these last three weeks had been on her too. "Jah, Meg has four, did you know?" she said playfully as she opened the sliding door. "Well, hurry on now." She rounded the vehicle to pay the driver. Joe was glad his mamm's playfulness had rubbed off on him. It had made his years easier.

The sound of young calves filled the calm of the evening. The smell of woodsmoke mingled with autumn rain and livestock met him immediately. It was good to be home. Or at least this much closer to it.

With careful movements, Joe opened the walker and saw it snapped securely, then took one slow, careful step out of the van. On two legs, he inhaled a long breath, letting much of his weight be supported with his arms and the walker. The driver, a quiet older man who hummed most of the way, retrieved his wheelchair from the back along with their other belongings.

He was tempted to use the walker all the way to the house but remembered Melissa's warning not to overdo it; but he had been sitting for over six hours, had he not?

From the barn his father emerged, along with Matt. Joe straightened as both men paused in their steps to take a look at him. Surely, seeing his crippled son standing practically on his own had his father taken aback. Joe smiled his way before taking a seat in his wheelchair.

Daed continued his way. "I thought the driver delivered a stranger to our door," Daed said, relieving Mamm of her suitcase. "Good to have you home, fraa." He winked.

"Nee, just a son trying to stand on his own two feet," Joe replied.

"It was a blessing to see. Welcome home, bruder." Matt reached out and patted Joe's shoulder. His sandy mop of hair poked out humorously under his hat.

"New haircut?" Joe teased.

"She's learning," Matt said with a blush. "I had hoped we could help you bury that chair when you returned, but it's good to see you making progress."

"It's just so I don't overwork anything."

"At least for the next few weeks," Mamm put in. "Doctor's orders. Joe will still need our help, of course."

"Our son has always been independent, Linda," Daed reminded her. It was his father who helped Mamm understand his need to live alone and start his own business.

As he sat carefully in his chair, he noticed three extra horses grazing in the pasture nearby. "Who's here?"

Daed traded a look with Mamm and then scratched his beard. "A few folks were eager to see you well."

Joe winced at the news. He was tired, eager to get his stomach filled and hopefully have a full night's sleep. Meg had been wonderful letting him and Mamm stay with them, being so close to the hospital, but Joe had barely slept in the twenty-three days he'd been gone.

"It's yer family and a few friends. Don't be a fusser. It makes wrinkles," Mamm quipped before making her way to the house.

That's when the door opened, and Leah stepped out onto his family's porch. In a lovely shade of bold blue, she looked as pretty as a spring morning and as untouched as a snowflake. He'd pictured this moment a few dozen times while lying awake at night. Longed to see her expression when he could stand as upright as the next man. But here he was, in the same chair he left home in.

But to Joe's delight, Leah's smile held no hint of disappointment. In fact, if Joe wasn't mistaken, those were happy tears.

Joe answered more than a dozen questions over a delicious meal of fried ham, yeast rolls, and garden cucumbers slathered in a sweet salad sauce. Leah remained a quiet observer, taking in how different Joe looked sitting across the table from her. He was thinner in the face, but those eyes still made her heart pitter-patter. She pulled her gaze away and forked more scalloped potatoes into her mouth. It was best not to be seen gawking. However, she had missed him every day he'd been away.

The Shetlers weren't like her own family. Where Leah's bruders showered her in embarrassment, Joe's flowered him in compliments. It was no wonder Lizzy had fallen so quickly for Levi, who sat scarfing down ham without chewing it properly.

The first time Leah had met Linda, she thought her to be just like every other Amish woman in the community, but as the evening went on, surrounded by her children and grandchildren, it was plain to see she had a funny bone to her, much like Joe. Linda's quick wit spurred many laughs, and she was never hesitant in giving out hugs.

"Why do you not tell peanut butter secrets?" Linda asked Karen's eldest kinner, who all shook their heads. "Because it will spread." With ten grandchildren, Linda was living her best life yet.

Matt's twins had taken to pushing a rolling desk chair across the sitting room floor while Leah helped the women clear the table. Her blackberry crisp had been far too big a topic after supper. Leah dropped a handful of forks into the dishwater and blushed when she noted Joe taking his third helping.

"He likes you." Joe's schwester, Karen, had four children to Matt's six and resembled Minister John more than his three sohns. Leah looked to the kitchen table where the men still sat talking over crops and livestock.

"I'm happy to see he has eyes for you. I don't listen to gossip and know just how Barbara can overreact."

Leah half smiled, glad to know Karen didn't think of her as a flirt. It still troubled Leah to know Barbara continued to avoid her.

For the rest of the evening, everyone sat around the sitting room singing old songs. Many Leah didn't know the words to, but she listened with open ears and tried learning them alongside the younger kinner. To be included made Leah's heart swell.

"Mamm does this at least once a month," Joe whispered beside her. "She and many of the other women fear the younger ones will not keep up our songs, so they invite friends over to sing."

"It's a great idea. I do wish to learn them." Leah meant it too. How busy life had been before, she thought as another song sprang out of the minister's mouth. Leah welcomed the slower community that took its time to teach old songs.

Joe's deep voice was another surprise. It blended well with Karen's next to him. Caleb looked nearly as uncomfortable as she was, but he too made every attempt to learn and participate. The Shetlers were a welcoming family with as much love for strangers as they had for their own.

Once the family began readying to leave, Joe suggested they sit on the porch. His cheeks were red from the warmth of a full house, and she too was happy to step outside in the cooler evening air.

Slipping outside, Leah was immediately met with an evening breeze. In the distance, a fiery sunset burned. The sounds of children's laughter filled the air near the barn as Matt and his fraa loaded up all six kinner in their buggy.

"You have a wonderful family, Joe."

"They're not for sale, if you're looking to buy."

"Perhaps we can trade then," she said with equal pluck. How she loved his humor.

"Remember, I've met Amos and Mitchel," Joe teased. "Caleb mentioned he checked the cameras."

"Jah, we both did. Your friend Bonnie is. . ."

"Very Englisch." Joe chuckled. "I know, but she has a heart the size of Alaska."

"She promised to let Caleb know if she found anything. . .suspicious, but neither of us have heard from her. Caleb even knocked on her door last week, but she wasn't home."

"I'm glad she didn't find anything, sort of."

"I know, but if she had, I'd worry less knowing it was all over."

"I was glad to see you when we arrived."

"Lizzy said that you would be. I shouldn't have come without being invited by you, but. . .she insisted." Leah sat on a short-legged stool next to him as they watched the sun dip below the hillside.

"I am thankful for it."

"Dok Stella left me messages each day on how you were doing. I'm sure she made it sound better than it was."

"It was. . .painful, but I got through. The first few days were the worst. I was afraid to see you, but at the same time, I couldn't wait."

"Why would you be afraid to see me?" *Of all the stuff.*

"I thought you'd rethink courting me," he said with a shrug.

"Joe"—Leah reached over and placed a hand on his—"you have done something I'm not certain I could have, and from what Dok says, you're the better for it. I know you worry how this will affect me. . .*us*, but I've never known you not in that chair, so anything else would just be. . .different."

"Danke, Leah."

His eyes locked tight onto hers. "For what?"

"For being a blessing to me."

The sound of Caleb bringing his buggy around said their visit had to be shorter than either of them wished it to be.

"I'm not so sure of that." Leah ducked her head to hide the warmth of her own cheeks. "I feel blessed knowing you."

"I just don't want you regretting this. I have to take it easy for a few days, but each day I'll only get stronger."

His hand touched her arm and her heart soared. "I know you will."

CHAPTER TWENTY-SEVEN

It felt good to be back in the outdoors shop. Caleb had done plenty of housekeeping, so there wasn't a hint of dust anywhere. With one glance at his books, Joe could see the young man had also kept each sale recorded. Hiring Leah's bruder had been a good decision, but even a hardworking employee needed a few days off.

Most Wednesdays the outdoors shop wasn't as busy as the rest of the week. Brad and his groups of boys had been happy too that Joe had returned.

"Not that I don't like the kid, but we come to shoot, so it's good to see you back," Brad said as Raelyn let an arrow loose, outscoring all three boys combined.

"Good to be back," Joe replied before turning to the young girl smiling at him. "A fine job."

"I'm the best!" She fist-bumped the air.

"Are not," Chasen said sorely from one corner of the target range.

Since Cain and Abel, envy was born. Joe understood sibling quarrels, and he even liked a little competition in his earlier years, but he'd not feed pride. "We are not to strive to be better than anyone but simply to hit our target," Joe said.

"But we shouldn't be sore losers either," Brad put in, then glared at his son. "You missed the last two shots."

Joe watched the boy's shoulders sag at the reprimand, and his heart went out to him.

"Next year I can see I might have a little champion on my hands after all." The father swooped up his dochter in a hug of congratulations. Joe had never witnessed such praise when Chasen shot well. It was none of his business how a man raised his children, but if Joe ever was blessed with a son and dochter of his own, he'd never put one child above the other.

The door in the front opened, its sweep rubbing the concrete floor revealing a new customer. "I'll be back." Joe left Brad with the children, wondering how best to address Brad's behavior at the indoor range. Chasen was a fine shot. In truth, it was only when Raelyn tagged along with them that he shot poorly.

"Bonnie! Good to see you." Today she wore bright red lipstick and a pair of dangling earrings that Joe was almost certain looked like feathers. If he wasn't mistaken, her hair had been colored recently too. The orange tint seemed completely unnatural.

"I'm so sorry, Joe." She marched straight to the counter and began emptying the contents of her purse all over it. "I should be fired. I'm the worst neighbor ever!"

Loose change, receipts, and tubes Joe suspected contained more of the flaming red lipstick rolled out and began to accumulate. "It's a blessing, not a job. What's got you all worked up, Bonnie?"

"I forgot," she said with an exasperated tone. "Your friends came by, and I was running late. Avon pretty much sells itself, and there were nineteen orders to put in when I returned home. Did you know that those sisters down the road, the three who make rugs and such, are some of my best customers?" Her penciled brow lifted. Joe wished she'd stop erasing her own and drawing in fake ones. Bonnie was a nice-looking lady who tended to try too hard to not be exactly what she was.

"I did not." Joe didn't want to know. He couldn't imagine what they could possibly purchase from Bonnie that fell within the rules of the church.

"That middle one is a bit chatty." She leaned on the counter in a more relaxed stance. "I've seen her riding with a different boy for the last two months. I thought you folks didn't do that."

"It's better to try on three pairs of shoes than pay too much for a pair that doesn't fit," Joe replied.

"I like that. I should write that down. You know, use it in my marketing." She began digging farther into her purse. Joe suspected for a pencil and paper and not for what she came to show him.

"Bonnie, what can I do for you today? Did Caleb forget to pay you for the month?"

"No! Oh, geez! My head sometimes goes in a few hundred directions. My doctor says it's because of the coffee, but I only drink three cups a day!"

Finally she pulled out an envelope.

"You caught them," she announced, handing over the envelope. "I know you said to call the sheriff if I found anything on your memory cards, but..." She paused, a worried look on her face. "I thought it was best to give it to you and let you do the right thing. I'm not the hero kind, and I've yet to pay the last ticket the good sheriff gifted me."

Joe opened the envelope and pulled out the three photos tucked inside. One was taken near the creek where Leah had been found, and two more were taken not more than twenty feet from the Wickeys' barn, where Joe knew the remaining three bucks were kept.

"I know it didn't capture their faces or anything, but..."

"One of them is Amish." The words left Joe's lips like a bitter medicine that would take some doing to be swallowed. Not only was Leah's attacker Amish, but he had returned.

"I'm sorry, Joe. I sure hope it's just one of the family's boys and not what it looks like."

Joe spread all three photos out onto the counter and gave them a closer look. The man in camouflage was broad shouldered. The baseball cap didn't conceal the light hair, but it didn't give any further clues to who he might be.

In the second photo, Joe got a clear view of his full body, and the holey denim pants had him mentally sifting through every customer who had entered his shop in the last three years. One in particular. Joe knew only one man who sported such a poor choice in clothing, and the thought nearly made him ill.

"Look closer. Is that a shoulder or just a blur?" Bonnie pointed out. "I tried enlarging it on my computer, but the pixels just made a mess of it."

Joe didn't know what pixels were, but he studied the image more intently, and sure enough, Bonnie was right. Unfortunately there wasn't enough of this one to determine any of his traits other than he wore a red vest.

"There are three of them," Joe muttered. A chill rolled over his shoulders. Three men had possibly taken part in Leah's attack. That was worse than knowing that one of the men was Amish. Joe tried to figure out his identity. Though many plain folk dressed similarly, there were subtle differences between communities. The man was lanky, and it looked as if his clothes were two sizes too big.

He'd have to go to the sheriff, but first, Joe knew he needed to show Gabriel Fender, their nearest minister. Hopefully he would know which of his flock was hiding among them.

"It's not one of Leah's bruders, but I do know who can figure it out. Danke, Bonnie. You have been the best neighbor a man could ask for."

With suspicions and assumptions, Joe tucked the photos into his pocket before informing Brad he had to close his shop for the day. An unexpected emergency.

Until the men were identified, Joe didn't know who he could trust.

"It will take too long in a buggy. I can drive you," Bonnie offered.

Though Bonnie insisted taking a buggy would take longer than accepting a ride from her, and Minister Fender lived less than twenty minutes by buggy, they pulled into Fender's Bed-and-Breakfast half an hour later.

Gabriel Fender had been a minister of Cherry Grove since Joe was in the fourth grade. When the community split, having grown beyond thirty families, he was now one of three ministers in what some folks were beginning to call the Locust Creek district. Joe liked the north, south, east, and west idea best, but what did he know of naming districts?

Minister Fender wasn't a tall man, and his rounded girth made him look even shorter than he really was. He also sported a long white beard, which often earned him second looks from small kinner in town during the Christmas season. Not quite seventy yet, Minister Fender saw over all his and Erma's needs, including running the only bed-and-breakfast in the county.

"My sister stayed here last Easter. She's a city gal." Bonnie put the car in Park. "Thought they were serving her cow brains for supper." Bonnie laughed. She had no filter but was otherwise harmless.

"Gabriel is allergic," Joe countered in return. "Nothing a minister dislikes more than cooked brains." He winked before exiting the car and securing both crutches tightly under his arms.

At the sound of an ax splitting wood, Joe crutched around the side of the house to find the minister with a small mound of hickory and red oak collecting. It was a fall chore that consumed most men's minds this time of year.

Seeing Joe approach, the minister set the ax down. "Hiya, Joe. Heard you got you a new set of legs."

"New hips, knees, and the sort, but they tell me there's still some flesh and bone in there." Joe grinned.

"What brings you by?"

"That trouble over at the Wickeys' deer farm—I think I know who is responsible."

"I see." Gabriel scratched his beard and drew closer. "Thinking and knowing are strangers to one another."

"I have a few pictures taken from wildlife cameras I set up along the Wickeys' farm." The minister lifted a bushy brow. Photos weren't permitted within the Amish faith, but once Joe explained the purpose of the wildlife cameras, the minister was ready to see what made Joe certain.

"Rueben knows of this?"

"He does. The sheriff too. I know Leah has been worried they may return. I had hoped it would ease her worries. I never thought they'd actually return."

"Mighty brave or really stupid. Have you shown these pictures to the sheriff?"

"Not yet. I was hoping to show them to you first."

"Why is that?"

"One may not be such a stranger." Joe still couldn't fathom any Amish man he knew being part of stealing a buck or hurting a woman. He pulled the photographs from his pocket and handed them to the minister.

"You can't see his face." Gabriel squinted, holding the sheet of paper at different angles. "But he is not one of ours," the minister said with certainty. Leaning toward Joe, the minister pointed to the straw hat in the photo. "No holes in the side, and the band is solid. That's not ours."

"Nee, it is not." Joe knew most of the neighboring communities fell into the same rules when it came to headwear. All but one.

"Komm ena while I fetch my coat and hat, and then we will call the sheriff. No sense in us traveling to town. Gas is getting too expensive."

Joe smiled as he followed Gabriel into the house. A minister didn't do the Lord's work without first dressing for it, even if he was full of jokes.

CHAPTER TWENTY-EIGHT

Moses was becoming quite the protector Joe claimed him to be. He barked at everything, even dead sticks and harmless rocks. His fascination with nipping at the horses' hooves trod too close to danger, but Leah found his adorable antics traits that would in turn make him the best watchdog ever.

It wasn't as easy convincing her family to her way of thinking after his latest episode of howling and sharp barks all through the night. Late summer cicadas had been the latest cause for stirring his nature and keeping the entire Wickey household awake.

After a quick breakfast of leftover buttermilk biscuits, fried pork, and oatmeal, Leah and Moses saw to gathering eggs. He had a remarkable habit of herding all the chickens to one corner of the fenced-in lot while Leah collected eggs from each nesting box.

"If you let him continue to chase the chickens, there will be no more eggs," Mammi Iolene quipped.

"He's a herding dog. Joe says it's part of his breed, and I never have to fend off the rooster when he goes with me," Leah defended. Jah, Moses was already making Leah's life sweeter.

"I don't know why Verna and Lizzy thought me best as head cook." Mamm strolled into the kitchen with two notebooks in her arms. A blend of sleeplessness and duty had her staring at her long list with overwhelming concern.

Hunting for a Husband

It was less than two weeks away from Lizzy and Levi's wedding. It was tradition for all the women of the community to help. Though they lived in the neighboring district, Mamm had been given the role of head cook. She'd be responsible for planning meals, handing out duties, and absorbing all the stresses that would otherwise be left for Lizzy and Verna to shoulder.

"Verna said they sent out eight hundred invitations. I don't even know eight hundred people!"

Jah, Mamm was weary from being up most of the night, and stressed, though for good reason. Leah wasn't sure she knew that many people either. Wanting to lift some of her mamm's burdens, Leah quickly offered to help with more than being a sidesitter.

"Mammi Iolene and I will help you. You remember when Cousin Irene almost wed?" It was probably not the best example, considering Mamm had planned two wonderful meals with the help of family and friends, only for Irene to have a change of heart two days before her wedding.

"Irene knows it's best not to marry the wrong person," Mammi Iolene replied. Her niece did no wrong in Mammi's eyes.

"I had Louise helping, and it was still a fine meal," Mamm said defensively. "Folks enjoyed the fellowship, and we sang songs and visited until well after dark."

"I'll see to the shopping list. I wanted to pick up everything for the sugar cookies I was assigned to bake." With a full sheet of paper tucked in her backpack, Leah harnessed Amos' horse and headed to Cousin Verna's bulk store. It was at the other end of the community, but recent rains had brought with it cooler weather as well as vast changes in the landscape as trees began turning from worn green to brilliant reds and bold yellows.

She kept a firm grip on the reins, as the horse was known to take the lead any chance he got, but after a few moments, she found herself relaxing. Clearly his training had done some good.

Wickey's Bulk Foods was a large, stretched-out metal building containing everything from straw hats to cheese. "Gut mariye, Laura," Leah greeted the youngest of Verna's kinner behind the counter.

"Hi, Leah." Laura offered a quick hello as she rang up deli meats for an older couple. "These come straight from Walnut Creek," she jingled. "You'll not find better at the local markets." Verna's youngest had the fairest complexion and the prettiest brown eyes, but her knack for tattling always took away from her fine looks.

Leah pushed the shopping cart down the baking aisle. She collected a forty-pound bag of baker's flour, a large bag of sugar, and three containers of powdered whip topping. Chocolate pieces were next on her list, followed by baking powder and a fresh brick of yeast. Once Leah had scratched off much of Mamm's list of supplies, she went in search of red jimmies. The little confections would be perfect on top of frosted sugar cookies.

Scanning the shelf for red sprinkles, Leah considered buying two containers instead of one. She could bake an extra two dozen cookies for Joe's shop. Thinking of Joe made her smile and reflect on the kiss they shared at the pond. Her face grew hot under the recollection.

"Laura tells me that you are courting Joe Shetler."

Leah snapped out of her dreamy state and straightened as newly married Barbara Smoker strolled down the same aisle. Surprise was not a word Leah wanted to say out loud, but she knew the look on her face said it for her.

"We are," Leah replied, wishing her voice didn't sound so uncertain. Under a black bonnet, Barbara looked twice Leah's age. Marriage quickly turned young girls into women. Her soft brown hair held hints of autumn.

"Here ya go, Leah." Laura came hurtling down the aisle next. "Lizzy said to send these with you too." She placed two boxes in Leah's cart. "It's the Orbeez for the centerpieces. Lizzy doesn't see just how busy I am now that she's spending less time helping here. Surely you have more time than me to see to them."

Just like Verna, Laura was becoming a fine delegator.

"I can see to them." The water-based, gel-like beads did make centerpieces more lovely, Leah thought.

"What are you two talking about?" Laura questioned. More than not, to hear any gossip she could.

"Leah and I were just speaking of her newest beau," Barbara replied.

"Oh, that. You missed the gathering last week."

Leah wasn't about to ask Joe if they could attend a gathering like normal courting couples where he couldn't partake in any of the activities but the singeon. In fact, she found fishing and visits on the porch less distracting as they got to know one another better.

"Joe and I enjoyed spending time with his family and singing. He just returned home as it is," Leah informed the two of them.

"Lizzy thinks you make a fine pair, but Elam was none too happy to hear you started courting. He's come to the last three gatherings hoping to see ya. I don't know why he keeps coming about, either. He doesn't talk to anyone else and just stands about watching everyone. It's kind of…odd." Laura made a face.

It was odd. Leah had given Elam no reason to think she was interested in him.

"There will be a singeon at my parents' place on Thursday. You and Joe should komm." Barbara further shocked Leah. It seemed that now that Barbara was married to Ruben Paul Smoker, she no longer felt the need to be so insecure around Leah.

"Perhaps we will. Danke for asking." Leah was grateful and hoped in time she and Barbara could mend the fence between them.

"Many are happy to hear Joe's surgeries went well. Joe has always been a verra kind sort."

"He has always had a look to him too." Laura snickered. "If he hadn't fallen off that bank into the river, I reckon he would have been taken up long ago." The sound of Verna calling her daughter back to the front of the store was the only reason Leah didn't tell her cousin what an unkind thought that was.

"She's one who speaks without a thought for her words first."

"Jah, and she has many thoughts." Leah chuckled.

"I'm sorry for thinking wrong of you. I saw you here alone and wanted to tell you that, and I hope you can forgive me for thinking the worst."

"You're forgiven, Barbara. I hope we can put this behind us. I'd very much like to make friends."

"I'd like that too." Barbara smiled. "Have a gut day, Leah. I shall hope to see you and Joe soon."

With lifted shoulders and a happy heart, Leah left the bulk store and headed toward Frannie's Material shop. This time of day, Leah suspected there'd be fewer customers for Frannie to fuss over, giving Leah plenty of time to sift through material.

Frannie Shetler was in her late thirties. More often than not, those not from the area might mistake her as a schwester to her own kinner, as young as she looked. Surely she'd married early yet to have three kinner Leah's age.

Veering right on Farrow's Creek Road, it was all Leah could do to keep Amos' horse from trotting right past the small shop that sat near the two-story white house. Much of the front of the property was gravel in small pea-sized stones, leaving the side and back yards for mowing.

A long metal barn sat just across the road. Leah noted two men standing next to a buggy, talking. One lifted an arm, and she politely waved back before slipping inside the material shop.

Inside was eerily quiet. That meant Frannie was inside the house seeing over chores. A long, wide table sat near a cold woodstove for cutting or, more often than not, tearing material being purchased. The high window over the door gave ample lighting to all the bolts of fabric nearby. Farther in the back was a variety of thermos bottles, pans, stockpots, and kitchen items on shelves. There was a toy aisle and one section with homemade cards. Some were stamp-style, while others were colored by younger hands, but all beautiful. Copies of the local Amish directory, as well as those in communities tied to someone in the area, sat high on a plastic shelf. Underneath, Leah spotted the Billy and Blaze books, a favorite of Amos' growing up, along with scholar readers, and coloring books for kinner.

Leah strolled into a narrow aisle at her right and pulled a bolt of dark blue material from the rack just as the front door opened.

"Sorry, I just put water in the canner to finish up applesauce and saw the buggy." Wiping her hands on her apron, Frannie went to her. "Looking to make a new dress?"

"I'm to be a sidesitter in mei cousin's wedding."

"Elizabeth and Levi, jah? The Shetlers are our neighbors, across the field there." Frannie pointed. "Linda has talked you up plenty. I do think she hopes a second wedding is coming soon enough."

Leah blushed at the comment but warmed, knowing Joe's mamm approved of her. It was every young woman's hope that her future mother-in-law approved of her.

"I embarrassed you," Frannie said, placing a hand on her shoulder.

"Nee, I'm fine. I'm looking for a dark blue."

"Enough for one dress?"

"And a shirt, jah." A little thrill of happiness went through her, knowing how much Joe would appreciate her gift.

"I remember sewing Otto's first shirt. My mamm fussed over me the whole way. It had one sleeve shorter than the other, but he looked so handsome in it." Frannie laughed as she pulled a rich, dark blue and instinctually measured the perfect yardage before tearing the fabric in a perfect line. She continued chatting about Otto, who Leah assumed was Frannie's husband she hadn't met yet.

"You do know Joe's favorite is elderberry pie?" Frannie looked up from folding the yards and grinned. "His grandmother used to make elderberry pie all the time. When she passed, I made a few, sent them over to their house after...you know." She ducked her head quickly. "I wanted to make him feel loved. He struggled at first with it."

Leah appreciated Frannie sharing that with her. It was nice to know Frannie did that for Joe after the death of his grandmother. "I knew he liked peanut butter. I've never eaten elderberry pie." Though she had heard Stella mention elderberries plenty when it came to colds and flu. "Danke. I shall see if I can find a recipe."

"No need to search one out." Frannie's tone hiked. "I can give you mine, and we have elder bushes out back. I picked all I need for jellies and the like for the season. You're welcome to have what's left."

"That is kind of you." Leah appreciated such kindness and anticipated trying the new recipe.

"The birds usually finish them off when I'm done. Let me run inside and get you that recipe."

When Frannie returned, she kindly shared her elderberry jelly recipe as well as a small ice cream bucket for collecting elderberries in. Who knew that much work was involved in making jelly, but Leah took in her every detail. Louise might consider adding elderberry jelly to her jam and jelly business.

After another short chat about which apples made the best applesauce, Leah gathered both cut yards of robin's-egg blue and dark blue material and bid farewell to Frannie. She wasn't as good as Louise at sewing, but she was determined to sew Joe at least two new shirts. Courting couples always wore matching colors when they were seen in public together.

Outside, Leah noted a second buggy pulled next to hers. She hadn't heard anyone enter Frannie's shop, but she quickly brushed the concern aside and sought out the elderberry bushes around the side of the material shop. Frannie was right, birds did love the round purple-black berries, but she worked hard to collect as many berries as she could in the small plastic container. Deep in thought, anticipating surprising Joe with an elderberry pie, Leah startled when someone called her name.

CHAPTER TWENTY-NINE

Joe sat at Gabriel's table with an empty kaffi cup between his hands when he heard the sheriff's vehicle pull into the drive. Gabriel stood and collected his black hat and jacket. Despite the warm kitchen and the comforts of his own home, today was all about business.

"All this should be taken care of in town," Erma muttered as her husband went to the door to welcome the sheriff. The minister's fraa had a tender heart.

"Komm in, Sheriff. Erma has a warm zucchini cake waiting."

"I can't turn that down, but don't tell the wife. She's been working on improving her cooking skills lately." The sheriff's deep chuckle filled the hallway.

"We all can learn by practicing more. Have a seat, Sheriff."

"Not everyone," the sheriff commented before taking a seat directly across from Joe. Not quite forty, with a hint of a Southern accent, the sheriff towered over the minister in the seat beside him.

"Your phone message said it was important and that you had evidence to share." Removing his hat and placing it upside down in the chair beside him, he nodded when Erma cut three slices of cake and set one before each of them. Spices of cinnamon and cloves warmed Joe's senses. Between seeing over his shop after a long absence and trying not to interfere with Brad's ability to bestow favoritism between his kinner, Joe felt as if breakfast had been days away. He lifted his fork, ready to dive into Erma's warm cake.

"I'll let Joe share that." Gabriel picked up his fork and began to eat.

Joe looked to the sheriff and put his fork back down. The cake would have to wait. "I put up wildlife cameras around the Wickey farm. I didn't think they'd caught anything, but they did." Joe removed the photos from the envelope and slid them closer to the sheriff.

One by one, the sheriff lifted a photo and examined it with no readable expression before setting it back down. "I see why you called me here instead of just bringing them down to the station. Do we have any idea who the straw hat belongs to?" He pointed to the figure who was clearly Amish.

"He's from the Pine Valley community, is the best I can say. They have a different way of doing things over there," Gabriel put in, then turned his focus back on finishing off his last bite.

"I believe it to be Elam Zehr. He's been visiting the area a lot the last few months. This one," Joe said, pointing at a photo of another man. The man was standing sideways, his face looking away from the camera, but Joe felt he was sure who he was. "Might be a fella who comes by my shop a lot."

"You run the camping and hunting shop over on Cherry Grove?" The sheriff lifted a brow.

"It's more of an outdoors shop. I offer books on hiking and fishing gear too," Joe quickly clarified. Gabriel had been skeptical at first of Joe's choice in livelihood, until Joe shared that folks loved the outdoors as much as he did. "Brandon Carlton never wears a pair of trousers without holes in them." It was signature for the young man, but that habit might cost him now.

Sharing that fact had Joe clenching his jaw. All this time and all those chats with Brandon about the deer farm up the road. His constant parade of questions and brushed aside remarks. Now Joe recognized them as clues to a puzzle almost finished. If Joe had only paid better attention. If he only realized what the young man had been up to, he could have prevented Leah from being hurt.

"I know Brandon and his family well. Let's say he tends to hang with some bad examples. How do you know the victim, Leah Wickey?" The sheriff sat back and began eating.

"Leah is a special friend. We're courting."

Erma turned too quickly for Joe to see her reaction to the news, but Gabriel and the sheriff both made little effort to suppress a grin.

"Well, then." The sheriff finished off his cake, thanked Erma, and stood. "I need to call this in and have them picked up for questioning." Pulling his cell phone from his pocket, he didn't waste any more time calling his deputies to meet them at the Carlton house.

"Danke, Sheriff, for helping in this matter. I don't like seeing folks hurt, but even we recognize facing the consequences of our actions," Gabriel offered.

"Would you mind coming along, helping me speak to this Elam fella?"

The local sheriff had been sheriff long enough to know that not all Amish families would be open to speaking with him, and hoped the minister would help be the buffer between the two worlds.

"I can. My driver dropped me off, and I could use a ride home anyway," Joe put in. Normally Bonnie was as patient as a cat on a grasshopper, but today she admitted to having three cups of coffee and was hoping to deliver her Avon books to local businesses.

Joe also wanted to hear what Elam had to say for himself.

"All right, then." The sheriff put his hat back on his head and headed for his car.

Joe had never ridden in a police car before. All the switches and screens, it was a wonder the sheriff could focus on the road at all.

"Putting up cameras was a good idea. The local warden often advises folks with big farms to hang them up since someone shot two high-dollar horses late in the night in a known spot for poaching deer."

"I only hung them so Leah felt more comfortable going outside. After the attack, she's been afraid." At least now that she had Moses, albeit too small to do more than nip at heels, she admitted to feeling safer.

"She has reason to be, but hopefully Brandon leads us to who's behind it. There's a third man, after all."

Jah, that's true.

"I didn't want to mention it until I knew your motives to helping the family, but we found a carcass a few days ago. Not the first one in our area, nor will it be the last. It's not easy investigating a murderer of critters, but the warden has a few friends. Access to things I don't. His buddy owns a large hunting reserve in Missouri. Some fine animals down there. I've seen the pictures." The sheriff winked. "They keep records of their DNA, and some even have tracking devices on them in case they wander past the fences."

"Rueben wouldn't have invested in that. We don't go to such lengths, even for a buck worth thousands in breeding stock."

"He did tag them, though," the sheriff revealed with a grin.

Joe suddenly remembered the talk Leah and he had at the barn when her family hosted church. "The bucks have red tags. The does have yellow," Joe said out loud.

"Exactly. We've been searching for weeks, and it wasn't until the warden went to investigate a carcass that we got our best clue yet. After the Wickey girl was found, we combed the hills and neighboring farms." The sheriff flipped on his signal to make a right turn. "I noticed the tags on the does and asked Mr. Wickey about them. Like the warden's buddy, he marked them for what he calls ownership. The warden couldn't find any bullet holes or arrows in the deer and, at first, thought it to be struck by a car, considering it had two broken legs. He went to remove it to dispose of, and that's when he found a red tag buried in the mud next to that carcass."

"So it was Legend?" Leah said it had been the most docile of the lot.

"It was. I just haven't told the Wickey family yet and hope you won't either. I'd like to get my hands on these fellas first."

"I'd like to see you get your hands on them," Joe muttered under his breath.

"I reckon you can tag along. After all, you care enough for her to have hung those cameras in the first place."

The sheriff was a laid-back sort, and once they reached the Carltons', it took him less than an hour to get a confession out of Brandon and have one of his deputies place him under arrest. The young man didn't even shake an eyelash to name Barry Anderson as the man in the red vest.

Barry was another disappointment, adding to Joe's anger. The owner of Bucks and Beards Hunting Reserve had been hinting about taking his business to the next level. Joe felt a fool missing all the signs and warnings that led to Leah's injuries.

"I should have known Barry was one of them," Joe told the sheriff as they made their way to the Wickey farm.

Joe leaned on both crutches as he stood on Rueben's porch while the sheriff revealed everything to Leah's family. He wondered where Leah was, glancing about for any sign of her. It would be good to see her face when news of two of the men responsible for hurting her had been taken in.

"These men," Rueben began stiffly. "They have much to gain stealing such an animal to start his own breeding stock. These are men of much, yet they steal from others. Hurt others."

"I suspect that's what motivated them, but I have no issue arresting a man of money as I do one without. The law is the law," the sheriff punctuated. "I do suspect Mr. Anderson to lawyer up and put up a fight."

"We don't fight," Rueben informed him.

"I know your people don't, but you don't have to. We've got a new prosecutor in town, and she's looking to make a name for herself, and the commonwealth is always searching for a cause. Neither man will see daylight for some time."

"And what of Elam? He asked me all kinds of questions about the deer. I thought we were freinden." Amos kicked the dirt.

"I could have done something too. Barry and Brandon both talked about your farm and asked questions, but I didn't suspect a thing," Joe shared. He could see Amos was sporting his own guilt for what happened to Leah.

"Well, we are still working to locate him. I've got deputies combing every Amish farm from here to Mason County."

If Elam didn't want to be found, Joe suspected he wouldn't. It was easy to hide among homes and farms of folks who didn't always welcome authorities beyond their doors. "Where's Leah?"

"She went to the bulk store this morning. Said she might visit Dok Stella and Viola and maybe Frannie's shop," Lilly informed them. "You don't think. . ." Lilly clasped a hand to her stomach.

"No worries, ma'am. That boy is hiding, I assure you, but I will drive toward the Material Shop to be certain she is there."

"I'm going too," Rueben insisted. He too was now filled with equal concern for Leah's safety. Giving the sheriff no time to resist, Rueben opened the passenger door of the sheriff's car and climbed in.

Joe sat in the back of the car next to Amos. The look on the young man's face was a mix of hate and regret. In the front seat, Rueben sat board stiff.

"You did not want to worry my fraa, Sheriff, but I see you too have concerns about this Elam."

"I do, Mr. Wickey. Finding your daughter right now is important. Both Carlton and Anderson are pointing the finger at that boy for hitting her. Of course, he might point the finger at them, but until we know for sure. . ."

"If Elam gets word you arrested both men, he might. . ."

"Run? I already thought of that, young man," the sheriff replied to Amos. "Deputy Browning is in Pine Valley now with a search warrant checking inside his family's home and outbuildings. Pleasants County isn't so big, and he can't hide for long."

A cold shiver ran up Leah's spine when Elam appeared out of nowhere, removing his hat from his head. He was drenched in sweat, as if he'd been pitching hay all day. His clothes appeared worn and dirty, his hair damp and combed to one side.

"Hiya, Elam. Hope you are well," Leah offered. Glancing into her bucket, she wondered if she had enough for the pie recipe. For a moment, she considered making an excuse about needing more thread and slipping back inside where Frannie still lingered. It had troubled her thoughts to know Elam had been going to youth gatherings in hopes that she would be there.

"I have been hoping to see you. To be sure you are all right." He drew closer. There was an urgency about him that didn't seem natural for two folks saying their quick hellos.

"I am. No need to worry about me." More unease continued to trickle over her the closer he came.

"What are you doing?"

"Frannie let me pick elderberries from her. I'm sure this is enough." Leah made a motion to leave, but Elam took a sharp step in front of her.

"Elderberries are a pain to pick. I can help you finish filling up the bucket." He pulled the bucket from her hand and brushed past her. "Can't leave a job unfinished. Might as well fill the bucket."

Leah let out a huff. She hadn't recalled him being so. . .pushy. Turning, she watched him work, swiftly racking the berries from the five-fingered heads easily. He'd done this before, she concluded, but now she was trying to determine how bad she needed elderberries at all.

"I heard they arrested the men who attacked you. I can't tell you how happy that makes me to know they will be put away for it."

Taken aback by the news, Leah gasped. "When?" Why had the sheriff not called and told her father of this?

"Just an hour or so ago," he revealed before pulling a large cluster head above him downward and cleaning it off too.

"Daed will be happy to hear of it. I should be going." Leah took a step forward, reaching for the bucket. "Danke for sharing such good news. I can rest much easier knowing it."

Elam let the limb, now free of the weighed down berries, bounce back before turning to face her. "I reckon the sheriff will want to talk to you. He might have questions only you can answer."

Leah's hand was growing tired, and he didn't seem to want to return her bucket anytime soon, but the idea of talking to the sheriff again almost made her nauseous. "But I didn't see them. Not really anyhow, and...I don't want to see them." To face her attacker, nee, she didn't want to do that. As happy as she was to know the men had been found, Leah couldn't bear to think of looking them in the eye. The very idea made her lightheaded.

"Komm, sit. You look as if you might fall down." Elam gently placed a hand on her elbow and led her to a picnic table sitting between the shop and Frannie's home. "It's okay, Leah. You can do this."

"Nee, I cannot." She looked to Elam, appreciating his concern. "I don't want to see their faces. One of them stole from us, and one..." Goose bumps raced down her arms and up her spine. "He...hurt me," she said in a soft, shaky tone.

Elam winced. "Just tell them what you can. My cousin in Indiana was a victim of a hit-and-run. They found the driver of the car that hit her bike, but she still had to identify him and answer questions. I'm sure they will just want the normal things. Who do you know that would hurt you? Who are your friends? They always look to those closest to you when it's an attack. Do you remember anything about the man who...hit you on the back of the head?"

"How would you know this?" He wasn't making any sense.

"Again, my cousin." He shrugged. "Remember, it was that last Wednesday in July. They will ask what you did that day."

"I can't remember what I do every day." Leah's voice pitched.

"Of course you can. You were doing laundry, like most Amish women, on a Wednesday, which is why you were barefoot while picking flowers. I was..." Elam sat the bucket of elderberries on the ground and stared at her intently. "Here all that day. Otis and his family went to visit family, and I drove by and saw all his pigs were out."

Elam wrung his hands together nervously. He didn't sound so sure, so how was she supposed to sound sure herself?

"Took me all afternoon, I reckon. Then I heard you were missing.

I figure we all know where we were and what we were doing that day." Elam stared at her intently. "I cannot tell you how relieved I was that you'd been found." Elam reached out and touched her cheek.

The burning touch sent Leah to her feet. "Elam, you shouldn't do that. You should know that I'm courting Joe Shetler. You are a fine man but not the man for me."

"I understand," he said, as if not willing to argue with her. Perhaps that was why Leah had never really had any interest in Elam. Though he appeared to be interested, he was more interested in her family's farm than learning what she liked to do on a free Sunday.

To her surprise, Elam reached into his pocket and pulled out a pack of cigarettes as if it were a natural thing. With practiced movements, he lit a cigarette and inhaled. Then he blew out the smoke in the air between them. His gaze grew darker, more intent. "Just remember where we were that day, Leah, and all will be well."

As if he had nothing more to say, Elam turned to leave, and suddenly Leah remembered one piece of evidence she thought unimportant. That scented memory that had haunted her dreams. Leah hated the smell of cigarettes, even though she knew many young boys toyed with smoking, and sometimes married men hid such from their wives. Elam's had a very distinct smell. The smoking scent put her stomach into turmoil because of the mint-like scent attached to it, and Leah hadn't told the sheriff about collecting flowers.

"It was herbs," Leah muttered.

"What?" Elam turned swiftly.

"You said I was barefoot, collecting flowers. It was mullein. That's an herb. I never told anyone that. Elam, you were there, jah? There was a man behind me. I didn't see him, but...he smoked. Are you the man who hurt me?" Leah blurted out.

Elam reached out, gripping Leah's arm tightly, neither paying any mind to the sound of a vehicle pulling into the gravel drive in front of Frannie's shop. He tossed his cigarette on the ground before shoving his face so close to Leah's that the smell of his horrid habit filled her nostrils. "You can vouch for me. I'd never hurt you."

Leah pulled from his grasp and thankfully he let her go. She was no match for him. "You pretended to be interested in me so you could steal from my family."

"It wasn't my idea. Barry made us do it," he defended. "And. . .I didn't pretend. No one pretends to like you. I just don't see how you ended up with Joe. He can't even take care of you."

"I'll never hurt her as you've done."

"Joe!" Leah wasn't sure if she was dreaming or not, because there Joe stood, on two legs, glaring angrily at Elam. Leah had never seen him angry before, but felt her shoulders ease knowing he was there once more. Anytime Leah found herself in a fix, Joe was there.

"Everyone knows what you've done. You can't run, and I won't let you hurt her again."

"Again?" Leah took a protective step back. "You are the one who. . ." She hugged her middle, hoping Joe was wrong.

"Leah, I'm sorry. It was an accident. You weren't supposed to be there!"

"Elam Zehr, I'd like you to come with me."

From around the corner, the sheriff stepped into view. Had he been there all this time? Behind him her father and Amos stepped out, and Leah felt her fast heartbeats slow. How did they all know she needed them?

Leah ran to her father's open arms, hiding her face in his chest.

"It's not my fault, Sheriff. I had to do it! You don't understand!" Elam's pleas did nothing to stop the sheriff from placing him in handcuffs.

"We'll sort that all out back in town," the sheriff interrupted.

CHAPTER THIRTY

Leah had been up since before the sun rose. Her excitement for Lizzy prompted her to hurry through morning chores and ride along with Mamm to Cousin Verna's. Mammi Iolene had declined leaving early, insisting it showed worry that everything was not as they left it the night before. Leah agreed with Mamm that all the cooks would arrive early to see to the wedding meal, and as head cook and Lizzy's sidesitter, they couldn't dally.

Now it was almost nine and time to find her place next to Lizzy in one of the reserved chairs in front. If not for spotting Cousin Verna slipping out of the cabinet shop building, she would have. Everyone had worked hard to ready it for the wedding meal. She hoped Verna hadn't been rearranging the wedding table again.

Leah hurried inside, along with Mary Elizabeth and Delilah.

"Best we see all is well before Minister Graber starts," Delilah said. Her own mother, Betty Marie, was outside stirring corn in one of the many heavy soup pots. "You know how he is about tardiness."

Leah didn't know. She had only met the minister a handful of times since moving here, and not once had he shared two words with her. "Verna probably put those crystal dishes filled with nuts on the wedding table again," Leah quipped and hurried to the front of the long room. She'd have no time to do so once the service started. Her duty was to be at Lizzy's side for the rest of the day, and it was frowned upon to walk out of a service unless one had small kinner. Yet Leah knew few batted an eyelash at a wedding, as there were many duties to spread about.

"I knew it," Leah grumbled. "And just after Lizzy settled how all was to be arranged." She hurried to set all to rights once more. Leah didn't mind upsetting cousin Verna any more than she had when she added silver paper stamp cutouts in the shape of horseshoes on the tables. Lizzy wanted Levi to have things he desired at his wedding too.

"I'm glad my mamm would never go over my head like that," Mary Elizabeth said while flipping blue plastic cups face down for the third time since they arrived. "She says it's easier to pour them facing up, but no one wants a cup full of ladybugs!"

The throng of ladybugs that had appeared just two nights ago were wreaking havoc on the community. Hopefully they didn't like cake.

There were nine rows of tables stretching from one end of the cabinet shop to the other. It had taken over two dozen men to see the heavier equipment moved out of sight and safely tucked away.

Dark tablecloths with silver vinyl ran down the center of each table. Small glass bubble bowls were spread out evenly on each table. White and blue Orbeez made for a delightful look, each topped with darker blue flower petals.

While the Glick sisters saw to turning cups face down, Leah went to the far corner. She continued rearranging the eck, or wedding table. It was shaped out of three tables making a flat-bottom V. Two chairs sat directly behind a three-layered white cake with blue and silver flowers trailing over its top and down one side. Two more chairs were placed on each side for the sidesitters.

The table linens had been Levi's mamm's. Leah had been the one to tack on the extra material in the front, adding a long table runner of lace at the top. It was as fine a table as she ever saw. Two crystal vases with bold and vibrant bouquets burst out among the white. Leah touched one of the petals and wondered how florists managed to find such dark blue flowers this time of year.

There was a large crystal dish with a pointed lid containing the wedding rings. Leah had not known of that tradition until Lizzy spoke of it. Neither Louise nor Beth had wedding rings at their weddings. The powdered sugar balls baked with nuts inside did look delicious, but more than that, as Lizzy explained, they were part of a tradition Levi had insisted on.

There were already cards in the card holder bearing Lizzy's and Levi's names as well as the date. Leah recognized her own mother's handwriting on one card and smiled just as she noted that the two large sheet cakes had been draped with paper towels to keep pests away. The cool morning temps would only last a little longer, as today was to be a rather warm day.

Once she was certain all was in order, Leah gave the eck a final scrutiny. Framed verses and poems were situated on every table, but a few dear to heart sat here. Delicate china dishes for all those serving in the wedding party sat in front of each chair. She and Joe would soon help fill those spaces. How kind of Lizzy to let her be with her today when she had many friends she could have chosen. Leah knew why Lizzy did so, and was thankful.

"I'm putting these at the very ends," Leah announced as she moved two crystal glasses filled with mixed nuts as far from Lizzy's view as possible. Lizzy didn't even want nuts served. She wanted candy. Leah suspected that although Verna had a way about her, she did want the best for her daughter's special day.

Leah's own mamm would likely be a rack of nerves until the day ended. She'd already worried herself ill that seventy-three pies would in no way feed everyone. Despite so many coolers of chicken waiting to be served, she insisted the menner could have spent more time cooking and less time chatting.

Two large tents had been set up just outside. Underneath were a few more tables for any overflow necessary to see everyone fed. Everyone was accustomed to eating in turns, but as two more buggies arrived, both filled as full as they could get, Leah felt some of her mamm's worries press on her too. There might be as many as five sittings before they could feed everyone.

Long white fold-up tables displayed trays of pies. Lizzy requested cherry, apple, and chocolate while buckets of fruit salad, ice cream, and pudding stayed cold in the nearby freezer buggy.

There were six three-burner stoves aligned in the center of one tent, as pots of sweet corn, noodles, and potatoes sat in long warming trays waiting to be served. In another row, three more stoves warmed bakers' ovens. Leah could smell the sage scent of stuffing being cooked, and her mouth salivated.

She had been so busy these last few days, she hadn't taken much time to eat a proper meal.

"They keep coming," Mary Elizabeth announced when a van pulled into the crowded drive. Not only were folks still arriving, but Leah also imagined Mamm was ready to declare that some folks would have to take smaller helpings. She was stern about fairness.

With all as it should be, Leah and the Glick sisters hurried into the barn and found their places ahead of the newcomers exiting the van.

"Where have you been?" Lizzy narrowed her a look.

"Seeing your wedding table wasn't sprinkled with nuts." Leah grinned.

"Danke," Lizzy muttered before the barn went strangely quiet.

Leah peered over her shoulder, and there he was.

Leah had visited with Joe last evening while she helped Linda and Karen set up tables for the final meal. Karen mentioned there would be plenty of yodeling at the final meal after the wedding, and Leah didn't even try to hide her enthusiasm.

Joe was dressed in black and the matching dark blue shirt Leah had sewn with her own hands. He was the most handsome man she'd ever seen. He was smiling as he moved through the crowd. Hands were shaken and kindness was given, but when he looked her way, she saw that mischievous twinkle that first stole her heart on a rainy May afternoon. He had a slight hitch in his gait, but as he drew closer, Leah felt the joy in her heart push a tear down one cheek.

Joe was standing on his own two feet, and he was making his way to her.

Months ago Leah had made a silly promise, and she had every intention on keeping it. However, Leah didn't want to wait to be the last unwed maedel in the community, and she certainly didn't want to wait until she was thirty to marry.

Minister Graber didn't believe in tardiness, even on a Thursday morning. It was a wonder the man had never been late to anything, considering he was the father of twenty-one kinner. Joe couldn't imagine what it took to ready so many each morning. Folks were still milling about the large barn that had been cleaned from walls to rafters for a happy wedding day.

The minister's voice began leading everyone in song, indicating the ninth hour and encouraging folks to take a seat. Soon voices lifted to the barn rafters in a sweet melody that always struck a chord in Joe's heart.

Peering over his shoulder, Joe glanced at his mother sitting perfectly content on the front bench with her hands firmly in her lap. Yesterday she'd been all worked up, worried that Daed wouldn't finish smoking the hams or that Matt hadn't spray washed all the barn floors well enough. How many times had she asked Karen to rearrange tables?

Looking at her now, you couldn't see it, but Joe knew he'd been blessed with a remarkable mamm. She'd not only seen him through his first steps, up a few mountains, and down some dark valleys. She battled fatigue, prayed relentlessly, and still could bring laughter to her family and joy into their hearts.

Joe grinned, turning his gaze on Minister Graber once more. Linda Shetler would be in tears before day's end. She'd been an emotional roller coaster when Karen and Matt married, and here Levi was the youngest of their lot. A mother's heart simply couldn't conceal such powerful love.

The late supper would be served at his parents' home. Joe helped Levi set up volleyball nets and tables. Daed had spent plenty on a new tent that Mamm insisted they needed anyway, seeing as they still had one child left to marry off. Joe agreed with his daed. Mamm had only been so worked up these last two weeks because she was holding her tongue so often. Most weddings took place at the home of the bride's family, the meal at her soon-to-be husband's. If the space was limited, then a close family member would offer up their home too. However, Verna Wickey had been firm that the noonday wedding feast be here. Joe's mamm didn't squabble over it. There was more space in the bulk store parking lot, but tradition had been broken, and Mamm's Old Order upbringing was deeply rooted in tradition.

Joe reassured his mother that when his day came, she could host both meals if that was what suited her. The light that flickered in his mother's eyes at that declaration had Joe thinking a lot of his own future. Leah cared for him, and each time her eyes caught his, the attraction that had first bloomed between them had become an intimate understanding of the love they equally shared.

Joe shifted on a folding chair next to Levi and his close friend James. Joe knew Lizzy could have chosen from dozens of lifelong friends aside from Delilah, but warmed knowing Lizzy had chosen Leah to be one of her sidesitters too.

A lot of matchmaking was done during a wedding. Aside from choosing haulers—the young men responsible for readying the wedding buggy and carting the newly married from one house to another—and choosing the little sunbeams, which often included nieces and nephews who displayed small hankies matching the wedding parties and handed out candy and favors in the afternoon, couples also chose which boy and girl should serve as table waiters. It was most interesting to see who would be paired up with whom.

Chrissy Keim had put up a strong protest against who was responsible for matching her up with Kevin Graber, the schoolteacher. Joe had always thought the woman shy, but the moment she spotted her name inked on the table server cards next to his, she'd been anything but shy about her thoughts on Lizzy's choice. However, today Joe knew she would silently do her part, as no one would interfere with such a special day.

His black vest was tight under his coat, and Joe gave it a yank. His new shoes were giving his feet fits. Daed had warned him not to try on new shoes today, but Joe wanted to look his best, not just for Levi.

Joe glanced at his father. John Shetler had delivered many sermons over the years, but today he sat up front, a witness to Levi taking a fraa. Behind him was his bruder Matt, taking up enough space for two men. Then there was Joe's eight-year-old nephew, Matthew. Like father, like sohn, Matthew squirmed on the bench seat. Matt never was good at sitting still. Twins Dora and Flora sat on each side of their mother across the room. Both were mocking her lifted chin as she peered over the kapp in front of her, pretending to pay attention to Minister Graber's words, their short legs swinging. Joe smiled at the identical pair.

He hadn't entertained it before. Didn't dare think of it. But now Joe felt the possibility within reach. The vision, clear enough to see. Daughters and sons with light hair and mischievousness driving their own mother mad with their antics. The vivid vision almost made him laugh out loud. Instead, his eyes traveled to Leah sitting next to Lizzy in her rich blue dress, white apron, and crisp white kapp. She was dressed as many of the young maedels were, in colors Lizzy had chosen for her special day, but Joe could make her out of the lot of them, catching her blue eyes in his gaze.

His heart beat a little faster when she floated a shy grin his way. Love had found him. *Him.* It was a wonder. Grace and mercy had been allotted to him in many second chances.

Leah had given him encouragement to face a different future. She believed in him without truly knowing him. She challenged the faith he had in himself. She'd given him a gift. A gift of possibility. A heart that was full.

He glanced at his feet, glad they both didn't stumble. His crutches were stashed in the buggy, in case the day wore on him. He no longer begrudged them and the freedom they offered. A freedom he'd been denied for over a decade.

He glanced at Leah once more and felt his chest squeeze. In his heart he knew, no matter what tomorrow delivered, he wasn't alone.

As the song waned to an end, Bishop Joshua Schwartz from the Miller's Creek district escorted Levi and Lizzy out of the room and toward the house where they could be given the best advice a bishop's wisdom could offer on the duties of marriage and what God had instructed for each of them. Joe wondered if Leah had thought about her own wedding, and then he did chuckled as quietly as he could. Had not she been hoping for a husband since moving here? It felt like years behind them, although not a year had passed since he first laid eyes on her. Even then, Joe had felt change had come to his life.

He was no longer opposed to change. In fact, he was ready to make a few more. Time was not promised, and what time he had was hers.

EPILOGUE

Two Years Later

March was certainly going out like a lamb. Leah had never remembered a more perfect spring day. Her wedding quilt hung under the porch eave, flapping in the generous wind. Inside, Mammi Iolene and Beth fussed over Louise's dinner rolls. No one made dinner rolls like Louise.

"I suspect they're done fussing over supper, and that ham sure smells ready to eat. Best fetch that husband of yours and your bruders," Daed said from a rocking chair nearby, bouncing his first of two grandsons in his arms. Malachi sported tufts of light hair like his mamm, but as his grandfather's namesake, by all accounts, favored the King lot.

Leah laughed and wondered just how long before her father's arms would be full of grosskinner.

Joe hadn't wanted to wait until one of them turned thirty either, and despite the snow that blew hard in November, Leah couldn't have been more pleased at all the wrong paths she'd taken to be where she was now. Joe said he'd add on to the house, but Leah liked the coziness of the smaller home. Now, that seemed a too-quick decision, as building on might be necessary sooner rather than later.

She hadn't shared the news yet, hoping today, as he celebrated his twenty-seventh birthday with their families, she'd have at least a moment alone with him to give him that special gift.

Joe had also welcomed Leah's green thumb, and as she glanced toward the shop, where the men had gone, she couldn't help but smile at perfect rows of peppermint, sage, and daisies.

Making her way over, she heard the sound of a wisp and thud between echoing voices. Here she thought Joe was showing Marcus the new rod and reels. Her brother-in-law seldom had time for fishing, but while visiting for the weekend, Joe assured Marcus he had a great fishing spot picked out.

Leah rounded the shop, finding the men clustered together staring at hay bales. She shook her head. She'd never understand what went on in the minds of men to find it a challenge to sink an arrow into a hay bale. There were so many more challenging things one could do with their day.

A whoop followed the impact of an arrow striking a bull's-eye. It was a silly game. No real sport in it, but she smiled anyway, seeing Joe in his element.

"It's time to eat," she called to them. Not a head turned as Joe was naming off different parts of the steel bow in his hands. Leah rolled her eyes, noting Mitchel drinking in his every word. At fifteen and youngest of the Wickey lot, Mitchel needed no influencers to convince him to take on a new hobby. He made friends fast and was already spending his spare time with a few boys Leah suspected got into more mischief than they should now that she no longer slept just down the hall.

"Hello!" she called out again, and heads turned her way. "I've come to fetch you for sup. . .unless you'd rather keep shooting a stupid hay bale over eating fresh peanut butter and elderberry pie." That got her husband's attention but not Amos', who was grinning suspiciously now.

"You know, if you can sink a stick in that hay bale, I'll wash dishes," Amos challenged with a cocky twinkle in his eyes.

Her husband stood grinning, waiting for her response.

While hunting for a husband, Leah had found everlasting love. He was the one she met during a storm. The one who brought new traditions into her life. He'd filled the holes of her grief and Beth's leaving and taught her that forgiveness released one from regret. Joe consumed all the chambers of her heart.

"Fine." Leah accepted the bow. Little did Amos know that just because she didn't find shooting arrows as entertaining as they did, that didn't mean her husband hadn't spent countless hours instructing her at the indoor range on slower days. Working alongside her man was frosting on the cake, just as Beth told her it would be.

With a glint in his eyes, Joe winked when none were looking. Leah readied the bow, pulling back the bow string and setting the safety before lifting it to her target.

"If he does dishes, I'm taking you on a walk to the pond later," Joe flirted.

Leah hoped there were kisses involved before she surprised him with his birthday gift. Studying her target, Leah let out a slow breath as Joe had taught her before letting the arrow loose. With the impact came complete silence.

"Best we get on now," she said, turning to see everyone's mouths open. "Beth will be thrilled that she isn't doing dishes."

Leah chuckled, leading the way home.

RECIPES

CHICKEN SKILLET

INGREDIENTS

- 2 tablespoons butter
- 1 pound chicken breast
- Salt and pepper to taste
- 1 onion, diced
- 4 garlic cloves, minced
- 1 teaspoon red pepper flakes
- 4 ounces cream cheese
- 1½ cups chicken stock
- 2 cups spinach or kale leaves
- 2 cups freshly cooked pasta

INSTRUCTIONS

In large skillet, melt butter. Season chicken with salt and pepper and cook until browned and done. Move to plate while making the sauce. In same skillet, cook onions, garlic, and red pepper flakes. Add cream cheese and chicken stock. Whisk until blended and allow to reduce. Then add spinach or kale. Once wilted, add chicken back into the skillet. Plate pasta and pour skillet chicken and juices over pasta.

PEANUT BUTTER PIE

Makes 1 pie

INGREDIENTS

- 3 cups milk
- 3 egg yolks
- 1 cup sugar
- ½ cup cornstarch
- ¼ teaspoon salt
- ½ cup creamy peanut butter
- 2 teaspoons vanilla
- 1 deep-dish pie crust, prebaked
- Whipped cream or Cool Whip
- Chopped peanuts

INSTRUCTIONS

In medium-sized saucepan, add milk and egg yolks; beat together with whisk. Turn heat to low. In small bowl, mix sugar, cornstarch, and salt; add to milk mixture. Turn up heat to medium and constantly stir until mixture comes to a low boil and thickens to a pudding consistency; then add peanut butter and vanilla and beat until smooth. Pour into a deep-dish pie crust that has been prebaked according to package instructions and cooled. Top with homemade whipped cream or Cool Whip and chopped peanuts.

MINDY STEELE, raised in Kentucky's timber country, is a bestselling and award-winning author who enjoys writing in favor of her rural surroundings. Mindy is a welcomed addition to the Amish genre. Her knowledge and respectful admiration for the Amish credits her ability to understand boundaries and customs, giving her readers an inside view of the plain life. Mindy's books are peppered with humor and sprinkled with grace, charming all the senses to make you laugh, cry, hold your breath, and root for the happily-ever-after. Mindy lives in northeastern Kentucky with her husband, Mike. They have five wonderful children and over a dozen grandchildren who give her plenty of inspiration.

OTHER BOOKS BY STEELE

The Heart of the Amish Series
Barbour Books
The Flower Quilter
Courting an Amish Bishop
A Stolen Kiss
Hunting for a Husband

The Miller's Creek Amish Series
To Catch a Hummingbird
The Butterfly Box
Cicada Season
Ladybug Landing

Stories
An Amish Flower Farm
His Amish Wife's Hidden Past
Christmas Grace

Novellas
A Brookhaven Christmas (Christmas Cookies and Mysteries Anthology)
The Christmas Cookie Thief
Leaving Lancaster (in *A Lancaster Amish Christmas*)

Romantic Suspense
The Mountain Protectors Series
Bones on the Mountain
Breaking McKinley's Curse
Deadly Sanctuary

Christian Fiction for Women

Christian Fiction for Women is your online home for the latest in Christian fiction.

Check us out online for:

- Giveaways
- Recipes
- Info About Upcoming Releases
- Book Trailers
- News and More!

Find Christian Fiction for Women at Your Favorite Social Media Site:

 Search "Christian Fiction for Women"

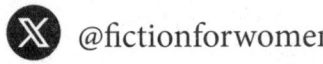 @fictionforwomen